The Seventh Blessing
A Tales of Gymandrol Novel

♡ Melissa Buell

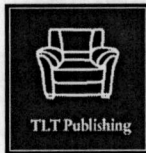

Melissa Buell

TLT Publishing

Chicago

THE LITTLE THINGS PUBLISHING, LLC

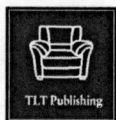

TLT Publishing

Chicago, Illinois

Printed in the United States of America

Cover Design by Matthew Maniscalco
Interior Design by Cameron Ruen
Edited by Farrah Penn
Published by The Little Things (TLT) Publishing

The Little Things (TLT) Publishing
Chicago, Illinois
Visit our web site at:
www.tltpublishing.com

ISBN: 978-0-9844013-5-2

Second Paperback Edition: August 2011

To my husband, Chris,

for all of your shoulder rubs, encouraging words,

dishwashing, and willingness to overlook

unfolded laundry.

ACKNOWLEDGEMENT

I'm so very thankful for the many people who have influenced me and helped me in life and in my writing.

My husband Chris - thanks for encouraging me, listening to my rants about my characters not doing what they were supposed to do, and giving me time to write. I love you...infinity plus one.

My boys - You both helped name characters and listened as I read parts of the story aloud. Thanks for being patient as Mama wrote. And wrote. And wrote some more. I love you a lot!

My publisher, Randi Ertz - I am still shocked that I got the call to join the awesome team of TLT Publishing. Thanks for being supportive, available, and ensuring that my book had the best people looking after it.

My editor, Farrah Penn - I am so blessed to have a fantabulous editor who also loves YA books! You helped me make my writing stronger and I appreciate that we were on the same wavelength with the story. Thanks for being amazing and patient!

My cover artist, Matt Maniscalco - I am excited and proud to have such a rockin' cover on my book. You were able to take my ramblings and translate them into a work of art. You captured Samantha and the library perfectly. A million thanks!

My critique partner, Allison Lakso - You inspired me to actually show my work to someone and look where that has taken me! I appreciate all of our e-mails back and forth and hours spent talking about writing and what characters would do. Because we know that they ARE real!

My "beta testers" who read the first version of the book: Bryan, Andrew, Amanda. Thanks for your comments about how to make the story stronger. And the characters more evil. And the situations more dire. Samantha does not thank you but I do.

My little sister, Tiffany - I lost my voice after reading the entire story out loud to you in one day but that (and you) helped me find the flaws and fix them. You inspire me to write good books for girls.

To my family and friends who encouraged me, read the book, and didn't laugh at me for writing.

To all the teachers and professors that I had who encouraged me to write and do my best. I hope this is a good end result. An "A" would not be turned away.

Of course, I could not do anything without Jesus Christ, the author and finisher of our faith. Hebrews 12:2

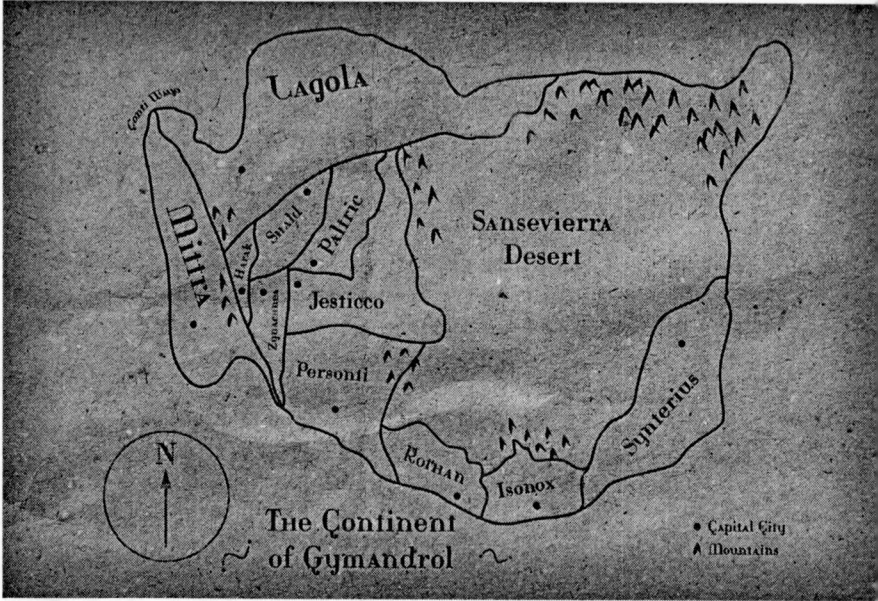

The Continent of Gymandrol

Lagola

Conti Way

Mittra

Braſt
Svajid
Paltric

Jesticco

Zyucarum

Personti

Sansevierra
Desert

Synterius

Rothan
Isonox

N

The Continent
of Gymandrol

• Capital City
⋀ Mountains

The Seventh Blessing
A Tales of Gymandrol Novel

CHAPTER ONE

*T*alia looked up from her scroll, turning to the cry of anguish that came from the adjoining bedchamber. *It will be soon now,* she thought with a smile, *but not too soon, I hope.*

She only had a few more lines to write before her remembrance of the Fairy Rebellion would be finished. King Bennett of Mittra and King Aspen of Synterius had asked Talia, as well as a few other trusted royal fairies, to write about this most pertinent historical event of the continent of Gymandrol. While she enjoyed writing, Talia did not enjoy the memories she was required to recall.

Retelling the experience brings it into sharper focus, she thought, trying not add too much emotion in her account. *But how does one keep emotion out of the war that killed many fairies and caused us to run to the human countries for safety?*

Talia's desk was covered with slips of paper, stacks of history books, piles of parchment and most importantly, her mother's diary. Each contained a puzzle piece of history that came from their people. History that was important to understand, so it would not be forgotten and repeated in the future. Talia opened her mother's diary, noting the leather binding was cracked from use.

The first entry was dated thirty years, when her mother, Tatiana, was admitted as one of the first female fairies in the Academy for Magical Abilities. Talia read her mother's accounts numerous times and had many committed to memory. However, she was searching for a particular passage today. One that would help tie everything together.

There are so many bits of history. It's hard to know what to keep and what to leave out, Talia thought to herself as she turned the pages. *The day Mother and Father met is important to me, but not to everyone else. Father's service to the king and Mother's service to the queen are both equally important. Father's death . . .* The page was well marked, dotted with dried teardrops from both Talia and her mother. *His death was very important. That must be in the account. Oh, here it is. The words of the Ancients.*

In Tatiana's careful hand were words handed down from the Ancients, the first fairies who used magic. The Ancients believed there was a magnified form of magic that was only apparent when they used their own language, not the everyday language used by humans and fairies alike. If Talia was able to understand why her mother wrote down these last words shortly before her own death, it would be the key to—

"To what? That's what I've been trying to find out for the last several years!" Talia exclaimed, surprising herself as her harsh tone echoed in the still room. She sighed, pushing her hair away from her face and stood up to pour herself a drink of water from the nearby pitcher.

Talia stopped short when she caught a glimpse of herself in the mirror that hung on the wall. A large splotch of ink was smeared across her cheek, and her ebony hair stood out like a cloud. Her shimmer, a telltale sign of a fairy's emotional state, sparkled merrily above her eyebrows. She managed to scrub her face and smooth down her hair before a piercing scream came from the bedchamber behind her.

A gray haired, wrinkled midwife tottered into the sitting room. Her eyes brightened when she saw Talia at the writing desk.

"Mistress Talia," she wheezed. "The queen needs you immediately!"

Talia quickly rose from her seat, feeling her forehead growing hot. She feared the worst for her queen. As she entered the queen's private bedchamber, she spied Queen Adelaide lost in a sea of blankets in the center of her enormous bed. Her face was white with beads of sweat gathering upon her brow, and her large brown eyes dimmed in pain. Talia approached the side of the bed with a smile, even though anger sparked inside her. *Do they not know it is the middle of summer?* Talia thought. *Who piles on blankets in July?*

"Dear queen, how can I be of assistance to you?" Talia gazed down at Adelaide's face, which was normally serene and delicately beautiful. She hoped the birth would come quickly, if only to prevent her friend from so much suffering.

"Excuse . . . the others . . ." Adelaide murmured between labor pains.

Talia turned to the ladies-in-waiting and midwives who were hovering nearby, waiting to be asked to help deliver Mittra's newest heir to the throne. She tried not to roll her lilac eyes at their restless pacing and frantic mutterings.

"Ladies, if you please." Talia smiled and gestured toward the door. She was relieved that they would not be in the room any longer to agitate the queen. They quickly left when they saw the purple shimmer on Talia's forehead and stubborn expression set on her heart shaped face. However, the royal midwives stood ready to argue their right to be there, which provoked another sigh from the fairy. "The queen would like some time alone. You won't miss the birth, I promise." When they filed out, she locked the door.

"Thank you, dear friend," Adelaide whispered, closing her eyes as another pain tightened across her belly. "This little one . . . is a fighter. The king will be . . . proud of his son," Adelaide labored to get the words out, trying to smile at Talia.

What will Addy and the king do if it is not a boy? Talia wondered to herself.

She removed all but one blanket from the bed in an attempt to make the queen more comfortable. "Not so hot, now, is it?" Adelaide gave a small smile as Talia proceeded to fan her. "What have the midwives given you? Or done to you?" Talia looked apprehensively at the queen. "No knives under the bed, right?"

She shuddered when she thought of the tradition of placing a knife under the bed in an attempt to ease the pain of labor. What if the knife stabbed through the mattress and cut the mother? She ducked under the bed, but found no evidence of such a tradition.

Adelaide laughed hoarsely. "No knives, though the old midwife, Rynthea, wanted to give me a special blend of herbs from her garden. No thank you, I said. She insisted, at which point I called for you. They do not help take my mind off the pain." Adelaide paused as her belly contracted again. "Oh, the stories they told! Childbirth stories should be outlawed during labor. I will ask Bennett to make a law of it." Talia laughed with Adelaide this time.

"I wish I could give you some fairy magic to bear the pain a bit easier, but I don't think that's possible, Addy." Talia could only call the queen by this familiar name when no one else was around. Her mother taught her that peasants do not call royals by their first names, let alone nicknames, in public. "I can heal, but it is not really healing that you require at the moment." She dabbed at Adelaide's smooth forehead with a damp cloth.

Adelaide smiled. "Save your fairy gift for the child. You could tell me a story, Talia. A fairy story, *not* one of a four day long childbirth. Is that what you have been writing on that ever-present scroll of yours?"

"No, not a story, exactly." Talia glanced at Adelaide's face. "The king asked me, along with Osric and Elan, to write down what we remember about the Fairy Rebellion. I am almost finished with my account. I fear that it is too emotionally based for historical standards, but I was only eight years old when it happened, so there is that."

"Females have a different perspective than males do, I have noticed, especially in my conversations with the king himself. I am certain that your account will be just as essential as those of those silly male fairies. Who knows what they have forgotten in their old age?"

Talia shook her head, smiling. "They are not old by fairy standards, Addy. Osric just turned ninety-three this year, and Elan is a good twenty years younger than him. Fairies do not age as humans do. But . . . I'm not saying that they are not silly." Talia winked. "They act like little boys, fighting to get the king's attention. My mother told me it has always been that way, even when she met them back in Sansevierra." Talia looked at the queen. "I shall read you my account if you think it will take your mind off the pain. If it distresses you at all, I will stop."

Adelaide nodded her head, closed her eyes, and breathed deeply as another pain rolled through her. "Go on, Talia. I have always wanted to know more about the fairies. We did not have any in Harak, so all I know is what has been whispered behind fans by the ladies at court. Well, until I came to Mittra and met you, my dearest friend."

Talia blushed at this admission from the queen. Who would have thought that a young fairy refugee would be the Queen of Mittra's personal advisor? *Certainly not me,* Talia thought as she hurried to the other room to fetch her scroll. She shook her head at the midwives, who were anxiously waiting to be called back to the birthing chamber.

"No, no. Not yet," Talia spoke softly to them. She murmured a charm to calm their fretful spirits, hoping it would also work on Adelaide. She noted the sudden look of peace on their faces as she closed the door once again. After taking a seat near the head of the bed, she unrolled the scroll to the beginning of her tale.

"Many years ago, back when Sansevierra Desert was not yet a

desert, there was a time when fairies and humans existed in separate kingdoms. The land of the fairies, Sansevierra, was surrounded by the human kingdoms that preferred to be near the edges and waters that encircled the continent. The continent of Gymandrol was surrounded by the Bisanthus Sea in the west, the Freesian Sea to the north, the Zuiden Sea in the south, and the Lantista Sea to the east. Humans seemed to be experts at sailing and navigation, while the fairies were content farming in the landlocked area of Sansevierra. This created a fair sense of trade between the two groups, who lived peacefully, side by side, for many years."

"It was here that the fairy King, Marchen, opened an academy for those with magical abilities. A young fairy named Dagan was admitted into the Academy. This set off a chain of events that was unforeseen by the admission advisory committee, and cataclysmic consequences arose for the entire continent of Gymandrol. Dagan illegally practiced 'darker magic' and began to gain followers who were enticed by the idea of overthrowing the fairy king. The wicked fairy and his faction led the rebellion that caused the downfall of the kingdom of Sansevierra, sending fairies scurrying to surrounding human countries for asylum…"

‡

Later, Talia sent a note to Osric, informing him that the queen was minutes away from giving birth. Osric rushed to the king's study with this urgent message. King Bennett flushed to the roots of his red hair and rushed out to the balcony on his castle, which overlooked the main square of the city. His royally handsome face shone as he exclaimed, "My kingdom, I am going to be a father very soon!"

"Huzzah!" echoed throughout the square from the king's loyal subjects.

Talia hurried to the entrance of the balcony where Galen, the king's personal guard, and King Bennett were waiting. She wore a huge smile on her face as Galen whispered in Bennett's ear. Bennett beamed and charged out onto the balcony.

Talia reached Galen and said, "The queen has born a daughter. We have a new princess!"

Galen's wrinkled face paled and he began to shake. Talia grabbed his arm and helped him into a nearby chair. "Stop the king," he croaked. "I took your smile to mean it was a boy . . . ."

Suddenly, trumpets sounded from the balcony. "My people," King Bennett began. "My wife has given me an heir! It's—"

Talia raced to the balcony, cutting him off. "No, your majesty," she whispered in his ear, ignoring the murmuring from below. "It's a girl."

"He's a girl?" King Bennett gasped.

The entire crowd gasped with him. A princess? Not a prince? What would the king do? Bennett shook his head as if to clear it and then made his way to the railing of the balcony, hands trembling slightly.

"My people, I have a . . . daughter. You have a princess. That is all." The king abruptly turned and left through the curtained doorway.

Talia motioned Osric over to her. The old fairy served as the king's secretary of state, and she wanted him to do damage control with the crowd. She made frantic smiling motions at him, hoping he would get the hint. Osric stepped forward to the edge of the balcony. She noticed that his hair, once blonde, was now mostly silver in the morning light. His distinctive silver fairy eyes dimmed with age, and his wrinkled face still bore a shadow of his former attractive self.

"This is an unforeseen circumstance," he began in a thin voice. "We should remember that girls are just as good as boys. The blessing ceremony will take place in one week, and you are all invited!" Osric waved his hands in a dismissal to the crowd and left the balcony.

Talia closed the drapery that covered the entrance to the balcony.

"Are you sure it is a girl?" Osric questioned, his silver shimmer scarcely visible.

"Of course, I am sure!" Talia retorted as her purple eyes flashed with anger.

Osric held up his hands in surrender. "I just thought . . .Well, maybe the next child will be a male. For the king's sake. And the country."

Talia felt her forehead growing hot. "Why is that, Osric? A female can rule in Mittra. It has not happened in many years, but it is possible." She stomped off, her shimmer sending sparks up into the air.

After taking a walk to cool her emotions, Talia approached the room where the Gift Givers, those fairies who helped name and give blessings to the royal babies, were staying. Each fairy was handpicked by Talia for their ability to bear the burden of choosing the appropriate blessing for each baby. The fairies knew their gifts could change the life of one of the royal family forever. Talia also knew that they were weaving a tapestry using their fairy magic to showcase the blessings the princess would receive. She stopped at the entrance of the chamber, appalled at the angry words spewing across the room.

"Since it's a girl, we need to choose different names. I love Humufia."

"No! Pirouette!"

"Ugh, like in ballet? Never."

"I like Demetria."

"That sounds a bit evil, dear."

"It's better than Musetta!"

"I love Brunilla."

"Isn't that a disease?"

"Halfrida was my mother's name. It's lovely."

"Not as lovely as Imelda."

Talia whispered a spell under her breath, and the room suddenly became quiet. She gave a satisfied smile. "Now that's better. Sit down please." All of the fairies complied. "The queen has chosen a name already. The princess shall be called Samantha."

The six fairies raised their eyebrows in dismay. When they opened their mouths to argue, nothing came out. Talia's silence charm was rock solid until she chose to lift it.

"I understand Samantha is not a typical noble name, but the queen wants to honor her great-grandmother by using her middle name. I will pass along a few of the names you suggested as a possible middle name. Have a good day."

Talia left, murmuring the countercharm when she was a few feet down the hall. *Now to send out the official invitations to the private blessing ceremony*, she thought as she headed to her room.

Born in the month of July, Princess Samantha would receive seven fairy blessings. This meant that seven Gift Givers would be invited to the private ceremony. Frowning, Talia wrote down Osric and Elan, the king's oldest fairy advisors. She would have to keep them quiet and offer them the position of the last two gifts given during the ceremony. Otherwise, who knew what they would do to "out bless" each other? She noted that Gahan, Phelan, Cesolia, Philana, and Evelina rounded out the list of fairies. Each was well schooled in giving appropriate gifts to a noble, especially to a first-born who could rule the country one day.

Talia sealed the invitations with purple sealing wax and the signet ring given to her by Queen Adelaide. She called a messenger to deliver the invitations while gathering all the items that were essential for a newborn baby.

‡

Three days later, Talia, Adelaide, and little Samantha arrived at the chamber where the private blessing ceremony would be held.

"Are you aware, Addy, what started the tradition of the private ceremony?" Talia questioned as they passed the rows of chairs that had been set out. They stopped as they approached the raised dais, framed by heavy drapes, at the front of the room. Adelaide shook her head, laying Samantha in the carved wooden cradle at the center of the platform.

"No, I have wanted to ask you about that. I remember when you first sent me the welcome letter after Bennett proposed to me. I was delighted to go to a new land but also scared, since I did not know anything about fairy customs. You will have to continue teaching me, Talia, just as you have these last five years," Adelaide replied, sitting in an upholstered chair behind the cradle.

Talia loosened the ties holding the drapes back, allowing them to cover the opening to the dais for a brief moment of privacy. To the left of the cradle stood a small writing table on which Talia placed a scroll, a quill, and a bottle of golden ink. She whispered a spell over the quill, which seemed to quiver in anticipation.

Talia smiled. "Do you see this ink and quill, Addy? When the blessings are announced during the ceremony, the quill magically records the gifts given to the child. This prevents error by clerks who might not be truly listening to the blessings that are given."

"As for the private ceremony, I can tell you a story my mother told me. It happened the first year we lived in Mittra. The first royal baby born was King Braddon's nephew, a lesser lord. What was his name? Lord Belton, bless his heart. And his nose. Elan's father, Soren, was the eldest fairy at the time. He was given the honor to announce the first royal fairy blessing."

"Unfortunately, the ceremony was in January, during a break in the coldest winter Mittra had seen in hundreds of years. Soren was not properly attired to be out in the snow and wind. Consequently, his nose began to run incessantly during the ceremony. When King Braddon asked, 'What gift shall you bestow upon young Belton?' poor old Soren was not paying attention and remarked to the fairy on his right, 'I wish this silly nose would just fall off rather than drip.' The crowd gave a resounding gasp of surprise when little Belton's nose fell right off his face! Several expensive fairy healers managed to get Belton's nose back on by nightfall, but his nose was never quite centered and tended to get blocked rather easily. Everyone felt this was a tragic waste of a fairy gift and quite a public scene for the royal family to endure. My mother and Osric advised the king and queen to have a private ceremony to ensure this spectacle would never happen again," Talia laughed at the memory, but Adelaide looked rather shocked.

"Has that happened in any private ceremony?" Adelaide asked worriedly.

"No, not that I remember. Every fairy is very careful now. After Soren's mistake, he was sent into retirement, and no one wants to be forced into that!"

Suddenly, Talia heard raised voices as the chamber doors opened and then slammed closed. She raised her finger to her lips and crept forward, pulling the drapes so that they were completely hidden. She placed her hand on the dagger hanging from her belt. *I hope this is not an assassination or kidnap attempt,* Talia thought, gripping the dagger's hilt as she peeked through a gap in the drapes. She relaxed when she saw it was just Osric and Elan. *Why must they argue all the time?*

Once King Bennett made Elan his war advisor, Osric felt the need to tell Elan how to do his job effectively. He also demanded that Elan come to him before going to the king regarding matters of state. Talia attempted to intercede when she could, but she was tired of being the mediator. She edged closer to hear their conversation without alerting them of her presence.

"All I'm saying is that it's too bad that the child is not a boy," Osric insisted.

"Yes, that may be so, but we still must give the child proper blessings. I do not know why you had to follow me in here. I wanted some alone time to think of the best gifts, but now I have lost my concentration," Elan complained as he crossed the room, standing just a few feet from the curtain surrounding the dais.

Talia noticed Elan's dark hair was beginning to silver at his temples, giving him a distinguished look. He was tall for a fairy, standing four inches taller than Osric. He maintained his strong looks even with spending so much time outdoors in the sun and wind. His wide shoulders gave evidence of his strength from working with the knights in the king's service. His silver eyes wrinkled at the corners when he smiled, causing both fairy and human girls to swoon.

Talia held her breath, but she knew that they would not be able to hear her if their volume increased, as it tended to do. She just hoped that they would not wake the sleeping princess.

"Well, I had a long list of blessings to give to the child, if it were male!" Osric boasted. His thin chest puffed out as he stood toe-to-toe with Elan.

"I am sure that your list was not as long or detailed as mine," Elan responded, his shimmer glowing brightly as he stared down at the older fairy.

"I would give the gift of determination. Whatever the child set out to do, it would be carried out to the end," Osric said proudly, his own forehead giving off a faint glow.

"I would give the gift of courage! He would never back down from a fight. That is a great gift," Elan nodded, pleased with himself.

"Courage? Please." Osric's voice rose as he circled around Elan. "I have more helpful gifts for a leader. I would give the gift of obligation, so he would always help those in need."

"Next would be quick reflexes. A *soldier* values things like that," Elan smirked as he crossed his thick arms over his chest.

Osric's eyes narrowed. "A *scholar* would appreciate the gift of learning languages easily. Much more useful, I would say. But then, I am a learned man." His silver eyes flashed at Elan, daring him to go on in this war of words.

Talia turned to roll her eyes at Queen Adelaide, but instead, she noticed the charmed quill moving across the scroll. *What is happening?* Talia thought, perplexed at the sight. She hurried to the table, and when she realized what was happening, her face lost its color. *Think, Talia! What would Mother have done? She would have had the immediate remedy and would not be hesitating, losing precious time. I never should have taken this position as Addy's advisor. The most important day of Samantha's young life, and I cannot even think properly. But I cannot walk away and leave this mess unsorted. I cannot fail the princess now.*

Talia frantically ran through the spells she had spent most of her life memorizing, pulling at a loose strand of hair. *If I simply charm them into silence, might that silence charm also affect the princess? Anything spoken is quite dangerous. What can I do to stop this? What gift can I give to her? These blessings can destroy her if she is not strong enough to bear them. A gift of strength? No, someone else might use it to control her.*

Suddenly, Talia remembered a blessing her mother used to say many years ago. Words from her mother's diary also came to her—words from the language of the Ancients. Talia recited them in her mind as hope bubbled up in her chest.

"A *soldier* would appreciate the gift of handling any weapon with skill and dexterity. As a *learned* man, I do not expect you to understand what good gifts are," Elan spoke mockingly to Osric.

Talia watched the quill write the sixth blessing down. She leaned toward the quill and spoke clearly in the tongue of the Ancients, hoping the words were correct, hoping they would register before Osric's response to Elan's comment came through, hoping that the tiny princess sleeping next to her wouldn't have a future filled with tragedy. The seventh blessing glistened up at her dazzlingly.

Talia stood up and turned to look at Queen Adelaide. The queen had risen from her chair, and Talia watched as her eyes scanned the scroll.

Adelaide's face turned as pale as the white lace at her throat. Her lips moved without sound, and her brown eyes became wide with disbelief. Talia hurried to her side, catching the queen's petite frame as she fainted.

She lowered Adelaide to the floor as the drapes were thrown back from the entrance to the dais. The small fairy ignored Elan and Osric. Instead, she took a small vial from the pouch on her belt and carefully poured a few drops into the queen's mouth.

Within a few seconds, Adelaide regained the color in her cheeks. Her eyelids fluttered open. "Talia," she began weakly. "The blessings? For Samantha?"

Talia hesitated, unsure of how to comfort the queen. "Your highness, Samantha has been given blessings, it would seem. I know that it is difficult to take in—"

Adelaide took a deep breath, cutting her off. "Difficult? My only daughter is given blessings meant for a prince, and you call that *difficult?*" The queen raised herself slowly from the floor. Talia tried to help, supporting her back with her hand.

Adelaide's eyes sparkled with anger. She turned to Elan and Osric, who were standing wide-eyed at the edge of the dais. "As for you two," Adelaide's voice soared in rage as the old fairies stood frozen in place. "Just wait—"

Forced into silence, she turned in confusion towards Talia, who wore a stern look on her face. "I am very sorry I had to charm you, my queen, but I know you would have regretted your words later. As they say, 'A royal should never have regrets.' I will take care of these two," Talia indicated Osric and Elan with a nod of her head. "You should get ready for the ceremony. The *real* ceremony. Everyone will be here soon."

Adelaide opened her mouth to protest, gesturing towards Samantha, who was still fast asleep. Talia shook her head. "She will be just fine. I will take care of the scroll and make sure these *wise advisors* are not present when you return."

Talia led Adelaide to the door on the far side of the dais. "I am so sorry, Addy," Talia whispered, her purple eyes filling with tears. "Go now. All will be well. Not perfect, but well."

Adelaide closed her eyes, sighed silently, and then turned to leave through the door. She looked back at Talia and patted her throat. Talia gave a small smile and murmured the counter spell. Before she left, Adelaide whispered, "Thank you, dear friend."

Talia turned, facing Osric and Elan with a grim look on her face. She gestured for them to leave the dais. Then, she walked down to the chamber where the guests would soon be arriving.

"What were you trying to do? The poor queen almost died of apoplexy! You are the king's most trusted advisors," Talia hissed, her shimmer sending purple sparks into the air. "Why would you argue over such stupid, meaningless things? Oh, I am sorry, not *meaningless,* because all of your bickering translated into gifts for Princess Samantha! What will you do now?"

Both fairies were a head taller than the diminutive Talia, but they seemed to shrink down under her wrath.

"Talia," Elan managed to squeak out. "It was wrong for us to be so... competitive and argue so vigorously. Is not there some way to remove the blessings? What did we even say?" Elan's face paled as he recalled his words. "Oh dear, she will be some kind of warrior scholar! Osric, how could you have done this?"

Before Osric could respond, Talia stepped between them. "Enough of the fighting! That is what started this whole mess. Yes, these are rather unconventional gifts for a princess, but we can fix this."

Talia purposely did not tell them about the seventh blessing. She hoped that no one would try to translate the language of the Ancients. She knew the quill recorded the last words she had spoken, but per fairy protocol, she had to put the fairy blessings in the Library of Records.

"Perhaps . . ." Talia mused. "Osric. Elan. I have thought of an opportunity for you to redeem yourselves." She hurried to the writing table and picked up the scroll, the gold ink sparkling in the candlelight. She returned to the two fairies, who were waiting earnestly. "Take this scroll and translate the blessings into the language of the Ancients. Hopefully, no one will take the time to translate them, and the secret will stay safe with us. Oh, and be sure not to label the top with 'Princess Samantha.' Think of something clever. No one is to know about this. Not even the king. Queen Adelaide will tell him when the time is right."

Elan and Osric looked at each other and nodded. Earlier, they thought they would certainly be exiled into the East by the king and queen. Now, there seemed to be some hope.

"One of the blessings is already translated," Osric said, looking closely at the scroll.

"One less for you to do," Talia replied, secretly willing him not to translate it.

"Yes, that is so," Osric murmured, smiling at his fortune. "You are most wise, Talia."

She waved her hand as if to brush away the praise. "Go now. I will invite a few apprentice fairies to replace you in the ceremony."

‡

Talia rubbed her eyes wearily as she climbed the stairs to her room. *This exhausting day is finally over*, she acknowledged with a slight smile. The public ceremony had gone much as Talia could have predicted. *What silly gifts,* the fairy thought with a spark of agitation. *I should really make a better list of princess gifts. Not that anyone will follow them,* she sighed to herself. Talia opened her door and set the scroll from the second ceremony on her writing table. Listed in gold ink, written by Talia herself, were the false blessings gifted to Princess Samantha.

Graceful dancer
A gentle giggler
The ability to sip soup quietly
A low curtsey while keeping her balance
Talented musician
Long fingernails
Petite

Talia snorted in disdain at the last item on the list. "How in all of Sansevierra do you expect to make the princess petite?" she demanded out loud, shaking her head.

She met Adelaide after the ceremony to discuss the items gifted. The false gifts seemed harmless, but she hoped they would be able to convince Samantha as she grew. Adelaide's anxiety lessened as they talked, to Talia's relief.

We will just have to hope for the best, she thought as she readied for bed, *and plan for the worst . . .*

CHAPTER TWO

Ten years later

" *Y*ou can't catch me because you're a girl!" Nolan, Prince of Lagola, laughed at Samantha, running toward a grove of trees.

"Oh yeah?" Samantha replied. "I'll show you that a girl can catch a boy, Know-Nothing-Nolan!" She hiked up her heavy skirts to her knees and sprinted as fast as she could. *Get him, get him, get him.* Samantha's thoughts sounded in time with her footsteps, and her blonde hair streamed from behind her as she ran.

She reached the first tree just seconds behind Nolan. She saw his long leg dangling down from the tree branch as he tried to climb out of her reach.

"Got you!" Samantha's voice rang out as she tugged on his leather boot. Nolan swung his foot back, the thick heel smashing against her mouth. Samantha tasted blood and dropped her hold on him, clutching her mouth. She willed away the tears that sprang to her eyes.

Nolan dropped down next to her and pulled her head up. "Let me see," he insisted, pulling her hands away. He cringed at the sight of blood running out of Samantha's swollen mouth and the tears threatening to spill from her emerald green eyes, but he did not want to get in trouble with his mother. "It's not that bad, Prissy Princess Sammy. Are you going to cry now?" He knew if he made fun of Samantha, she would chase after him again, which would cause another fight. Then they would *both* be in trouble. It seemed to make sense in his head.

Samantha felt a rush of anger overtake her as her head buzzed with rage. She spat out the blood onto Nolan's boots and punched him in the stomach as hard as she could. Nolan gasped, bending over slightly. After a moment, he straightened and glared at Samantha. His deep brown eyes narrowed in irritation.

"Oooh, Nolan got punched by a girl! What are you going to do?" jeered his younger brother Acton, climbing out of another tree.

"He won't do anything because he's a big sissy!" heckled his youngest brother Ellery, who stayed hidden in his tree.

"I am not a sissy. Just watch!" Nolan took off after Samantha, who had already started running. Samantha knew that Nolan could not stand to be teased by his little brothers, and she had just given fodder to the fire. *And now I'll pay for it*, she thought as she ran as fast as she could toward her family's home in Conti Wayo.

The thick forests surrounding Conti Wayo helped keep the castle cool, making it the ideal summer home. The only negative aspect was that Nolan lived on the other side of the stone wall every summer, too.

She saw a huge mud puddle inside the courtyard and veered left to avoid it. *I need to get inside before Mother sees me with all of this blood all over my face*, Samantha thought. *The dinner guests will be here soon, and I still need to get ready. Talia is probably already looking for me—*

Samantha felt something hit her side, cutting off her thoughts. She flew into the air, landing on her belly in the middle of the puddle. She pushed herself up in the filthy mud, shaking her head. *What hit me?* She turned to see Nolan smirking in the mud next to her, thick muck dripping from his dark hair.

He picked up a handful of the soggy dirt and dribbled it on the top of her tangled hair. Then he stood up, poising to run away. "See what happens when you mess with me? This is your warning, your highness!" Nolan's laughter echoed through the courtyard as he dashed off.

Samantha pulled herself out of the puddle, shaking in anger and embarrassment. *Stupid, stupid, boy! Oooh, I cannot wait until I can get Talia to charm his stupidness away! I need to get inside before anyone sees me.*

She pushed open the heavy wooden door that led into the grand foyer and headed toward the stairway, which would take her to her bedroom. Before she got there, a round of shrieks stopped her.

"Samantha Culdania Faeryna Talia Jacqueleen! What do you think you are doing?" Queen Adelaide's voice rose several octaves, and her face paled so much that Samantha feared she would faint.

Samantha turned to see all of her parent's special guests standing in the foyer, frozen in shock at her presence. *I don't look that bad, do I?* She turned to the oversized mirror on the wall, gasping at her own reflection. Her large green eyes peered back at her muddy face, taking in her swollen mouth that was still oozing blood from the small cut on her lip. Her pale yellow gown was now muddy brown, while her bodice was spattered with her dried blood. Her long blonde hair was disheveled and streaked with clumps of muck, twigs, and flakes of leaves.

She whipped around, facing her mother with clenched fists. "Mother, I can explain. Nolan and I were outside, and he was not being nice to the other children. So I told him that he must behave himself, and then he insulted me! He said I couldn't catch him because I was a girl! So then I caught him, but he kicked me and then pushed me in the mud—"

"That is quite enough from you, young lady!" Adelaide's voice rang out as she interrupted her daughter. "A prince, like Nolan of Lagola, would never do such a thing to a princess. Remove yourself to your chambers *immediately.*"

Samantha ran as fast as she could up the carpeted stairs to her room, refusing to care about the spectacle she made as she fled. She crashed through the tall doors and collapsed in a heap on the rug in the middle of the room, sobbing out all of her frustration of the last few hours.

Stupid Nolan! It's all his fault! Samantha pounded her fist into the patterned rug, wishing it was Nolan. *Why does he have to be so mean? It was bad enough that he put worms in my soup last night and crickets in my bed the day before that. But this is public humiliation, and I will never ever forgive him for it!*

Samantha knew this was not the proper way for a princess to behave, but she could not always do exactly what her mother wanted. Thankfully, she had Talia. Talia would understand Nolan's ickiness, and she would not scold her for her dirty gown. She would probably laugh with her and help her wash up while telling her a story of life back in Sansevierra.

As if she could read her thoughts, Talia entered the room, gently closing the door behind her. Samantha felt Talia kneel down and survey the scene.

"Oh, Sammy. What happened now?" Talia's soft voice caused Samantha to tear up all over again.

"It was Nolan! It's always Nolan. He is such a stupid, stupid, BOY!" Samantha cried so hard that she thought she would throw up. After a moment, she felt Talia's hand begin to rub her back.

"Shhh, it will be fine. He will grow up and get over his boyishness, and you will grow up to enjoy his attentions," Talia replied, amused at Samantha's dramatic sensibilities.

"Never! I will never want him to pay attention to me," Samantha sat up, exposing her filthy gown. "I wish I could throw mud in his face. Let's see how he likes it."

Talia's dark eyebrows shot up as she eyed her dress. "Now I

understand, Sammy." She gestured to the mud stains. "I can see why both you and your mother are so upset. I will call Bergette to draw a bath for you. Your parents would like you to come down as soon as you are presentable, which could take a while." She stepped closer, taking in the dried blood, cakey mud, and her bruised mouth.

Samantha sighed as she walked toward the bathing chamber. "It really is hard to be a princess, Talia. I would not wish it on anyone."

‡

"We have no choice, Bennett," Adelaide insisted later that evening in the couple's private sitting room. "Samantha just cannot control herself around the Lagola boys. I have tried, Talia has tried, and numerous governesses have tried to make her less of a tomboy. I really do not know what to do about our daughter except take her back to the castle in Halat and engage her in more princess appropriate activities. Perhaps being back in the capital with polite society will be the push she needs. Bennett?" Adelaide asked in an irritated tone, noticing her husband's inattentiveness.

King Bennett leaned back in his favorite chair, stroking his beard. It had once been fiery red, but now it had streaks of grey through it. "I do hear you, my dear. I am just . . . thinking. Is it bad that she plays with the boys, climbs trees, rides horses, and plays with practice swords? I find it rather charming. And refreshing, if I may tell the truth. Most princesses are silly beyond comprehension, always giggling and talking about their new gown or other nonsense." Seeing the ire building in his wife, Bennett hurriedly retreated. "Not saying all princesses, of course! You were not like that, my dear. It just seems that most royals had fairies bless their children with such ridiculous gifts. Do you not wish sometimes that Sam was given something more . . . reasonable?"

Adelaide clutched her hands together to cover her sudden nervousness.

Talia warned me that I should say something to Bennett about her true gifts, but I fear it is too late to admit that I kept something from him. "What do you mean? Are you unhappy with the gifts she was given?"

Bennett sighed. He stood up and walked to the window, which overlooked the wide expanse of grass outside the castle. He was familiar with the land and knew the field led to the low wall, separating Mittra from Lagola. "They are fine, of course. But what kind of man will she attract by, what was it? Giggling gently or sipping her soup quietly? Really, Addy. I had hoped for more serious gifts. You do realize," his voice dropped as his face took on a grim look, "that she *could* rule Mittra. A ruler needs to have strength and courage. I hope she will make a wise choice. Maybe returning to Halat is what is needed for her. She can undergo 'princess lessons,' as you like, and 'leadership lessons,' as I would like. We will hire all the best tutors to come to the castle. I will arrange it with Osric and Elan. Why don't you speak with Talia? I am certain that between three of the cleverest fairies, we can achieve a princess whom the whole country will love and admire."

Adelaide rose from her seat near the window and stood by Bennett's side, gazing out into the night. "I trust your judgment, Bennett. I will go speak to Talia now and arrange matters as quickly as possible."

Bennett kissed her forehead before she left the room and then stood there, pondering what life held for his only child.

‡

Samantha snuck into stable before breakfast the next morning, eager to visit her horse. The head groom allowed Samantha to ride a gentle black mare named Shadow when she visited Conti Wayo. Shadow loved munching on the carrots and lumps of sugar Samantha brought her from the kitchen. This morning was no exception. While Shadow snuffled the treats out of her outstretched hand, Samantha stroked the long black mane and whispered to her borrowed pet.

"I have to leave today, Shadow. Mother insists that I return home to become a 'proper princess.' I can't tell you how very tiresome *that* shall be. I shall have a dancing tutor, an etiquette tutor, a language tutor, and I'm sure many others! At least Talia will be with me. I know she will help me remember my lessons and help me practice them until they are perfect."

She sighed, leaning her shoulder against the warmth of the horse. *I wish I could stay here. I would ride, swim, run, and climb trees whenever I want to! Why can't Nolan and his family leave? Then I can stay here without Mother fussing that the boys are a bad influence on me. Or am I a bad influence on them?* It was hard to recall all of the points Mother made before Samantha was allowed to go to bed the night before. *Either way, this feels like a punishment. I wish—*

Samantha was startled out of her reverie by the appearance of Edric, Nolan's older brother. He waved a hand in greeting, his grin revealing straight, white teeth that stood out in his tanned face. All of the princes from Lagola had inherited their father's square jaw and dark hair, but Edric had his mother's hazel eyes. *I think the big difference between Edric and Nolan are their eyes. Edric's are very friendly and kind, always waiting to see me smile. Nolan's eyes are mischievously narrowed, always waiting to see if he can make me cry. The other girls might think Nolan is better looking, but Edric is the better friend.*

"I thought I'd find you here," Edric said in a happy tone. "Do you want to go for a ride?"

"No, thank you, Edric. I only have a few moments before I need to return to the castle. We are leaving this morning."

Edric's face registered his shock at her words. "*Leaving?* But you have only been here for a month! I thought you were staying for three, just like last year."

Samantha laughed gently at his expression. "I thought so too, but

Mother changed her mind after the scrape I got into with Nolan last night." Seeing the confused look on Edric's face, Samantha frowned. "I take it he didn't tell you? Well, your weasel-worm brother picked on one of your cousins, and I told him to apologize. To make a long story short, I ended up with a muddy gown, a bloody mouth, and the punishment of returning to Halat. He ended up with a punch in the stomach. I should have given him a black eye . . ." Samantha trailed off, thinking of how she would still love to punch Nolan in the face.

Edric bent over and clutched his belly. He laughed so hard that tears streamed from his eyes. "Oh, Sam! I would have loved to see that fight. I will apologize for my brother. He should have gotten my peacemaker gift, not me. I will teach him a lesson for you, how about that?" He patted Samantha's shoulder and led her from the stable. "What are you having for breakfast?"

"Ugh! All you boys think about is your stomach!" Samantha faked a groan as she entered the castle with Edric.

"Well, I am fourteen. I'm a growing boy, you know."

"Come on, I'll feed you," Samantha smiled up at her friend, who was her familiar defender against his younger brothers' torments. "You have to write to me, okay? I need some connection to the world outside of princess lessons and propriety. Tell me how you and your brothers are and sketch interesting things for me in your letters. Promise?"

Edric smiled down at her. "I'm not the best artist, but I will send you letters when I can. You're not the only one who has to have protocol lessons. My father is insisting that I put away childish things and spend more time learning how to run a country. When you get discouraged, just think how I'm training to be a *king,* and then you can have a laugh."

Samantha felt a familiar smile tug at her face as her laughter rang through the hall.

‡

25

"Really? Thank you, Father!" Samantha squealed in delight as she threw her arms around her father's waist. "I love Shadow. I would miss her most out of all the things I have to leave behind in Conti Wayo. How did you know?"

King Bennett looked down at the adoring face of his daughter and smiled. "Ragnol, the groom, told me that Shadow is the only horse you ever bring treats for. Just keep the sweets to a minimum if you want the horse to be any good for your training." He ignored the looks Adelaide shot at him.

Samantha stared up at him. "What training?"

"Well, you need to train in order to ride properly. It also would not hurt to know how to defend yourself on horseback, just in case anything ever happened. Elan will take over your training once you reach Halat," Bennett told her, patting her hair.

"I do not think defensive training will really be necessary, Samantha." Adelaide's voice was forceful. She smiled, trying to hold her composure in front of the servants. "Maybe only one lesson from Elan will be sufficient. She will not be a warrior, will she?" Adelaide laughed hollowly at her rhetorical question.

"Well, my dear, there is the old legend of Queen Einara of Mittra. She led her people to battle when she was a princess. She was engaged, but her betrothed died in battle. She was heartbroken and declared she would never marry another. The people of Mittra loved her so much that she was made queen, even without a husband. Einara was the first warrior queen of Mittra. Who knows when we might have another?" Bennett winked at Samantha. Adelaide just turned her head sharply as she entered the covered carriage. "Keep an eye on Mother, won't you?" Bennett whispered to Samantha. "Try not to upset her while you complete your lessons. Just do your best. You are a good daughter," Bennett pulled her into a brief hug, which surprised Samantha. Her father was not usually demonstrative toward his family, but she did not mind this sudden show of affection.

"I will, Father," Samantha whispered as she squeezed him back. "I'll be the best warrior princess I can be." She returned his wink, hurrying into the carriage.

"Goodbye, my dears! I will follow behind you in a week or so," Bennett called as the carriage started down the pebbled path toward Halat.

☦

"I cannot do what she wants me to do, Taley," Samantha complained. Four years had come and gone, and her mother was still the cause of her frustration. She slumped down on the couch in her private sitting room, folding her arms.

She liked the way Talia had decorated her room. It had been tough to convince Adelaide to change the pink and purple wall hangings and overstuffed furniture, but Samantha enjoyed the softer shades of light blue and yellow. She appreciated the way the morning light filtered in through the white curtains hanging at the large window, and the built-in seat beneath it gave her a perfect place to read. The mahogany writing desk was replaced by a more delicate one, carved out of a lighter wood. Across the surface of the desk were several scrolls, a few sheets of paper, and her favorite quill. Two couches sat facing each other, flanking the fireplace, which crackled faintly in the morning chill.

Talia looked up from her seat on the opposite couch, her hands full of embroidery. "Do what, Sammy?"

Samantha pushed herself up and leaned toward her friend. "I cannot do all of the things Mother wants me to do in the perfect manner she wants me to do them. I thought that once fairies blessed you with a gift, that characteristic came easily to the one blessed. All of these princess lessons are going to make my head pop! I can't 'giggle gently' for one thing. If something is funny, I laugh! My silly fingernails will *not* grow long because I keep breaking them during practice with Elan. I do not know how to make myself petite, other than hunching over, which makes Mother clear her throat at me. I am already taller than Mother, and I am only fourteen years old! Elan says that I have my father's 'muscular frame' but I don't want to look like my father. I feel like an overgrown oaf! Oh, Taley, my life is unbearable." Samantha turned and buried her face in a blue striped pillow on the couch.

Talia rose and went to the desk, collecting a few items. She carried them with her to the low table between the couches. "Sam, dear, sit up. Stop pouting and listen to me. On this scroll, I want you to make two lists. The first one will be all of the things you dislike about princess lessons, or being a princess, or just things you dislike in general. The other will be what you *do* like to do, what you are good at, those kinds of things. I will clear your schedule for the next hour so you can do this." Talia pressed a kiss to Samantha's temple and patted her hand. "Just for the record, you are not an overgrown oaf. You are tall and slender and though you *do* have muscles from all that work Elan is making you do, you just might use them one day. But I am sure Queen Einara had muscles too, and she was able to use them to protect her country in battle. You're also quite beautiful, you know."

Samantha huffed as she stomped over to the mirror. "I wish I could be beautiful like you and Mother. Mother says my chin is stubborn looking, but Father calls it determined. I just call it pointy. I wish my face wasn't so long and my nose didn't turn up at the end." She stuck her tongue out at her reflection.

"I will bring you some hot chocolate to help you think about the list," Talia said before she left the room, closing the door behind her.

Samantha picked up the familiar black quill and spun it in her fingers, thinking of all of the lessons she endured for the last four years. *The negatives will outweigh the positives,* Samantha thought as she divided her paper.

Things I Detest About Being A Princess

- _Dancing. Especially with my dance tutor, Yalens, who steps on my "ridiculously large" feet and then blames me for it! (I heard him talking about my feet to my painting tutor.)_
- _Giggling in a ladylike manner. My etiquette tutor tells me it is proper to hide my giggle behind my hand while fluttering my eyelashes. (This does not look coy, like she believes. She simply looks like she is trying to hide her mouth because she has food stuck in her teeth. She should look in the mirror sometime when doing it.)_
- _Ridiculous gifts given by well-meaning but silly fairies._
- _The tapestry in my bedchamber that portrays my fairy blessings. Ugh. Even after I redecorated my suite, Mother refused to let that go. She said it is a daily reminder of all that I should be._
- _Mother and her princess lessons. She knows I ~~dislike detest loathe~~ absolutely HATE the lessons, but she insists that in order to make a match with a worthy prince, I must be an ideal princess. I do not think a prince would be happy with a fake princess, but I do not know if he would be happy with the real me, either. I do not even know the real me._

Things I Do Like About Being a Princess
I am sure there are a few things I like . . .

- _Riding Shadow. My horse is my second best friend, next to Talia._
- _Talia. I should have listed her first. (Sorry!) If I wasn't a princess, she wouldn't be with me and my family._
- _Training with the knights and soldiers. This is only because of Elan and Father. Mother was very unhappy when Father agreed with Elan's idea. He thought that I should take some of my so-_

called aggression out on the training field. I have to wear a heavy helmet and armor to disguise who I am, but I do not mind.
• *Learning languages with Osric. This might sound boring, but I find that I am a very quick learner. He was not very surprised at this, though. I think Osric is proud of me. He always asks how I am doing with Elan's lessons as opposed to his lessons. I told him that they are completely different. With Osric, I am a scholar. With Elan, I am a warrior. Or so I like to think.*
• *Being a scholar-warrior. Maybe I won't be as powerful or kind as Queen Einara in the old legend, but I do want to be the best Samantha I can be.*

I hope this satisfies you, good Talia. Thank you for being my friend and listening about my so-called unbearable life. I realize now I can try to bear it.

Love,
Sam

✝

The next morning, Samantha awoke at dawn, washed, did her stretching exercises, braided her hair, and then dressed quietly in her training gear. She preferred to get ready by herself because her maid, Bergette, always made tisking noises and disapproving faces when she thought Samantha could not see her. Samantha found the routine of dressing in her harness a soothing exercise, though she could not explain it to anyone other than Elan. The fairy had smiled when she spoke of it, saying, "So it is with me," and that cemented their friendship.

She smiled at herself in the long mirror that hung on the wall in her bedchamber. Her eyes grazed over the silver hauberk that covered her body from her shoulders to her knees. *This is so much more fun than dressing for a ball,* she thought as she took each piece down from its assigned place in her wardrobe. *My other wardrobe, as Mother calls it.* Samantha rolled her eyes. Each piece of her harness had been lovingly made by fairy armor smiths, overseen by Elan, who was overseen by Osric, who was overseen by Talia. *Now the cuisses,* Samantha thought as she strapped the padded metal pieces to her thighs, *and then the vambraces.* She fastened the leather coverings to her forearms.

She lifted the cuirass over her head, marveling at the clever manner in which Elan had instructed the smiths to make it. It hinged at the shoulders, allowing her to dress herself, and weighed very little, though still very strong. Samantha knew it had something to do with fairy magic, but she did not fully understand it. *And that's fine with me,* Samantha thought with a grin, *as long as I get to wear it!*

"And now the pauldron," Samantha whispered, rolling the word in her mouth.

She loved the sounds of the words, feeling them deep within her. They were so foreign from her princess vocabulary, and she was delighted at the chance to practice with the other knights in the training yard. *Does Mother even know what a pauldron is?* Samantha asked herself while she attached them to her shoulders.

After placing the couters to her elbows, she picked up the sack from the bottom of her wardrobe that contained her helmet, arming cap, and gauntlets. Her eye fell on a small packet of letters that were almost hidden in the back of the cabinet. She shook her head. "Not today. Today is too important to read those," she murmured, walking to her bedchamber door.

As she passed the tapestry woven by the fairies at her birth, Samantha stuck out her tongue at it, just as she did every day. It was a childish gesture, but it made her feel a bit better when she thought of her princess lessons that would inevitably follow her lesson with Elan. She opened the door just as Bergette was lifting her small fist to knock.

The young maid jumped back, a startled look on her face. "Oh! Princess, you are already awake and . . . dressed. I was coming to help you. You need only ring and I would be here right away—"

Samantha touched her arm softly. "It's fine, Bergette. You know that I like to have some time in the morning to myself. I will just have a little breakfast and head out to the yard." She crossed the room to the low table between the couches, picking up a plate with a single piece of toast and a peeled orange. "Thank you, Bergette! How thoughtful," Samantha smiled warmly at the maid, who nervously pleated her apron between her fingers.

Bergette bobbed down in a curtsey. "I know you never eat all of the food Cook sends up, so I reminded her to send up a little bit of food. After a bit of grumbling, she sent this tray. But she insists that you eat a hearty lunch!"

Samantha threw her head back and laughed. "Tell Cook that I will eat an enormous lunch after today's training session. Elan wants me to test for a squire today. I hope I can eat this without vomiting." Seeing the look of alarm on Bergette's face, Samantha hurried to relieve her. "I am not ill, just nervous. I'll be fine when it's all over and done with."

I hope.

‡

"Now, Sam, I know you love Shadow, but you might want to think about trading to a different horse. Just for jousting purposes," Elan assured her, patting Shadow's neck.

Samantha sat in the high backed saddle used for jousting matches, wrinkling her nose in distaste. "Do you think Shadow is not good enough, Elan? She is a champion mare. Excellent bloodlines! Is it because she is a female?" she teased with a gleam in her eye.

Elan waggled his index finger, as if to scold her. "You are an impertinent whelp, and I do not care who your father is! No, it is not because Shadow is a female. The truth of the matter is that you are growing taller and will soon outgrow Shadow. If all of your training is in earnest, and you seek to be like the queen in the legend, you must open your heart and receive another mount. A mount that can carry you into battle. A mount that will serve to help protect you from the enemy—"

The ringing of Samantha's laughter interrupted Elan's dreamy speech. "I'm sorry, Elan. I truly am. But if you could have seen the look in your eye . . . Were you imaging a battle? Was your horse your faithful and true companion?"

Elan's silver eyes took on a tragic look and his dark head drooped slightly. "I hope you never find this to be true for yourself, Princess, but others may fail you. They may purposely hurt you. They may even try to kill you. Your horse will never do such a thing. It is an extension of you, if properly trained. That is what I seek to give you. Will you not allow this?"

Samantha swallowed, his words piercing her heart. "If you feel it is that important, good Elan, I will trust you to find me a new mount for training. May I still keep Shadow until that day?"

Elan nodded, beaming at her. *See that Osric*, he thought as he walked toward the quintain, *my gifts are useful for the girl after all.*

Apart from Talia, both fairies never told anyone what happened during Samantha's blessing ceremony. Elan had been wary, yet excited when Bennett tasked him to train the princess in "leadership skills," as the king put it. It had been Elan's idea to enroll her as a page, and she accompanied one of his older knights, Sir Cabot.

Cabot was kind and respectful to the knights, squires, and pages who trained in Mittra, but the same could not be said about all knights of the realm. Cabot had been knighted at age twenty—a typical age for most knights in Mittra and its surrounding nations. He had served under

King Braddon for the first ten years of his knighthood and then swore allegiance to King Bennett when he took the throne sixteen years ago. Now at age forty six, Cabot was ready to retire from active knighthood and work with Elan as a training instructor.

Elan had talked with Cabot extensively before handing the majority of Samantha's training over to him. He recalled their first conversation that took place four years prior in the castle.

"You do understand, Cabot, that this is a *princess*. The princess of Mittra, in fact. The only one," Elan spoke, staring at the knight who sat across from him in Elan's private office.

"Let me see if I have this right," Cabot replied. "King Bennett wants me to train his daughter to be a warrior, and Queen Adelaide wants her to have 'proper princess lessons?' Hmmm . . ." He stroked his short black beard thoughtfully. "What says the girl about this proposal?"

"*The girl* is Princess Samantha, Sir Cabot. Please remember that," Elan glanced at Cabot, who looked appropriately contrite. "I believe she views this as an adventure. Almost an escape, it would seem, from her princess 'duties,' as she referred to them. There was some reference to Queen Einara, who you well know served this country in time of need. Perhaps you can model the princess's training after Einara's training— given that there are any records of it. She will, of course, start as a page and work her way up to a squire. Our goal is to make her a knight. That is, if she is good enough. I will not allow the training requirements to be relaxed simply for a princess," Elan told him, his shimmer glowing brightly for a moment.

"I agree, Sir Elan. I will put her through the same training exercises. She will be treated like any other page that wants to enter the path to knighthood. Just one thing—does she cry much? If there is one thing I cannot take, it is a weepy female." Cabot gave an exaggerated frown, but Elan just laughed.

"No, she's not much of a crier. Well, perhaps in private," he paused, as if trying to remember. "I will ask Talia about that. I do know she is tough and holds her own with the boys. Funny story about that. Did you hear about the summer in Conti Wayo . . . ?"

Elan shook his head, freeing it from the cobwebs of memories. He walked toward the head groom of the royal stables. "Maccus! I have need of your expertise in horseflesh. As I am sure you have noticed, Princess Samantha is outgrowing her mare. I have convinced her to switch to a larger, stronger horse. I think that the princess would benefit from a rouncey. What do you think?"

Maccus, a stooped shouldered man with gnarled fingers from years of hard work, turned into the stable. "Old Dusty here used to be a great warhorse, the finest destrier ever bred by my father." He stopped at the first stall, patting the dun-colored horse's nose and offering a carrot from his pocket. "Some of the best warhorses Mittra has seen came from these two. You're thinking a rouncey for the princess, hmm? Be about the right size for her with the way she's been growing. Not meaning no disrespect, sir," he rushed, seeing the crossness on Elan's face. "It just that we've all noticed that the princess has been growing. Like you said, she'll need a new horse. Let's see . . ." He paused as they reached the last stall. "Here we are! Windstorm would be my choice. He's fast, he's light, and he's got a good spirit."

Elan gave an approving smile as he approached the gray horse with the white mane. "He's what, fifteen or sixteen hands high?" he asked, patting the gelding's neck.

"Sixteen and a half, actually. It'll give the princess some room to grow, but she won't have a far drop when she falls off. *If* she falls off, of course," Maccus backpedaled, sweating at Elan's glare. "As you can see, he's a gelding, so you don't have to worry about him being too aggressive."

Elan kept his face solemn as he finished his perusal of Windstorm. "I agree, Maccus. Windstorm will be Princess Samantha's new horse."

Elan gave Maccus a slight smile before returning to his position in the training field, observing Samantha's practice runs at the quintain.

The quintain was used in tilting exercises by the knights, pages, and squires. A center post measuring twelve feet high was topped with a horizontal pole measuring six feet long, which turned in a full circle. A shield hung from one end of the horizontal pole and a heavy sandbag hung from the other. Each rider was to ride his horse quickly toward the quintain, lowering his lance diagonally across his body. The goal was to strike the shield squarely in the center while avoiding the sandbags that spun around on the arms of the quintain. This activity required strength, precision, and speed—all necessary components for a successful knight.

Samantha practiced at tilting so much she dreamed about it at night. She took to the lance quickly, which surprised Cabot and the other knights watching her. She had been told it would be difficult to master, and that she should not feel badly if she did not do well at first. Samantha felt deeply satisfied that she had been able to prove them wrong. *Just because I'm a girl doesn't mean I can't do things of this nature,* Samantha wanted to say but refrained from speaking her mind. Instead, she practiced more vigorously, pushing herself harder than anyone else. She did not want the male pages to feel like she was getting preferential treatment because she was a girl. And a princess.

She knew refusing to wear a dress to the training field bothered her mother. Thankfully, her father had interceded on her behalf, stating that she would be more likely to be injured wearing unsuitable clothing instead of proper gear. Samantha was grateful for her time outside, feeling alive, doing what she liked to do.

Elan motioned her over to the gate where he was standing. "I have found you a proper horse. His name is Windstorm and I know for certain that you will love him. Maybe not as much as Shadow here, but Windstorm will be a much faster runner and you can train him for tilting. What do you say, Princess?"

Samantha scowled. "Princess? Elan, you promised you would call me Sam on the field. It makes me seem . . . less princessy."

Elan's eyes sparkled. "I do not know if you have noticed, *Sam*, but you are a princess."

"It seems so, doesn't it?" She sighed. "But out here, everything seems *right*. In my other lessons, it feels like I am swimming through syrup. Heavy, cloying syrup. Don't laugh, Elan," Samantha shot him a look of annoyance.

"I'm sorry, I just pictured you swimming in your best ball gown..." Elan's voice trailed off into more laughter, this time with Samantha joining in. "You do not care for any of your lessons? Not even with Osric?"

"Osric's lessons are the only ones I enjoy in the castle, now that I think about it. He is teaching me languages now, did you know? I seem to be good at it. Can you imagine that? I am actually good at something that my mother *approves* of!" Samantha gave a hollow laugh.

Elan reached up and patted her hand, seeing the pain in her eyes. "Sam. Give your mother a little grace. You do see that you are a rather ... unconventional daughter, do you not?"

She thought for a moment before cracking a smile. "Unconventional? Yes, that is one word to describe me, I suppose. I will take that as a compliment, dear Elan. But I would rather be out here than in there, and I do not know how to reconcile that in my heart."

Just then, Sir Cabot called Samantha over for her final practice turn at the quintain. She gave Elan a brief smile and a wave before trotting off. *I am sorry that I gave you the gifts that I did, little Samantha. But I am also quite happy with the way you are turning out.* Elan sighed. *Time will tell with this one. I do rather like this Sam over Princess Samantha myself.*

‡

"How are you feeling, Dawes?" Samantha whispered later in the stable. Dawes, caring and kind, was her good friend as well as fellow page.

"Do you really need to ask?" Dawes groaned and rolled his eyes at her. "Have these last four years taught you nothing? I am always sore and tired and—"

"Whiny," Samantha supplied with a wicked grin. "Wasn't it fun, though?" She laughed at the horrified expression on Dawes' tanned face. His chin length brown hair was mussed from wearing his helmet, and his chocolate brown eyes were tired and red-rimmed. She noticed he had smudges of dirt marked on his thin face. Samantha remembered one of the ladies in waiting had said Dawes would never be as good looking as his older brother, Palmer. While Palmer's features fit his face, Dawes' nose was a bit too large and his eyes were closer together than his brother's.

Her older cousins, along with several other visiting princesses, always talked about swooning at the sight of a handsome man. They even went on to say that their hearts began to beat quickly when one entered the room.

"Just from seeing someone?" Samantha had asked them. "Doesn't it matter if he's brave or knowledgeable or good?"

They just laughed while her older cousin, Lacene, whispered, "Just wait until you're older, then you'll understand."

Samantha did not care for Lacene and her silly, simpering princess ways. Whenever Lacene arrived, she had all the furniture in her room rearranged and complained about the lack of closet space. Once, Samantha told her that if she didn't buy so many gowns, she would have more space. Lacene had stared at her, her eyes wide in horror at the thought of not having several changes of clothes for one evening. Thankfully, she only had to see those relatives once a year, during the winter season.

"Sam? Why are you staring at me? Is there something on my face?" Dawes stared at Samantha as she snapped back to the present.

"Nothing. Sorry, I was just . . . remembering something." She smiled at him. "So, when do you think they will let us know how we did on our squire examination?"

"I thought Elan said Sir Cabot would announce the results at dinner tonight. Do you think I made it?" Dawes asked, ceasing from brushing the horse he borrowed for training purposes.

"I'm sure you did, Dawes. But if you didn't, that's fine. You can just try again in the spring. Can't you?"

His face sank. "*You* can. You're still young, and *your* parents have money for you to continue training. Well, obviously because you're the princess and you can do what you want . . ." Dawes trailed off at the stormy look in Samantha's eyes. "Not that you are abusing the system or anything. You're good, Sam. You'll make it. But me . . . I don't know." His eyes dropped, but not before Samantha saw the bleakness in them.

Samantha knew that this was one of the most important days of Dawes' life. They frequently talked about what would happen if Dawes failed his squire test or if Palmer failed his knight test. He didn't know what would happen if one of them was maimed during training.

Samantha left Shadow's stall and stood next to Dawes. "I know this is very girly of me and not at all what a future squire would do, but I'll do it anyway." Samantha reached out and gave him a comforting hug. Dawes awkwardly patted her back, instantly pulling away.

"Er . . . Sam, you're not getting any romantic ideas, are you?" Dawes looked even more horrified at this thought than he did when contemplating failing his examination.

"Eww, no! Sorry, Dawes. You're one of my best friends, not a potential suitor. Here." She stuck out her hand. "Let's make a pact. I will never want to marry you, and you will never try to kiss me. What do you say?"

"I'll make that promise, but you have to shake like a man. Or . . . at least like a squire." He spat into his open hand and held it out to her. Cringing, Samantha spat into her own hand and squeezed his hand with hers.

"Disgusting. Boy spit." Samantha wiped her hand on the straw that sprinkled the stall floor. "I thought I was done with spit when I left Nolan and his brothers in Conti Wayo. Did I tell you about the time I held him down and spit in his eye?"

‡

"But, Taley, I think I should dress like the other pages tonight." Samantha scowled at her reflection in her bedchamber, crossing her arms over her chest. Her long golden hair lay down her back, except for a few braids that were pinned around her head. Talia had said it resembled a coronet. She wore a deep blue satin dress with embroidery on the high bodice and sleeves, which even she had to admit, was very pretty.

Talia raised her eyebrows. "Sam, dear, you have missed one important distinction between yourself and the other pages. You are a girl. *And* a princess. Do not sigh at me, Samantha. Even Queen Einara wore gowns, so you have no excuse. You should be proud to dress like a princess. Earlier this morning, you looked and smelled like a stable boy. Look at you now! Your father and your mother will *both* be proud of you tonight."

"You don't think I look too . . . girly?" Samantha gestured toward her chest.

Talia began to laugh. "Is that what is concerning you? You know that all young girls change and become more womanly. No one will treat you any differently on the training field for it. You are too covered up with armor for anyone to notice. I think . . ." Talia's eyebrows came together while she thought. "I think that most people seem to separate the armored

Sam from the gowned Samantha. Not that you are two different people, Sammy. Do you understand?"

Samantha turned around, squeezing Talia into a hug. "That's it! You've said it perfectly. I feel like I am two separate people, and I don't know which one is the real one and which one is the false one."

Talia blinked back tears and touched Samantha's cheek. "That is what your journey of life is to be, Sam. Finding out who you are inside. No one can do that for you. You never know, but you might have a quest just like Einara had when she was a princess." She stood up. "Come on down now. I happen to know that there will be an announcement that will make you and Dawes very happy."

CHAPTER THREE

Four years later

"*H*appy birthday, Sam!"

Samantha's eyes were not fully open when she reached under her pillow for the sheathed dagger hidden there. She rolled out of bed, still clutching the dagger, and took a defensive stance. A burst of laughter and a shriek of alarm forced her to open her eyes wide. Her mother stood shocked in the bedchamber, along with Talia and her father, who wore expressions of amusement and pride. Dawes lingered outside the doorway, a shy smile apparent on his face.

Samantha's face burned with embarrassment. "Ummm, good morning? I'll just put this away . . ." She slid the dagger back into its hiding place while Talia held out a dark blue robe. Samantha slipped it over her long white nightgown, belting it at the waist.

Bennett beckoned her into the sitting room. "Come, Sammy. We have all of your favorite things to eat."

Samantha followed her father, freezing at the sight of a huge table that was placed where her couches and table had been. Dozens of candles were scattered around platters that were heaped high with her favorite foods: sweet pastries, roasted pork, fresh fruit, scrambled eggs, spicy sausages.

She gave her parents a bewildered look. "But . . . why? I mean, I'm thankful for all this, I really am. But what about the ball tonight? You can't give me so much in one day!"

Adelaide stepped close to her daughter and gently touched her hand. "Samantha, dear, I know you do not care for balls and banquets. Your father has pointed out that tonight is more for me, truth be told. This morning is for you. So eat up! You are free from lessons for today, and you may go for a ride with Dawes for as long as you choose. Given that you have a chaperone, of course," Adelaide said sotto voce.

Samantha leaned forward and threw her arms around her mother. "Thank you, Mother! This is a wonderful beginning to my birthday." She couldn't help noticing how tall she was against her mother's petite frame. Holding back a sigh, she said, "Let's eat!"

"When you have finished eating, you may open your gifts here in private," Bennett informed her, glancing at Adelaide.

"You already have the gift from Father and me," Adelaide said, "the gown for tonight's ball, the jewels, and the new slippers. We ordered three pairs in case the others get worn out by all of the dancing tonight."

"Yes, I am so glad to own shoes that will fit my feet without pinching them. I do hope my feet have stopped growing. It's quite ridiculous and expensive, I know, Mother," Samantha laughed, shaking her head.

"You will have to open enough meaningless presents tonight," Dawes began, but stopped when Samantha pressed on his foot under the table. "Er, that is . . . we wanted to give you the gifts you would be sure to love here in private!"

Adelaide nodded her approval, while Bennett and Talia covered their smiles. "You must be sure to comment appropriately tonight during the gift ceremony." Samantha rolled her eyes. "Do not roll your eyes at me, young lady! Talia, did we not cover eye rolling in etiquette class? Yes, I thought so. In any case, Dawes is correct. Our guests may not understand some of your gifts. I do not fully understand them myself," Adelaide admitted, wiping her mouth daintily with her napkin.

Bennett took over the conversation. "I believe what Mother means, Sam, is that we are very proud of you and your studies. Who would have believed that a princess of Mittra would be on the road to knighthood? And such a beauty too!" Bennett grinned proudly, but Samantha squirmed under everyone's scrutiny.

"Please, Father," Samantha held up her hands as if in defeat, "Don't embarrass me any more on my birthday. I am no more accomplished than any other squire. Sir Cabot is very kind to me. He says I do not have to leave my home to go on the tournament circuit, as other squires and knights do. Dawes, on the other hand, is ready to leave with Palmer after the tournament tomorrow. He is a great squire and will be a great knight one day." She held up her goblet of apple juice toward Dawes. "To Dawes, a great squire and friend!"

Dawes flushed with pleasure and held up his own goblet. "No, Sam. To *you*, the only princess I know who can ride and punch as well as she can dance." Laughter sounded from everyone in the room, except Queen Adelaide.

Adelaide glanced suspiciously at Samantha and Dawes, a look of displeasure on her face. Talia took note of it and murmured a charm, causing her to focus on the happiness in the room. When Samantha looked at her mother to see her reaction at Dawes' toast, she was mildly surprised when she caught the broad grin on her face. Talia winked, confirming Samantha's unspoken question.

Oh Mother, there is nothing going on between Dawes and me. He is as good a friend as he ever was, and my heart does not beat any faster for him than it does for anyone else. Samantha knew Dawes had no romantic interest in her. He had bluntly told her that after relaying the story of meeting a lady-in-waiting from Harak last week. The lady wanted to know why Dawes spent so much time with Samantha, and Dawes had informed her that she was "just a princess, and my fellow squire. Also, she often smells like a horse." Samantha had punched Dawes for that comment during the retelling of the conversation, and he duly apologized.

"Open mine first!" Dawes urged, pushing a small square box toward her.

Samantha carefully removed the dark blue ribbon from the box. "I'll save this. I love the color. Let's see what you managed to find for a girl like me." She peeked inside. "Oh no, Dawes, you did not!" Samantha narrowed her eyes at her friend in false outrage, lifting a small bottle of perfume from the package.

"I'm sorry, Sam. But you do sometimes smell like a horse!" Dawes ducked as she threw the empty box at his head. "Talia helped me make this perfume. It cancels out the stable scent and replaces it with vanilla."

"Great. So now everyone that smells me will want to take a bite out of me!" Samantha declared in mock distress, dabbing a bit of the fragrance on her wrists. "Oh, Talia, it smells so good. Thank you. And thank you, Dawes. I'll just ignore your previous comment."

Talia passed her a fabric wrapped package that glistened faintly in the candlelight. "Something else made with fairy powers," Talia smiled, watching Samantha eagerly open the gift.

"A new quill! And ink. And a . . . blank book?" Samantha looked up at Talia.

"The quill has been charmed to work with the ink, and it will write down whatever you would like to say," Talia explained. "The book may be used as a journal for your thoughts. If you are busy or do not have the time to write yourself, you may dictate and the quill will record it for you. I hope it will be useful for you, Sammy."

"Of course it will be! You know I love to read and write," Samantha told her, watching Bennett and Dawes drag a covered object from the far corner of the room. "Oh, what's this?"

"Sam, you are such a blessing to us, and I know you will be a blessing to Mittra," Bennett told her. "This is a surprise from Elan, Cabot, and me. Addy, dear, I am sorry I did not tell you about it, but I wanted it to be a surprise to you as well." He pulled the cover off the gift, and Samantha and Adelaide both gasped.

"Oh Father!"

"Oh Bennett!"

Confusion set in as both Samantha and Adelaide stood up, talking over one another. Bennett was taken aback at the amount of noise his gift generated. He lifted his eyebrows at Talia, but she shook her head with a small smile.

"No silence charms from me," Talia said. "You need to hear this, I think."

"A harness, Father? A knight's harness? But I am not fully a knight, yet! I do not take the test until the fall. I have two more months of training before Elan will allow me to test—"

Adelaide's voice screeched over Samantha's. "Bennett! What were you thinking? I was hoping that tonight's ball would put an end to your dreams of knighthood for our daughter. You know that I wish for Samantha to make a match this evening. She is now eighteen years old. I expected her to have numerous proposals by now! Do you know why they have not? Because all eligible princes have been put off by this … this warrior princess that you have created! It was *not* supposed to be like this. I do not care about the tales of Queen Einara. I care about *my* daughter—my *only* daughter. I trust her to be married soon. No more of this knight business. Do you hear me?" Adelaide collapsed into her chair, shaking with sobs.

Dawes discreetly let himself out the room, but not before his brown eyes caught Sam's, wishing she could leave as well. She gave him a wistful half-smile and turned to her father, wondering how to diffuse the situation.

"Father, I love the gift. I appreciate everything you have done to encourage me in my pursuits, but I don't want to hurt Mother. I will attend the ball tonight, of course, Mother," Samantha said, facing the table. "I will dance with whomever you choose for me. I will perform to the best of my abilities and act according to your training. I suppose I will be a . . . perfect princess," Samantha choked out the last words before running to her bedchamber. Talia quickly followed her.

Bennett took a step towards his wife. "Adelaide, this is too much. You have no right to demand so much from Samantha. She has done everything you asked," he thundered, his eyes filling with a fire Adelaide had never seen before. "Her training as a knight is the only thing that makes her happy. Can you not see that?"

"*I* demand too much? You have been the one to push her in these 'leadership lessons,' to tell her the tales of Einara. You have not let her be the princess that I want her to be! Do you not understand the stigma of an unmarried daughter?"

Bennett crossed his arms over his chest. "Unmarried? Samantha is only eighteen years old! I do not doubt that she will be married soon. Why are you so distressed, Adelaide?"

"Many of her younger cousins in Harak are already married. She will soon gain the reputation of being an old maid. I was seventeen when we were married, you know. My parents had quite despaired of ever marrying me off. I was the fourth daughter and did not have a large dowry," Adelaide spoke softly, staring at the tablecloth.

Bennett relaxed his stance. "Addy, my dear. Come here." He waited until she stood in front of him, and then he gathered her in his arms. "You were not an old maid when I married you. I was taken with your beauty when I visited Harak on my goodwill tour."

Adelaide gave a small smile. "Don't you mean your 'wife hunt'? Oh, I overheard you men talking one evening. Did you ever wonder why my father gave you such an easy quest? He was desperate to be rid of me!"

Bennett's shoulders sagged. "And all these years I thought that he just really liked me," he complained, grinning. "Addy, will you not relent a bit with Sam? She is a good girl, even if she likes things more seemingly suited for a boy. That does seem a bit strange, does it not? I would think that with all of the fairy blessings she received, she would shy away from her knight duties."

Bennett missed the look of horror in Adelaide's eyes. *Does he know? Does he suspect?* Adelaide asked herself for the thousandth time since Samantha's secret blessing ceremony. She shook her head. No one could know. The secret would remain safe in the Library of Records. Talia, Osric and Elan had all sworn an oath of secrecy, and she knew they would never break it.

Adelaide smiled at Bennett. "I will try to be more lenient and understanding. Will you encourage her in her princess duties?"

Bennett returned her smile. "You strike a hard bargain, Addy. Yes, I will. See to Sam, will you? I must attend to some matters of state with Osric. Elden is supposed to arrive soon. He and the boys should have gotten here last night. I do hope that is well with them."

Once he left, Talia met Adelaide outside Samantha's bedchamber. "She is lying down for a bit of a rest, Addy. It is for the best."

Adelaide looked guilty. "Should I not go in there and apologize?"

Talia shook her head. "I do not think she is ready to hear it yet. Wait until she's had time to work off some steam. A long ride will be good for her today."

Adelaide nodded, leaving the room in deep thought.

‡

Samantha cautiously opened the door to her suite, glancing around before exiting into the hallway. Her plan was to sneak into the library to hide from the numerous guests milling about the castle, waiting for the ball tonight. *And avoid your mother*, a voice in the back of her mind nagged. *Yes, that too*, Samantha acknowledged with a slight frown.

She could not help overhearing her parents' conversation. *At least now I know why Mother is so hard on me—she's eager to marry me off. I just wish it didn't hurt so much.* Her stomach was still aching from crying, and she was thankful that Talia told her mother not to come in. *I don't want to see anyone right now. I want to sit and read and not think about tonight. Dancing with strangers is not my idea of a birthday celebration. Especially dancing with men who want a princess from Mittra for a bride.*

Samantha reached the library on the third floor without being seen by any guards or ladies-in-waiting. She slowly eased the door open, praying the hinges would not creak as they sometimes did. She breathed a sigh of relief when she realized she was alone in this place of serenity. Her feet sank into the deep carpet, and she inhaled the scent of old paper and ink.

Osric's study was connected to the library by a short hallway. They often visited the library for books and scrolls that were pertinent to the lesson he was giving her. She wandered up and down the tall rows of books, running her fingers along the spines. *History of Mittra, History of the Continent, Customs of Foreign Nations . . . everything Osric has taught me for the last eight years.* Osric's door was closed, so she ventured toward the scrolls on shelves near the door. They had always been off-limits to her before. As Osric had explained, they were handwritten, one-of-a-kind, never to be duplicated works of art. Samantha secretly thought that Osric just did not want her to touch them with her hands, which were often dirty from her outside lessons.

She subconsciously checked her hands before touching the engraved plaques on each shelf. The high shelves, out of reach even for her, held scrolls of the personal history of the ancient rulers of Mittra. She smiled when she saw three entire shelves filled with tightly bound parchment, bearing the placard "Einara, Queen of Mittra."

Just imagine what I could learn from reading about her, Samantha thought as she reached for a scroll. Before she grabbed it, a familiar name caught her eye. *They already have a shelf for me?* A tingling sensation coursed through her, and her eyes lingered on it for a moment, anticipating finding out what had already been written about her.

There were three scrolls lying next to each other on the shelf, directly under the shelves of Einara. Each roll of parchment was tied with a dark purple ribbon, and a small tag hung from each ribbon. The first tag read in golden ink, "Samantha, Princess of Mittra: Parentage, family tree." *Boring.* The second scroll's tag read, "Blessings Ceremony." Heaving a deep sigh, Samantha slipped off the ribbon and unrolled the parchment. There, in Talia's own hand, were her seven blessings.

I do hope that Talia told the fairies to pay more attention when they give their blessings. I wonder if other royals have to practice as much as I do, or if their fairies did a better job giving them gifts? She quickly replaced the ribbon and the scroll, moving to the third roll of paper. This tag was empty. Her pulse quickening, Samantha unrolled the parchment and then froze.

"The tongue of the Ancients?" she burst out, quickly covering her mouth with one hand.

She hurried over to the desk by the window, where the noontime sun was already streaming in. She laid the scroll down with paperweights on either end. Closing her eyes, Samantha recalled her lesson with Osric a few years ago about the ancient fairy language. He had been teaching her the history of magic in Mittra and even spoke some of the words of a charm so that she could hear the beauty of the language. When she showed interest in it, Osric wrote down the alphabet for her and allowed her to decipher a few simple phrases. He had been delighted at her perfect answers, exclaiming, "Wonderful, Princess! You have quite the gift for languages." He then became very pale and called a halt to the lesson for the day. *And he never did teach me anything more*, Samantha thought.

She opened a drawer and removed a fresh sheet of paper, a quill, and a bottle of ink. She placed the new parchment next to the scroll and concentrated on the lesson from Osric. To her surprise, the letters and words easily came back to her. She began to translate the wording, taking her time to make sure each word was correct before moving on.

Two hours passed before she rose from the desk, pale and shaking. She automatically rolled the scroll and replaced it on her shelf. She cleaned her workspace, folding the translated parchment into a small square and sliding it into her pocket.

She would never remember the walk back to her suite. Her thoughts were fully consumed by the strange words that she had discovered, hoping it was all a dream. The feeling of the crackling parchment in her hand made her head begin to buzz. *Maybe this afternoon never happened. Maybe there was no scroll in the library. Maybe I didn't translate a language that I don't even truly understand. Maybe my whole life is the same as it has always been.*

Bergette noticed the dazed look in Samantha's eye as she helped her wash and dress for the ball. "A big night, isn't it, miss?" she asked brightly as Samantha sat in front of her dressing table mirror. Bergette started to arrange her hair. "Any ideas on how you would like to wear your hair?" When Samantha didn't reply, she continued, "No? Well then, I will do my best."

Talia tapped on the door to the bedchamber and entered with a smile on her face. "Oh, Sam, you look beautiful! Bergette, I do love her hair up like that. She won't have to worry about it being in her face." Talia noticed the lack of color in Sam's skin and quickly dismissed Bergette. "What is it?" She took one of Samantha's hands, noting how cold it was.

Before Samantha could respond, Adelaide swept into the room

wearing a full length copper colored gown that set off her brown hair and brown eyes perfectly. "Samantha, dear, it's time to go downstairs and meet your guests. Oh, you do look lovely in that color! Stand up and let me take a look at you."

Samantha rose and stood before the full-length mirror in her room. The deep red gown was a sharp contrast to her fair skin and honey-colored hair. The long sleeves were fitted on the upper arms, which flared slightly from the elbow to the wrist. The bodice was high enough to be modest for Samantha, but low enough to be fashionable. The skirt was floor-length with a very short train, though Samantha would have preferred no train at all. Her figure had gained more curves over the last few years, which was unfashionable compared to her slim, petite mother and the rest of the court ladies. Samantha was unable to starve herself to fit into her stays, and Elan and Sir Cabot insisted that she eat to keep her up her strength for training. Samantha was surprised to see how much she liked her hair up in curls with her silver tiara resting gracefully on the top of her head. Her emerald green eyes were fringed with thick, dark lashes, untouched by a smudging of kohl. She wished for the narrow, regal nose of her mother rather than her own nose, which turned up slightly at the end, giving her an impish look. Her lips were full, and she felt her smile was wider than what was popular. Seeing the paleness of her cheeks, she pinched them and gave Talia a faint smile.

"Just a few nerves, that's all, Talia," Adelaide assured her, ushering Samantha into the sitting room. "Now, Samantha, I know this is your first ball where you are the guest of honor. Let me remind you of a few things . . ."

Samantha's mind wandered as her mother spoke, and she became aware of the small piece of parchment clutched in her left hand. *How do I get rid of this without them seeing? I am sure they do not know about it. Talia wouldn't lie to me my whole life, and neither would Mother. Right?* Seeing her mother's frown, Samantha forced herself to pay attention.

"Your father promised Elden that you would dance with Edric first, so be sure to be attentive and ladylike. My, that boy looks just like his father—"

"Edric is here? You've seen him?" Samantha exclaimed, her previous thoughts cast aside. "Finally! I have not seen him in eight years. He must have changed." She laughed at herself. "Here I am, talking like an old woman. Mother, may I be excused?"

Samantha gathered her skirts with her hands and hurried from the room, but Adelaide followed right behind her. "Princesses never run, Samantha! Do not show that you are anxious to see him."

Talia spotted a small square of parchment lying on the floor by the doorway and unfolded it. *Sammy must have dropped this as she left. I will take it down to her. Oh, my . . .* Talia managed to sit on the nearby couch before the sudden dizzy spell overtook her. After a few minutes, she was able to think clearly. *This must be why she was so pale. But how in all Sansevierra did she manage to get this?* She examined the writing more closely. *It is in Sam's hand.*

The fifth entry on the paper answered Talia's question. *Osric's gift of language. Of course. I was wondering if that would emerge as her other gifts have. I hope this will not consume her thoughts tonight.* Her eyes landed on the last blessing. Her blessing. Talia gave a satisfied smile. *Osric must not have taught her the original language of the Ancients, only a more modern version.* She noted only two words of her blessing had been translated; the words for "princess" and "magic." *Those are the same in both dialects, so that must have been fairly easy for her. I need to try to explain things. How do I even start to explain why we've kept this from her for so long?*

But before she could come up with an answer, she rushed down the stairs, submerging herself in the crowd of guests.

‡

Nolan poked his head around the heavy wooden door, relieved at the absence of chattering females. He eased the door closed, letting his eyes scan the wide row of shelves filled with books and scrolls that marched down the length of the room. He stepped to the left and began looking for something to read to pass the time before the ball began.

He sighed as he ran his hand through his thick chestnut hair, frowning slightly at the length that brushed the top of his collar. *I need to get it cut,* he thought, *hopefully before the ball tonight.*

He chose a random book from the shelf and idly flipped through the pages, slowly walking down the row of books. He already had six fanatical girls begging for him to dance with them that evening. His normally smiling lips curved down into a frown and his russet eyes had a shadow of disgust in them. Silly girls throwing themselves at any eligible bachelor! Edric said it was his fault for charming them, but Edric knew he could not help it. He rolled his eyes and huffed, "It's a fairy gift. It's not like I asked to have the gift of convincing speech."

The faint sound of a quill scratching on paper caught his attention. He crept along the wall, spying a slight movement by the large window at the far end of the room. *I do hope it's not another husband-catching girl,* Nolan thought as peered through a gap between the bookshelf.

The sight of the young woman sitting at the writing desk made him stop and stare. Her long blonde hair spilled loosely down her back and shone as the sun streamed through the window, giving her an ethereal glow. Her face was turned down toward the desk, but he could see her profile. He took in her smooth cheek, slightly rounded chin, and skin that was slightly more tanned than most ladies he met. She glanced up and he held his breath, worried she might see him staring at her from his hiding place. Her finely arched brows pinched together as she pursed her full lips, as if in deep concentration. He felt his heart beat faster. It was as if he could see the joy of life in her emerald eyes.

"Beautiful," he whispered, drinking in her loveliness. He shrank back behind the bookcase and crept from the library. He quietly opened and shut the door, trying not to disturb the library's occupant.

Once in the hallway, he leaned his head back against the wall. *How to meet her? I suppose I'll have to wait until the ball tonight. I've heard the rose garden is very romantic in the evening.*

Nolan glanced down, surprised to see the book he had taken from the shelf still in his hand.

"Nolan!" his brother, Edric, called out. "There you are. Father asked me to find you to make sure you are ready for the ball. He wants you to look your best while you sweet talk the foreign ambassadors tonight." He stopped, glancing at him. "Why do you look so . . . strange? And I don't mean your hair."

Nolan pushed himself away from the wall, walking toward his brother. "Edric, I have just seen an angel. She's the most beautiful woman in the world. I can only hope to see her tonight at the ball." Nolan handed the book to his brother and then gave a little hop in the middle of the hallway.

Edric laughed at the dreamy look on his brother's face and shook his arm, grabbing his attention. "Another girl to add to the collection, eh little brother? Don't you have enough admirers for one trip?"

Nolan scowled. "This one is different. Would you mind returning that book for me? It's some dull history book. Not the kind of reading I appreciate the way you do."

Edric flipped through the book with interest. "I might just borrow it for myself. But I'll be sure to officially check it out, unlike you. Let's go downstairs before you do any more dancing out here."

Nolan allowed his brother to lead him away from the library before he shot him a mock angry look. "Hey, what was that about my hair?"

CHAPTER FOUR

Samantha spied Edric in the grand foyer beside his father, chatting amiably with her parents. *He really did grow up!* Samantha laughed to herself, admiring his familiar features. She remembered how they were once boyish, but he had grown into his regal, masculine face complete with a square jaw and straight nose. His black hair was a bit longer than before, but his smile was as kind as ever. *Mother was right. He looks so much like King Elden! I'm sure he'll rule Lagola just as well as him one day.*

Samantha worked her way around the edge of the crowd, keeping her head down and hunching over so no one would recognize her. Edric excused himself from the conversation and headed toward a curtained niche lined with windows that let in the warm summer air. *Perfect,* Samantha thought, revising her plan.

Samantha snuck behind him, raised herself up slightly on her toes, and covered his eyes with her hands. "Guess who?" she whispered playfully in his ear.

Edric spun around and grabbed her hand, looking her up and down with a shocked expression. "Can it be? All I see is a princess in front of me. Where's that muddy faced little girl I played with in Conti Wayo?" Edric teased, pulling her into a hug.

Samantha beamed up at him. "Eight years, Edric! That's a long time to be away from your friend. And you are not the most faithful pen pal, you know."

"Speaking of pen pals, did you ever get a letter of apology from my brother?"

"I'd really rather not talk about Nolan tonight." Samantha sat down on a low bench by the windows, and Edric joined her. "Goodness, but you look old! If I'm eighteen, then you're . . . twenty-two? Is that right?"

Edric smiled with pride, rubbing his jaw. Samantha noticed he had faint stubble covering it. "Yes, I am twenty-two, and my father has decided that it is high time for me to find a bride. His words, mind you." His dark brown eyes smiled down into hers. "Do you want to make it easy on me and just say yes?"

Samantha gave a loud laugh and quickly covered her mouth. "I don't think so. You are my friend, and a great one at that. But you don't make my heart flip or my toes curl or any of those other silly things my cousins assure me happens when you meet the man you are to marry." She fluttered her eyelashes at him while he looked on in bemusement. "I need to be able to tell my tutor that I tried fluttering my eyelashes at a man when he proposed marriage. It will make her so happy!"

Edric chuckled. "You look ridiculous. I only proposed before the fluttering began. Well, if you won't marry me, will you help me find a wife?"

"Of course! Though, I am not a very good matchmaker. So, buyer beware . . ."

Samantha saw her mother eyeing the two of them from across the room. She sighed. "Edric, my mother has noticed me speaking with you, and I know she has it in her mind that you will be proposing tonight. Along with many other men, if she has anything to say about it. That's the whole purpose of this ball, you know. I, too, am supposed to find a suitable spouse. Preferably this evening. Evidently, I am doomed to be a spinster at the ripe old age of eighteen." She gazed with unseeing eyes into the large room, oblivious to the glittering jewels, bright colors of gowns, and flashing eyes of potential suitors.

Edric rose and held out his hand to help her up. "There does seem to be an awful lot of men here tonight. Specially invited *single* guests?" he teased as they walked together toward the ballroom.

"Knowing my mother, definitely." She heard the musicians stop playing and watched her father walk to the front of the room. "Did your mother come with you?"

"No, she stayed home with the boys. She sent a beautiful present, though."

Samantha felt a rush of relief, knowing that she would not have to see Nolan. But suddenly, a strange sense of loss swept over her. *You detest him. Be glad he's not here,* she scolded herself. She felt Edric shake her arm gently and looked up to see everyone smiling at her.

"She is just a little shy," Bennett laughed with the crowd. "My daughter, Samantha." He paused as a round of applause sounded through the ballroom. "Escorting her tonight in her first dance is the heir apparent of Lagola, Prince Edric."

Edric bowed low to Samantha. She began to remember all of the dance lessons she was taught over the years and was determined not to make a fool of herself. *I'll show Mother I can do something with all of her training.*

Samantha felt Edric leading her to the center of the room, but stiffened, faking a smile. She could feel everyone's eyes on her.

"Relax, Sam," Edric whispered. "Just enjoy dancing with your friend before all of the scary bachelors demand a dance with you."

Samantha began to laugh quietly, feeling her body relax. "Thanks Edric. I'm glad I have you as my first dance partner. Will you be able to fend off the scary bachelors?"

His eyes twinkled. "I seem to remember that you can hold your own in a fight. But if you have need of a second, Nolan can fight for you. He's much more experienced with hand-to-hand combat than me. Being a peace-maker has certain advantages, like unbroken noses and unsoiled clothes."

The music for the first song ended and they both gracefully bowed toward each other. "It's too bad Nolan isn't here, then, isn't it?" Samantha replied sarcastically, stepping off the dance floor as other couples began to dance.

Edric looked confused. "What do you mean . . . ? Oh! No, Nolan is here. Mother stayed home with the younger boys. Acton and Ellery are down with influenza. Nolan is around somewhere. I'm sure Father has him in some ambassadorial role with all of his smooth talking skills. Sam, what's wrong?"

She felt her body go cold. *Nolan is here? How dare he show up on my birthday! And he has never, ever apologized to me for that last summer in Conti Wayo.* She realized Edric was staring at her, so she gave him a small smile.

"I think I just need some air. And water. I'll be out in the garden," she murmured as she made her way through the well dressed guests dancing around the room.

As soon as she reached the marble railing that surrounded the balcony outside, she filled her lungs with deep, soothing breaths of the warm evening air. She could smell the scent of the roses growing in the garden beneath her. Glancing back toward the ballroom, Samantha took a few steps deeper into the shadows, wishing to remain somewhat hidden from her guests, and more importantly, her mother. The scene in the library rose unbidden to her mind, and she glanced down at her hand. *The list!*

Where did it go? And what exactly did it mean? She closed her eyes, trying to remember.

"Determination, courage, helping others . . ." she gasped, suddenly recalling the first three items. A surge of emotions swept through her. She hit the cold railing, balling her hands into fists, as a flood of memories threatened to overtake her. Fighting with Nolan, sticking up for the younger children, never backing down from insult or injury during her training, surprising everyone with the skills she had in her lessons. *Well, some of my lessons,* she admitted with chagrin.

Then it hit her. She struggled to regulate her breathing, feeling an intense pressure near her heart. *My princess lessons were exactly that— lessons. I had to learn how to be a princess because my blessings were false. Mother and Talia were the ones who arranged them . . . .*

"They knew! No, not you, Taley! Not you . . ." Samantha whispered raggedly, feeling her legs going numb and threatening to give out from under her. *I will not faint. I will not embarrass myself.* Relief swept over her when her legs felt steady once again. *Is that my determination kicking in? Do I really want to test all of these things now? I should go back to the party.*

Suddenly, a tall form appeared next to her. She had to tilt her head slightly to see his face, which was shadowed in the dim light. The dark hair and square jaw looked familiar. *He's a lot like Edric, but his nose isn't as straight. It almost seems like he's been in several fights and had it broken. Oh!* A roaring sounded in her ears, and she worked to control her fists, which were twitching and sending signals to her brain. *Nolan is here. What do I say?* She did not trust what would come out of her mouth at this moment, so she waited for him to speak first.

"Why are you not dancing? Or do you prefer the romance of the moonlight and the rose garden?" Nolan's voice was low and husky as he leaned toward her.

Samantha kept her face down so he would not recognize her. "I do not enjoy dancing very much, truth be told. I much prefer the gardens."

"Walk with me then, pretty lady," Nolan suggested in a flirtatious tone.

Samantha glanced up, watching him squint his eyes tightly shut before blinking rapidly. "Something wrong?"

"No, just a slight headache. At least it was a headache, but it seems to be gone now. Come this way," he urged, taking her hand and pulling her toward the short flight of marble stairs that led down into the garden. Once again, his eyebrows lowered in pain, but it was gone as suddenly as it appeared.

Samantha allowed herself to be drawn into the garden, though every fiber of her being fought her on the decision. *Make a plan, make a plan*, she told herself as they passed the large fountain in the center of the garden.

"Are you new to the castle scene?" Nolan asked. "I don't recall seeing you at any recent balls or tournaments in Lagola. Are you a cousin of Samantha's?" He tried to get a better look at the mystery girl's face, but she shyly kept it averted from his.

"No, not a cousin. You haven't seen me lately because I usually stay at home." A sudden thought came to Samantha. "Were you not in the ballroom to see your brother dance with the princess?"

"No, unfortunately, I missed the princess's grand entrance. My father had me speaking to some of his friends on matters of state. He finds my gift . . . useful. Though, it seems to be paining me at the present." He stared up into the night sky, glancing at the silver moon and brightly shining stars.

He does not recognize me! Have I really changed that much? Edric knew me right away, but I've also sent him sketches of me over the years. Maybe he never showed Nolan. I need to distract him.

"Do you see that marble statue over there?" she asked, pointing towards the south end of the garden, away from the castle. "The one of the lady on the horse? Do you know the story of Queen Einara?"

Nolan turned toward the statue that glowed faintly in the moonlight. "I do recognize it. Would you like me to tell you the history of Queen Einara? She was a great warrior . . . ."

As soon as Nolan turned to look at the statue, Samantha scooped up a handful of mud from a nearby flowerbed, using her body to shield the weapon from Nolan's view. Out of the corner of her eye, she caught a purple shimmer of light and froze. Her mind raced to Talia, knowing what she would tell her. *She'd say that a royal should never have regrets. Would I regret this revenge on Nolan? Not revenge, justice! What would happen if I smashed mud in Nolan-the-man's face, not Nolan-the-annoying-boy's face? Embarrassment, shame, public admonishment. What could I then say? He did it to me eight years ago when we were children? Those should not be the words of a lady destined for knighthood.* Samantha's cheeks burned red with shame, and she quickly looked around for a place to hide her ammunition.

The marble fountain was only a few steps away, and she hoped she could rinse her hand before Nolan noticed. He was still reciting the history of Queen Einara with great gusto.

Samantha darted to her right, slipping on a wet stepping stone near the base of the fountain. Nolan lunged toward her, arm extended, but he also lost his balance on a slick stone, following her into the fountain with a loud splash. She opened her mouth and let loose a peal of laughter. Nolan's jaw dropped, and Samantha saw the shock in his eyes mingling with a flash of remembrance.

"Sammy? What? How—I mean—where? Let me help you," he finished, heaving himself out of the lower basin of the cold fountain and shaking himself a few times. With a grin, he extended his hand to Samantha, and she felt her breath catch in her throat when she placed her hand in his. She knew her palm, slightly calloused from training, was different from other ladies he had surely met. He apparently had no apprehension of holding tightly as he helped her out of the water. Samantha did not emerge very gracefully, but how could one expect a person to gracefully emerge while wearing a long gown and several waterlogged petticoats?

Samantha shook her head, feeling her hair tumbling down from its pins. She managed to pick out her tiara before it slid off her head. She turned it in her hands for a moment before looking up at Nolan. His hair was still dripping, a lock plastered to the side of his temple. She lifted her hand automatically to smooth it away, but caught herself before she touched him. Bringing her hand down awkwardly, she cleared her throat.

"Sam—"

"Nolan—"

They both stopped and smiled at each other.

"What were you doing, falling into that fountain?" Nolan teased her, testing the waters, as it were.

"What, women don't fall into fountains in Lagola?" Samantha grinned.

Nolan caught her hand again, aware that other guests might appear at any moment from the ballroom. "Samantha, please tell me one thing before you go. Why didn't you ever answer my letters?"

Samantha glanced down at his hand, feeling the weight of it almost burning into hers. "I didn't answer because I didn't read them," she admitted in a whisper.

Nolan increased his grip on her hand. "Why didn't you read them?" His voice was low, matching hers. "Do you hate me so much that you could not bring yourself to read a letter from me?"

Samantha pulled her hands away from his grasp and clasped them together in front of her, shivering slightly. "Not hate," she murmured. She glanced back up, feeling tears threatening to spill over. "Maybe I . . . despised you. I felt I had a good reason for it. You really were a wretched boy." Samantha sniffed, wiped her eyes, and gave a short laugh. "You asked why I was in the fountain. I was washing off my hand from the mud I was planning to throw in your face."

Nolan's jaw dropped again. "You were actually going to throw mud in my face? Naughty princess! What will your mother say?" he teased, taking a step closer to her. "And are you always so brutally honest about yourself? Not something most ladies learn."

Samantha could feel her cheeks burn from his words. "I realized that the mud would be retaliation for a ten year old girl, not justice for a now eighteen year old kni—I mean, lady." *Idiot!* she admonished herself. *You almost said knight! No one else is supposed to know about that. I promised Mother I would be a lady tonight.*

Nolan's eyes brightened with understanding. "You never read my letters because of that last day in Conti Wayo. With the mud puddle. And the," he closed his eyes for a moment, "Kick to your mouth. I remember you were bleeding. I was worried about it, but I couldn't tell you that. Did it leave a scar?"

Samantha held her breath as he touched her chin. He moved her face closer to his so that he could examine her lower lip. His eyes suddenly met hers and she could not look away. She felt the warmth of his fingers, heard the hushed sound of his breath, and watched his gaze flicker back to her lip before he suddenly stepped back. Her rapidly beating heart seemed to be out of sync with the rest of her body, and she had to remind herself to breathe again.

"The letters said that I was, no, I *am* sorry for torturing you so. Edric made sure I saw the light, as older brothers seem naturally able to do. I don't suppose that anyone ever told you that boys only tease girls—"

Nolan was cut off by a cry from the balcony.

"Samantha Culdania Faeryna Talia Jacqueleen!"

"Oh no, not again," Samantha murmured at the sound of her mother's agitated voice. She looked around, spotting several guests gawking at the dripping wet pair.

"Your majesty," Nolan called out. "It is my fault entirely. I caused the princess to, er, misstep, and she fell into the fountain. I attempted to grab her to prevent such a fall, but I fell in myself. Please don't blame her."

Adelaide's hands gripped the balustrade, the line between her eyebrows smoothing out while her lips tightened into a frown. She could not say anything, but shook her head slightly. Samantha looked over at Nolan, her eyebrows arched. He whispered, "Fairy gift. Sometimes has that effect on people."

Those words shook Samantha free from her romantic reverie. *Or whatever you call this thing that just happened with Nolan.* "Fairy gifts," she muttered, remembering the issue she had to discuss with her mother and Talia. Samantha managed some semblance of a curtsey toward Nolan, who gave a bow and slogged over to her mother on the balcony.

‡

Samantha wore a robe thrown hastily over her shoulders and paced back and forth in the short hallway outside her father's study. She could just make out the music from the ballroom and knew that she must return to her guests soon. Samantha sighed, thinking about the confrontation she was about to endure. She already knew what her mother would say, how her father would respond, and the looks Talia would give to her. *At least I got to finally talk to Nolan tonight! Only eight years later. I should have read those silly letters. Then I wouldn't have had to carry this hurt for so long. At least I was able to be honest with him, and he actually said he appreciated it. I didn't have to act like a princess and measure my words carefully. I told him exactly how I felt and did what I felt like I should do.* She stood there stunned for a moment. *I was comfortable with . . . Nolan?*

She searched her memory and realized that she could count the people she felt comfortable with on one hand. Talia, Dawes, Edric, and

Elan were the only people who saw the various facets of her personality and did not admonish her nonstop. *And I haven't even seen Edric in years, I've only written to him.* Could she add Nolan to the list of people she trusted? She shook her head violently.

"Never! He is too . . . ugh, everything! He knows how handsome he is. Plus, he's too confident, and he has that silly fairy gift. Though he does smell good . . . Stop it!" she chided herself, feeling her cheeks warm when she remembered how close his face was to hers just minutes ago.

She was relieved when Talia opened the door to the study and called her inside, if only to put away her strange thoughts of Nolan. The situation in the room was much like she would have predicted. Her mother was sitting in a high backed chair near the fireplace, her mouth pulled down in a familiar frown. Her father stood beside her, resting his arm across the top of the chair and wearing a stern expression on his face. *Be strong, Sam, be courageous*, she told herself as she stood before them, feeling a swell of resolve and strength in her body.

"Samantha, I have been told of the incident in the garden. It is unseemly for a princess to behave in such a manner—" Bennett began.

"Unseemly? It is disgraceful! It is outrageous! I demand that you issue Prince Nolan a public apology immediately, and then you shall be on restriction for a year. Maybe longer—"

"Mother, Father. Please listen to my explanation before you discipline me. At first, I was trying to pay Nolan back for all of the grief he gave me that last summer in Conti Wayo—"

"No excuses, Samantha," Adelaide interrupted, rising from her seat. Her cheeks flushed with anger. "You never take the blame for your reprehensible actions. Prince Nolan would never do something to warrant such behavior from you."

"Mother, why don't you believe me? You always take the opposite side that I am on," Samantha fought against the urge to run from the room in frustration. "You should be on my side for once in my life! He always got me into trouble over and over, and you never see it that way. But I decided to let it go tonight. I knew it would be revenge, not justice."

"Why won't you leave it alone? Why do you need to right all of these perceived wrongs in this world?" Adelaide's voice was laden with sarcasm.

Samantha answered wearily, looking down at her mother, "You know why, Mother. It's one of my gifts, isn't it? Justice for all, helping others that are in need, something like that."

Adelaide, paling, gasped in dismay while Bennett looked confused. She whipped around, staring right at Talia. "You promised that you would never tell her!"

"Mother, she didn't tell me," Samantha rushed to explain. She dropped to the floor, touching her mother's hands. The coldness and shakiness shocked her momentarily, but she continued on. "I figured it out on my own. I was in the Library of Records today and found my scrolls. Osric had given me a brief lesson on the tongue of the Ancients, and I was able to use that to decipher the wording in the scroll. It's actually one of my blessings. Learning languages . . ." Samantha's voice trailed off at the sight of her father's face, which was quickly turning from a bright red to a deep purple.

"Adelaide!" Bennett's voice boomed through the room. "What is this about? A secret blessing ceremony? You knew about this and kept it from me?"

Samantha turned to Talia for support. Talia nodded to her in dismissal and then hurried to the queen's side. The last image Samantha saw before she fled the room was Adelaide's normally composed face covered with tears.

✝

Later that evening, Samantha emerged from her bedroom. She had spent the last hour or so in a quiet corner with a cool glass of water, trying to control her racing mind. Bergette was able to fix her hair into place as she slipped on her second-best gown, uncaring of how she looked at the present time.

She made her way to the full ballroom, hoping that she would go unnoticed. She snorted at herself. *You're a head taller than all of the girls, and you're wearing a shiny tiara! No, you're not standing out at all.* She tried to ignore the murmurings as she passed the guests sitting along the walls. She sighed when she reached the raised dais at the back of the room, which was reserved for her.

Across the room, the musicians were gathered to accompany a traveling minstrel, who had arrived to sing a birthday song for Samantha. Elan approached Samantha and bowed. She smiled and invited him to sit next to her.

"I have heard this fellow is quite good, Sam. Let us sit back and enjoy the music, shall we?" Elan asked with a keen glow in his silver eyes. She noticed his shimmer looked brighter than usual.

A smile played on her lips. "No chastising, Elan? I thought that you'd have been commissioned to instruct me to behave more like Queen Einara."

Elan snorted. "I saw the whole thing. You should have given him what he had coming. A good solid punch would have been my preference. But his jaw looks rather solid, and it would have broken your hand, I'm sure. That would be a shame, seeing as you can now train fully as a knight," he finished with a whisper as the minstrel began to sing.

Samantha swallowed back her laughter as the flamboyantly dressed musician came near to the dais. His light brown hair was worn long and his clothes were ill-fitting, almost like they were made for a much larger man. He strummed his lute while glancing furtively around the room, like a ferret. He opened his mouth and a faint noise came forth, completely discordant with the musicians.

"Louder, man! We cannot hear you back here!" a voice called from across the room.

The minstrel closed his mouth and shut his eyes tightly. A noise, similar to one a cat would make if its tail had been stepped on, sounded throughout the room. Samantha and Elan looked at each other with wide eyes as the clamor increased. Samantha clamped her jaw shut and stared at the ground, refusing to laugh at this poor fellow. Osric hurried across the floor as quickly as his joints allowed him and grasped the musician around the upper arm, pulling him from the center of the room. Elan jumped up to give assistance when the minstrel began to struggle. He continued his caterwauling while being escorted from the room by several of the castle guards.

Elan returned to the dais, facing the crowd. "I am sorry that you all had to witness that . . . er, noise. It seems that the minstrel we hired became ill and his servant tried to fill in for him. Not a very good substitution, I must regrettably say. Musicians, if you will?"

The room filled with music suitable for dancing and couples flashed quickly before Samantha's eyes in a flurry of color. Elan offered his hand to her, and she gratefully took it. *I don't really care for dancing, but it's better than being stared,* she reflected as Elan spun her around on the dance floor.

Suddenly, a handsome man with hair the color of sun-bleached straw tapped Elan's shoulder. A smile lurked on his lips. "May I cut in, sir? I am Prince Linden of Synterius. I was to have a previous dance with the princess, but she was unavailable then. Is she available now?" he asked, looking directly into Samantha's wide green eyes with his pale blue ones, obviously enjoying the element of surprise.

Samantha felt a tug in the pit of her stomach at the boldness of this handsome man. Elan released her, and she seemed to float into Linden's arms. Now that she was closer, she examined his face through her lowered lashes. His icy blue eyes emphasized the sharp features of his long, thin nose and slightly pointed chin. He was only about an inch taller than her, but she noticed he stood with his shoulders properly pulled back to appear taller. His chest and arms were well-muscled, and he was quick on his feet as he led her about the dance floor.

"Do I pass inspection?" Linden murmured into her ear.

Samantha jumped back slightly. His arms held her firm as a smile settled on his lips. She watched his eyes search hers. "I didn't mean to be rude, Prince Linden. Please excuse me. I just . . . I've never seen you around before and . . . actually there's no excuse. I was curious to see what you looked like." Samantha's honest gaze met his surprised look.

He laughed. "So, the tales are true! The Princess of Mittra is unusual. Well, in light of your honesty, I will be honest as well. I was curious to see if the gossip proved to be right about you. I saw you were on the dance floor, and I thought I would stake my claim first."

"Your claim, sir?" Samantha replied playfully. *Am I flirting with this man? Talia, where are you?*

"Claim on your friendship. Until you want me to put a claim on your heart, that is," Linden whispered huskily as he twirled her under his raised arm.

Samantha became aware of how close their faces were, and her breath caught in her throat. From afar, a sight caught her eye from the side of the dance floor. Her mother was speaking quickly to Elan while gesturing toward her and Linden. Her breath came back in a rush, and she remembered all of her lessons on courtly manners.

"Sir, you speak too boldly. We have only just met, and I am quite certain your mother would not approve of your speaking like this," she gently reprimanded him while gazing down at the floor, concentrating on moving her feet in the correct patterns of the dance.

"My dearly departed mother, bless her soul, most certainly would not approve, but I am swept away by your beauty, Princess. Please forgive me. I would throw myself at your feet even now, if that would appease you."

Samantha heard the last notes of the song swelling, and with contradictory feelings, she curtseyed to Linden. "Do not throw yourself on the floor. You'll only get your pants dirty, and I'll look foolish yet again tonight. I must say goodnight and see to my mother. She is casting looks in my direction that are quite pointed."

Linden, instead of bowing, took her hand once again and pulled her close. "May I introduce you to my cousin later?"

Samantha frowned at his forward behavior and stopped dancing for a moment. He tugged her along on the dance floor and she looked at him, shocked into moving with him. "Stop dancing, sir! I am sure I am committed to dance with someone else now."

Linden gave her a sly smile. "No one would dare cut in while I am dancing with you, princess. Or do you not know of my reputation?" His blue eyes took on a chilling gleam.

Samantha shivered, pulling away from him once again. "I do not care to know of your reputation or anything more about you, actually."

"I am a dragon hunter," Linden continued, as though she hadn't spoken at all. "And I always catch my prey."

"Samantha, there you are!"

Nolan's face appeared behind Linden, and he placed a large hand on his shoulder, yanking him backwards. Nolan stepped between Samantha and Linden, sweeping her away. "Sorry Linden, old friend. She was promised to me. Find a new partner."

Samantha gasped at the icy glare in Linden's eyes as she and Nolan spun away. She thought she heard Linden say, "Just wait . . ." but she could not be sure.

Nolan directed her toward the door that led into the room filled with presents. He released her as soon as they were through the doorway, dropping the heavy draperies for privacy. Nolan glanced over at

Samantha, who was trembling in the center of the room. He muttered something about Linden under his breath as he walked toward her.

He threw his short cloak around her shoulders and tied it securely at her neck. Only then did he look into her eyes. "What did he say to you? Do I need to break his nose?" Nolan asked gruffly, only partly teasing.

Samantha shook her head, clearing it from thoughts of Linden. She tried to pull her lips into a smile. "Don't break his nose. At least not yet. He's the only man who wanted to dance with me tonight. That has to count for something, right?" She remembered the chilling look that washed over him when he spoke of catching his prey, and she shivered again. "Is he really a dragon hunter, Nolan?"

Nolan led her to a long couch set against the wall and made her sit before he answered. "He has the reputation of one, but no one has seen him actually kill one before. He talks a big game. Don't worry. Edric and I will keep you safe."

Nolan walked back to the doorway, pulled back the curtain, and motioned to someone. "Talia is coming to stay with you. Those fairies can do some damage if they need to." He winked at her.

Samantha looked up from her seat on the couch and smiled shyly at Nolan. "Thank you for, um, saving me out there. I know you'd rather not do that." Samantha glanced down and waited for him to leave.

Nolan suddenly lifted her chin up with one finger and held her gaze. "You're a smart girl, Sammy. You always have been. But, just so you know, Linden was not the only man who wanted to dance with you tonight."

With that, he turned and left the room without looking back.

☦

Samantha nodded at her last guests of the evening and hurried up to her room, unsure of the emotions swirling through her. The initial attraction to Linden was completely different from the feelings Nolan brought out in her. *Not that I have feelings for Nolan! Linden seems to be a much better choice. I don't feel the urge to smash mud in his face.*

Suddenly, she pictured Nolan's handsome face covered in mud and could not help but laugh. Her laughter was cut short when she thought of Linden's strange behavior during the second dance with her. *Maybe he was just feeling competitive? A bad night? Hopefully tomorrow will be better.* The tournament would be exciting for all attending, and Samantha would be able to see both men tomorrow.

"Not that I am comparing them or anything," she muttered to herself as she opened the door to her suite. "I just want to see them in a different situation."

Samantha sighed as she settled herself in the window seat, thinking of what she would say when she saw her parents tomorrow. *Father will be fine, but Mother? And Talia? Can I insist on the truth from them?* Samantha was struck by a sudden thought that made her gasp, almost giving her physical pain. *Who can I trust anymore?*

Silently, the tears streaked down her face until she fell asleep.

CHAPTER FIVE

*T*alia paused outside of Samantha's sitting room door, listening for any noises. Believing no one else to be inside, she opened the door and entered the room quietly. The room was gently lit with the diffused glow of the rising sun. Talia was startled to see a figure curled up on the window seat. Samantha was still wearing her gown from the previous evening, now badly wrinkled, and her hair hung in tangles around her face.

The small fairy sat at the opposite end of the window seat, waiting for Samantha to wake up. *Poor thing. Why did she sleep out here? Was she waiting for me? Or Addy?* She sighed unknowingly as she gazed out the window.

"Why, Taley?"

She turned her head to see Samantha staring at her with grief and disappointment in her eyes. "It seemed like the best choice at the time, Sammy," Talia said softly, feeling her eyes well up with tears.

"Lying is never the best choice!" Samantha burst out. "You have always told me to be honest in all my dealings. I expected the same from you. And my mother."

Talia's shimmer dimmed so much Samantha could hardly see it. "Sam, everything that you've said is true. We all thought we were protecting you and the kingdom. I do not know what else we could have done."

Samantha looked up sharply. "We? Who else knew of this, and how did it even happen? My whole life is a lie!" She struggled to stand but her legs, bent from being cramped in a small space, refused to obey her. She fell the short distance to the floor and began to sob as if her heart was breaking.

She felt Talia rub her back, just as she used to do after a particularly grueling princess lesson. Her sobs lessened and finally ceased. Samantha gave a small hiccup and raised herself up from her sprawled out position.

Talia smiled. "Shall I start at the beginning? As you know, Elan and Osric have always been competitive . . ."

✝

Samantha met with her parents, Talia, Osric and Elan in her father's study later that evening. The first several minutes were a confusion of apologies, tears, raised voices, hugs (given by Samantha) and, finally, assurances of forgiveness. The only one who remained aloof was Queen Adelaide. She remained in her seat at the far end of the large table, eyes cast down, refusing to speak to Samantha. Bennett spoke into her ear, his eyes wide with worry, but she would not be swayed.

"Well," Bennett addressed the company from the head of the table, "I am unsure of how we proceed from here. What would be in the best interest of both Samantha and Mittra? Shall we look over the list of Samantha's *true* blessings?"

Osric brought out the roll of parchment with the ancient words on it. "It might take me a few moments to translate this."

Talia held up the paper with Samantha's translation on it. "It seems that one of your gifts took a strong hold, Osric," she commented as she passed the paper to him with a smile.

Samantha blushed as Osric grinned at her, his shimmer suddenly glowing brightly. "I remember teaching you the tongue of the Ancients just once. Indeed, it was enough!"

Elan cleared his throat. "Let us not overlook all of her prowess *outside* of the library, eh, Osric? Sam, er, Princess Samantha is almost a knight. Training is almost complete. I wish you could have entered the tournament today!"

Adelaide suddenly stood up and slammed her open palm on the table. "Enough! Though the secret is now out, it must remain here. The whole reason for the secret was so no one could use Samantha as a weapon." She turned toward Samantha, looking at her for the first time that day. "Do not forsake all that you have been raised to be. A princess. A proper lady above everything else—including this knight business. Life is not a game. You must be married before this is discovered." Adelaide turned to leave the room but stopped at the sound of Samantha's voice.

"And continue to lie, Mother? To deny who I am? That has not worked so well. I am still without a suitor, even hiding behind my princess façade. I would rather be a real person and marry a man who accepts me as I am and loves me anyway!" Samantha's voice was razor sharp and rang out clearly in the still room.

Adelaide, her back still to the room, spoke, "Then you will never marry." Then, she left the room before anyone could object.

An embarrassed hush hung in the air until Bennett broke it by clapping his hands together. "That's enough! We will proceed as we always have. Samantha," Bennett addressed his daughter kindly, "You may be accompanied by Talia to the tournament grounds with Elan as your escort, of course. In your squire attire, please. Honor your mother by not appearing as 'Princess Samantha' down on the field," he said with a wink. "You are all free to go. I have to set some matters of my house in order."

Samantha rose and gave her father a shaky smile. *Why can't Mother be more like Father? Why must she speak so hatefully to me? It's not like I chose my fairy gifts!* She took a deep breath and tried to clear her mind from the emotional cobwebs clinging there.

Elan came over and patted her shoulder awkwardly. "If you can be ready in fifteen minutes, Squire, I will wait for you and Miss Talia at the side entrance."

"I will be ready," Samantha promised, practically running to her room down the hall.

Bergette was straightening up the sitting room when Samantha burst in.

"Will you please help me, Bergette? I need to dress for the tournament immediately!"

Bergette flew into action, not making any comments or rolling her eyes for the first time that Samantha could remember. She withdrew Samantha's vest, shirt, and pants from the wardrobe, handing them to her lady as needed. Bergette pulled the bag with Samantha's helmet off the floor with a grunt, and a flash of white flew out with it.

"What's this, miss?" Bergette questioned, holding up a bundle of letters with one eyebrow raised.

Samantha felt her cheeks turn warm as she reached for the letters. "Just some old letters. I forgot they were in there," she murmured as she slid them into the drawer of her dressing table. Then, she sat down in front of her mirror.

Bergette's eyes gleamed with recognition but remained silent as she braided Samantha's hair, coiling it in a bun on the back of her head. She gave the bun a little pat of satisfaction and met Samantha's eyes in the mirror.

"Not wanting to speak out of turn, Princess Samantha, but I have known you since you were a small girl." She paused, waiting for Samantha to stop her. When she did not, the maid continued. "I've also seen the princes from Lagola grow up over the years, and I have friends in Lagola still who keep me informed. Even though we've not seen Prince Nolan in several years, I think he's grown to be quite handsome. He is not the same little ruffian who used to soil your gowns and such. Oh, I know about all those things. Little boys love to torment girls they secretly like. Didn't you know such things?" she laughed at the surprise that sprang into Samantha's wide eyes. "Of course not, not having brothers of your own. I know this tournament is important to you, being your first one and all, but be cautious around those two princes."

"What two princes, Bergette?" Samantha asked, her stomach unexpectedly clenching.

Bergette waggled her index finger as Samantha rose, grabbing her bag. "The servants have eyes and ears, don't we? You know I mean Prince Nolan and Prince Linden. Rumor has it that Prince Linden was likely to challenge Prince Nolan to a duel."

Samantha laughed. "A duel for interrupting a dance? No one would be that foolish!"

Bergette laid her plump hand on Samantha's arm. "The guards have told me that there is some bad blood between those two. Something about a dragon hunt. They are very competitive, and I don't want you to get in the middle of a bad thing such as that. You will be careful, won't you?"

Samantha bent and hugged her maid, who looked shocked at the gesture. "I will take all you say to heart, Bergette. Oh my, I'm sure Elan is waiting!"

‡

"But, Taley, won't the guests from last night recognize me?" Samantha whispered as they approached the random assortment of tents on the tournament grounds. "My father specifically said I must not bring shame upon my mother and be seen as the princess, but I can't go wearing my helmet when I'm not on a horse!"

Talia looked over at Elan, who smiled and nodded. "Elan and I talked it over. We have a plan. We'll both work together and create a haze about you so that no one notices your face clearly. Just a vague sort of shape. No one will be able to tell the color of your eyes or give a good description of what you look like. Is that agreeable to you?"

Samantha grinned. "Agreeable? Of course! Then I will really be free to walk about and see all that is happening here on the tournament grounds. Oh, but what of my voice?"

Elan frowned. "I don't know any spells for that at the moment. I should have thought of that."

Talia shook her head. "I didn't consider that either. Just try not to talk very much. Your voice is not low enough to pass for a man's, and you are too tall to be considered a boy. Ready, Elan? Stand still, Sam . . ."

Samantha stood still as a ticklish feeling swept over her face. "I feel sort of tingly. Did it work?"

Talia and Elan both nodded, silly grins on their faces.

"We can see through it if we concentrate on your face, but no one else should be able to," Talia assured her.

Samantha burst out, "I see Dawes up ahead! I suppose Palmer is here as well. I'm sure Dawes is excited to be his brother's squire for his first tournament."

The small group reached the red and white striped tent without incident. Samantha peeked her head into the closed opening and then pushed the flap back wide with a gasp.

"Palmer! What happened?" Samantha rushed into the tent, kneeling beside the knight lying on a blanket on the dirt floor of the tent. "Taley, remove the haze spell, please!"

Palmer looked up, his handsome face creased in pain. "Stupid horse.

He decided he didn't want to practice today, so he threw me off. And then he stepped on my leg. Dawes went for a doctor but if it's broken, there's no way I can enter the tournament."

Palmer looked past Samantha at Elan and Talia. "Fairies can heal, can't they?"

Elan nodded. "To some extent. I've never mended a broken bone before. Have you, Talia?"

"No, but my mother told me tales of other fairies doing it with rather … disastrous results. Headaches and stomach flu are much easier to heal. May I check it?" Talia bent down at Palmer's nod.

Samantha looked on with bated breath. "What happens to your position in the tournament if you can't compete today, Palmer?"

Palmer spoke through his clenched teeth, his dark hair falling into his eyes. "I'd have to drop out and try to get into the tournament circuit next year. That's the problem. My family needs the money from this event so that I can enter again . . ." his voice faded as his face contorted in pain.

Talia whispered a spell over him and his brown eyes slowly closed. "At least he'll sleep for a while, pain free. The leg is broken. Palmer cannot compete today."

Dawes entered the tent just as Talia was speaking. His face turned a ghastly grey and he gave a yelp. "Can't compete? But, he needs to! We need the money." He began to pace back and forth in the small tent. With wild eyes, he turned toward Samantha. "Sam, think of something!"

Samantha narrowed her eyes at him. "Like what, Dawes? How am I to get your family money right now? It's not like I can enter the tournament for him." She watched his eyes go wide. "Why are you staring at me like that?" she asked warily, looking from Dawes to Elan and back again.

Elan smiled and stroked his beard. "You do have your birthday present. Dawes, run and fetch it!" Dawes nodded and ran out of the tent with a grin on his face. "You can wear Palmer's colors. I'll squire you myself once Dawes returns. Are you feeling well, Sam?"

Samantha sank to the ground, face pale and sweaty. "Feeling well? No, I can't say that I am, Elan. My mother would kill me if she found out I am entering the tournament!"

Talia knelt beside the princess and took her cold hands into her own. "Sammy, you don't have to do this. I've made a promise to your parents to care for you. You could be severely hurt out there. Elan, do not encourage her or make her promise to do something she does not want to do. You can see she is unwell at merely the thought of it!"

Samantha glanced over at Palmer and sighed. "But if it will help Palmer and Dawes . . . I must help. Yes, Elan, I have you to thank for that gift," Samantha grumbled at the fairy with the proud look on his face. "Talia, I should be fine. As long as no one knows it's me out there."

"The haze should hold up for quite a while, even through the awards ceremony," Elan responded. "To earn the prize money, you must at least place. Third place is your aim," he assured Samantha as she stood up again, leaning slightly on Talia.

"Third? I always aim for first, Elan," Samantha retorted with a wicked grin. "You should know that; you trained me."

‡

Thirty minutes later, Samantha was in her shiny new armor, saddled on the back of Windstorm with Palmer's colors draped over the horse's body.

Elan checked her equipment over one last time. "You appear to be ready to go, Sam. Just remember to lock your lance into your saddle and sit up straight. Just like practice."

Samantha gave a small smile. "Except that I don't feel like vomiting before practice. Okay, I'm ready for the spell again. I'll put on my helmet after you make sure the spell works."

Dawes approached the group a few moments later. "Excuse me,

Master Elan. Have you seen Sam?"

Samantha began to laugh from her perch. "Up here, Dawes!"

Dawes gazed up at the knight in the bright armor with a confused look on his face. "Sam? Why do you look like a man but sound like a girl? Are my eyes going bad?" he spun around towards Elan and Talia. "Tell me I'm not crazy!"

Elan patted Dawes' shoulder. "No, squire. Just a bit of fairy magic is all. A bit of fog to confuse those who look at Sam, just as you did, so that the princess does not get into any trouble with the queen."

Dawes looked relieved but worried at the same time. "Oh good. Sam, I just wanted to wish you good luck. I know Palmer would say the same if he was awake. The doctor set his leg a few minutes ago, and he passed out from the pain. I think I'll go stay with him for awhile, but I'll watch you when it's your time to compete." He paused and then burst out, "It should be me taking Palmer's place! If I was only good enough, you wouldn't have to do this, Sam. You're going to be the queen one day, and if anybody finds out it's you out there . . . I'm dead! Your mother will murder me and then torture me and then leave my bones for the wolves to pick over!" He punched the fence post and then cradled his sore hand.

"Dawes!" Samantha spoke sharply in a regal voice. "Stop it at once!"

Dawes, Talia, and Elan all stared up at her. Elan found his voice first. "Well done, princess. I do see the Queen Einara in you."

Samantha placed the helmet on her head but left the visor up. "Thank you, Elan. That felt good. Now Dawes, I'll do my best for your family. *You* must be calm and sensible, or I shall be a wreck as well." She nodded to Elan and Talia. "Thank you, both of you. I could not do this without you. And seeing as this is probably my last time to compete in a tournament before I am forced to marry or locked in an attic, I'll put everything I've got into it!"

‡

Windstorm moved restlessly at the rails of the tournament grounds, and Samantha patted his neck soothingly. "We're next, boy. Just like practice. We've done this before. You just run fast and I'll do the rest. I hope . . ." she whispered as she watched knight after knight run down the field toward the brass rings tied to the cross-arms near the stands, eagerly reaching for the small ring with their lance. Each knight had five runs, and the ten knights with the most rings moved on to the next round.

Once Palmer's colors were waved, Samantha rode Windstorm out to the middle of the field to salute the royal box. The empty chair next to her mother set off a dull echo of *fraud* in her mind. *You are not a knight, you are a princess. You should be up there!* She took a deep breath as her father raised his hand and nodded to her. *Keep it together, Sam. This is not for you. It's for Dawes. It's for Palmer. Do your best.* Windstorm softly nickered at her, and she smiled inside her helmet.

"Let's go, boy!" Samantha murmured as she pressed her heels into the horse's sides.

Windstorm responded with a burst of speed. Samantha sat up in her saddle and automatically lifted her right arm, aiming for the center ring. *It seems so much smaller out here. Focus, Sam. Yes!*

The applause from the crowd echoed in her helmet. She felt the sweat run down her neck. *One down, four to go . . .*

‡

"Excellent job. Really well done!" Elan praised her as she joined the other knights in the corral.

Samantha raised her visor and reached for the cup of water Talia held up to her. "Thank you, Elan, but I should have had that last one. The wind blew it just as I was aiming for it. Very unlucky."

A herald blew three short notes on his trumpet and then announced with a booming voice, "The ten knights who will continue on will be . . ."

"Did you make it, Sa—um, Sir Palmer?" Dawes corrected as he rushed up to the corral fence. The other knights shot him dirty looks.

"Shhh! We're waiting to hear," Samantha hissed, motioning for him to stay back.

". . . Prince Linden of Synterius, Prince Nolan of Lagola, and Sir Palmer of Mittra. Please assemble at the far end of the field immediately."

Samantha handed the cup down and returned the wink Elan gave her. "Once more into the fray," she murmured as she took her place at the end of the line.

Pages and squires rushed out to the field to set out the next target. It was a quintain that had a rather small target and a rather large sandbag on either end.

"Not just like practice," Samantha mumbled, considering the right way to approach this part of the competition. "Windstorm, I must ask you once again to run like your namesake. Oooh!" she groaned with the other knights and the onlookers. The first knight failed to outrun the spinning arm of the quintain and was knocked out of his saddle by the heavy sandbag.

"Sir Diggory is out," the herald announced dispassionately.

Samantha caught sight of Dawes lurking among the other squires near the quintain. Even from afar, she could see him pacing and biting his nails. *Yuck, Dawes! Do you even know how dirty your fingers are? Stop pacing! You're making me nervous.* She waved at him and he looked straight at her. She held up her hand, motioning for him to stop. He froze and ducked his head in embarrassment.

Samantha glanced over to the rider in front of her, his face hidden by his visor. *Could that be Nolan? Or Linden?* She had been too overwhelmed to look for the colors earlier. She remembered to lower her own visor just as the rider looked back at her. *I believe that the fog is working, but I'd rather not test it out here,* she thought as the other knight nodded at her. She nodded back and then turned her eyes over to the royal box. Her father was chatting with King Elden while her mother sat with her ladies-in-waiting, silently observing the tournament. *Don't look, Sam. It's almost your turn!*

The next three knights easily hit the target and avoided the sandbag, securing their spots in the next round of competition. The fifth knight missed the target completely and was booed off the field. The sixth knight barely hit the target when his horse reared up, dumping the knight off his back and cantering away.

Samantha refused to laugh along with the crowd and patted Windstorm instead. "Almost, boy. Keep it steady. If you don't dump me off, I'll give you extra oats!" she promised while the seventh knight evaded the sandbag, hitting the target.

Samantha noticed King Elden turn from his conversation as the knight with the blue and silver colors rode out. *This must be Nolan!* She didn't realize she was holding her breath until he defeated the quintain. He raised his hand toward his father, who began to clap loudly.

Would my parents applaud for me if they knew it was really me? I'd like to believe so . . . Last competitor before my turn. Oh, dear. That sandbag looks like it really hurts.

"Let's not do that, Windstorm. Ready? Go!" Samantha dug her heels in and her horse shot across the field. Lifting her lance and tucking it under her arm, she lifted herself up in the saddle and leaned forward, exactly as Elan and Sir Cabot had taught her to do. She struck the target exactly in the middle and squeezed Windstorm again for an extra burst of speed to avoid the sandbag. *I made it through one more round. I'm actually enjoying this more than I thought I would. Maybe I'll be able to give Dawes and Palmer something when this is all over.*

The herald came forward once more. "The remaining six knights will have one hour to rest and water their horses before the next event."

‡

85

"Last go round, Sam," Elan said in an encouraging voice. He removed her armor to allow her to rest and stretch. "Just do exactly what you did last time and you'll make it into the final three!"

Samantha groaned as she lifted her arm and turned it in circles. "Why do these lances feel so much heavier than the ones in practice? My arm is incredibly sore! No, Taley, don't use magic to heal it. No one else has magical fairies with them."

Talia smiled in appreciation at Samantha. "You are incredibly honorable, Sammy. Not many knights would turn down fairy magic."

Samantha sighed. "Why start to cheat now when I've come so far without it? I must get back out there."

She left Palmer's tent with her helmet under her arm, heading toward the corral. She paused when she heard raised voices behind the tent. Peering around the corner, she saw Linden and Nolan standing toe to toe, angry looks on their faces. *Bergette was right! There's something between these two.*

"I was dancing with her first, Lagola. Don't you dare cut in again." Linden glowered at the other man. "Understand?" His voice strained as he pointed his finger in Nolan's face.

"The lady was done dancing with you, Synterius. I heard her say it myself. If you mess with Princess Samantha, you'll answer to me. Do *you* understand?" Nolan's voice was menacingly soft. His eyes narrowed as he looked down at the shorter man.

"You don't own her, and I don't recall hearing any announcements last night. Don't you have enough women following you around, or do you need another trophy for your collection?" Linden sneered. "Just what I thought. I'll see you out on the field, Lagola. When I take first."

His broad shoulders pushed past Nolan. Samantha watched as Nolan scowled at his departing figure. She turned to avoid eye contact with either man, but in her haste, she accidentally dropped her helmet. It clattered as it rolled under a tent door.

Nolan spun around and saw a figure kneeling on the ground, reaching into the tent next to him. "Can I help you?" he asked gruffly as the knight stood up, looking down at his helmet.

"No, sir. I'll just be going on my way," The knight started to turn when Nolan caught his upper arm.

"*Samantha?*"

She glanced up at him with fearful eyes, not daring to speak again. *What about the haze? Did it wear off?*

"Why are you down here on the tournament field dressed as a *man*? Do your parents know you're here? This is no place for a princess!" Nolan's voice grew louder and louder and the pressure on her arm increased.

"You're hurting me!" she mumbled, pulling her arm away. "And keep your voice down!" She huffed and crossed her arms. "Yes and no. My father knows I'm down here, my mother does not. I was disguising myself so no one would know I'm the princess."

"And . . .?" Nolan demanded, crossing his arms and staring down at her.

"And nothing!"

"Then why are you sweaty and dirty?" he challenged. "And smell like a horse?" he added after pointedly sniffing the air around her.

Samantha gasped at him. She pulled off one of her gloves and smacked him across the face with it. "That was incredibly rude! Did I say that to you? Because you smell bad, too!"

Nolan grabbed the glove out of her hand and threw it behind her. "I am a knight and have been in a competition," he growled. "It's expected. Tell me now or I will tell your mother what you've been doing!" His face contorted with pain and he gritted his teeth.

"What is your problem?" Samantha demanded, glancing over her shoulder for any onlookers.

"My problem is you! Whenever I talk to you, I get a massive

headache. No, that's not what I meant . . ." Nolan sighed, rolling his eyes.

Samantha could see the herald climbing the steps to the platform. "I'll talk quickly, so listen. I was just helping Sir Palmer."

"And how do you know Palmer?"

"He's Dawes' brother."

"Who is Dawes?" Nolan asked, exasperated.

"Dawes is a friend! Really, I must go," Samantha insisted as Elan motioned rapidly to her. "The tournament is starting again. Don't you need to go as well?" She hurried away without waiting for an answer.

"A friend? What kind of friend?" Nolan called, scowling at the curious looks others shot him as they passed. He pulled out his amulet and frowned at it. "So much for cutting through fairy magic. Worthless trinket!" He stuffed it back into his pocket. "Squire! Bring out my helmet!"

‡

"Miss Talia, now they have to tally up all of the scores for all of the events. If a rider was thrown off, did not retrieve the rings, or missed the quatrain, points are deducted. Sam has done really well, but I don't know if she'll place . . ." Dawes began to gnaw on his fingernails once again, pacing in front of Palmer's tent.

Talia whispered a spell, and Dawes' face eased into a relaxed smile, his eyes half closed. She watched as his hand fell away from his mouth. "She has done quite well. You need to keep a calm head, Dawes. Nervousness won't help Sammy at all. Oh, I see the herald."

Talia and Dawes surged forward with the crowd of pages, squires, and knights, anticipating the news.

"Hear ye! Hear ye! The top three knights will be awarded their prize by the lovely Princess Samantha! When you hear your name, please come forward."

Talia turned with wide eyes, searching the crowd for Samantha and Elan. *There! By the corral!* She frantically motioned to them, and they came running over.

"Taley, what is it?" Samantha gasped. "Does my mother know?"

"No, but she soon will if you don't change into a gown and clean up!" Dawes exclaimed. "You're supposed to give the winners a prize!"

Samantha's mouth dropped open as her face paled. "I'll need a bit of fairy magic to accomplish that! But . . . did I place? Or, rather, did Sir Palmer place?"

The foursome turned to hear the herald's next announcement. "First place goes to Prince Linden of Synterius, second place to Prince Nolan of Lagola, and third place to Sir Palmer of Mittra. Please advance toward the royal box."

Talia and Elan huddled together for a quick moment. Elan looked up and stared at Dawes. "Yes, that would work. Quick, to the tent, man!"

Dawes felt Elan dragging him toward Palmer's tent. "But, what are we doing? Shouldn't we help Sam? Master Elan, what is happening?"

Elan pushed Dawes into the tent and began to throw Samantha's armor at him. "Stop talking and put this on. This is helping Samantha. And your brother, too, for that matter. How can 'Sir Palmer' accept a prize from Princess Samantha? Only one way. You are now Sir Palmer."

Palmer stared up at his brother. "You competed for me? I thought you said that you couldn't do it—"

"I'll explain later," Dawes muttered. He managed to throw the hauberk and cuirass over his head, and then began attaching the vambraces to his forearms. "Is this enough? I don't have time to put everything on!"

Elan tossed the helmet to the squire and frowned at him. "I'll put the fog over you as well, but be sure to keep your helmet on. It wouldn't do for this to fail now. Quickly run over to the corral and mount Windstorm. And don't fidget or chew your fingernails or any other thing that 'Sir Palmer' wouldn't do." Elan spoke the words for the spell and clapped

Dawes on the shoulder. "Go now and don't embarrass your brother!"

Meanwhile, Talia and Samantha hurried into a tent intended for the ladies-in-waiting to rest in from the heat of the day.

"Remove your outer clothing. I'm sure I can find a suitable garment somewhere in here," Talia opened a trunk and shook out a dress, frowning at it. "It will be a bit short, but it will have to do."

Samantha undressed and dressed in record time. She uncoiled her hair from the sweaty mass on the back of her head and wiped her face and hands with a wet cloth. "I'm ready, Taley. Work your magic!"

Talia's eyes closed for a moment. She wrinkled her nose before she began to whisper strange words. Samantha realized that she could understand them. *A dress for a princess, let this be. Fitted, polished, wrinkle free. Hair of gold, tangled and dirty. Cleaned and combed, bright and pretty.*

Samantha raised her eyebrows at this. "*Pretty?*"

Talia scowled. "Can you think of a better rhyme right now? Now hold still."

Samantha held her breath as she felt a rush of wind surround her, pulling her in several directions at once. Just as suddenly as it started, it was finished. "How do I look?" she whispered, feeling slightly dizzy.

The fairy smiled at her. "Presentable. Now we must hurry out to the field!"

The two emerged from the tent, walking quickly toward the royal box.

"Talia! What about 'Sir Palmer'? How do I give him an award?"

Talia hushed her. "Elan took care of that. Look, there they are!"

Three horses stood in front of the royal box, their riders all wearing helmets. Samantha could see Linden and Nolan's faces, but the third rider kept his visor down. She glanced at the hands holding the reins and saw the fingernails chewed down to bloody stubs. It was Dawes. She struggled to keep the smile off her face as she walked onto the field. She crossed to stand near Osric, who was standing near the table that held the prize money.

"Prince Linden," Samantha called out. The prince dismounted, bowing first toward the royal box and then to her. "Prince Nolan. And Da—Sir Palmer," she finished, her cheeks flushed.

Osric murmured in her ear, "Gentlemen, thank you for competing today."

"Gentlemen, thank you for competing today," Samantha echoed in a loud voice.

"Allow me to bestow a gift upon you," Osric intoned, and Samantha repeated.

Linden stepped forward as she held out a small purse filled with coins. "For you, Prince Linden," Samantha said with a curtsey.

"Would you care to bestow any other gift upon me?" he questioned in a low voice, a spark shining in his eyes.

Samantha's stomach twisted as she saw Nolan step forward, a fury in his eyes. "I warned you off, Synterius!"

Linden spun around to face him. "As I said before, you don't have any right!"

Both men lunged at each other but suddenly froze in mid-air, arms extended out. Samantha turned to see Osric muttering as Elan ran out to the field, his lips moving rapidly.

King Bennett stood up. "Gentlemen! That is quite enough. Save your aggression for the field, please. Osric, Elan, if you will?"

The fairies nodded to one another, their shimmer bright as they uttered the counter spell. Linden and Nolan both fell to the ground.

Linden rose first and growled, "Just wait until your fairy friends aren't around to protect you, Lagola. I'll break your nose again!"

Nolan laughed in derision as he stood up. "Anytime, Synterius. It's happened before, but like a wise man once said, 'You can fix a broken nose, but you cannot fix stupid.' *I* don't walk into my own dragon trap."

91

Linden's pale face flushed. "You dare say that to my face?"

Nolan drawled out, "You want to have the reputation of a dragon hunter, but the only thing you've caught is yourself . . ."

Linden threw himself at Nolan with such speed and ferocity that the fairies did not have time to act. Samantha stood there in shock, holding the money bag, unsure of what exactly to do. She glanced up at her father, whose mouth was gaping wide. Linden and Nolan continued to punch one another savagely as they rolled in the dirt.

Huffing, Samantha threw the bag to the ground and ran over to the edge of the field where a bucket of water sat. Lifting it carefully, she hurried back to the two figures wrestling on the ground.

"Stop it," she cried but to no avail. She tossed the water onto the men. They instantly fell apart, spewing out the water that filled their lungs. "Is this any way for two grown men to act in front of a princess?"

Samantha noticed the complete silence of the crowd. She raised her eyes once again to the royal box with trepidation. Her father stood there in astonishment while her mother's eyes rolled back in her head as she fainted. King Elden stood up beside his friend and gazed down at her for what seemed like eternity. Slowly, deliberately, he began to clap. Bennett shook his head as if to clear it and began to clap as well.

The applause gradually filled the stands as other men rose to their feet. Samantha kept her eyes on her father, avoiding the looks from the doused princes or the audience.

King Bennett raised his hands for silence and then spoke. "It seems we men must be reminded by the fairer sex what is appropriate behavior. Gentlemen," he spoke sternly to Nolan and Linden, "Though I hesitate to use that term at the moment. Please receive *only* your prize money and leave the field. Sir Palmer," Bennett spoke to the helmeted knight. "I appreciate your decorum in front of my daughter. That concludes our tournament today!" He fixed his eye on Samantha and tilted his head in a gesture she knew meant, *Come here now.*

Samantha sighed and stepped off the field, consciously keeping her eyes from meeting anyone else's. *Mother will have my head for this. Even when I try to do something right, like keeping two men from killing each other, I make myself look like a fool. I should just lock myself up in the tower so no one has to deal with me. Stupid girl!*

She lifted her eyes up and saw Palmer's striped tent. "Well, I might be a fool, but at least I was able to help a friend," she consoled herself, walking towards the large tent reserved for her father and his honored guests.

CHAPTER SIX

"Samantha."

"I'm so sorry, Father! I know you specifically asked me not to dishonor Mother, and you know I would never try to dishonor the crown or our family's name. If I could show you why I did what I did—"

Bennett cut off his daughter's frantic speech. "Samantha, stop for a moment. I am not going to sentence you to death."

She raised her eyes up to his. "Or lock me in the tower?"

He stroked his beard. "Now there's a thought . . ." He burst out with laughter at the worried look on his daughter's face. "Lock you in the tower for stopping a fight? How would that be just? No, no. I was thinking that it might be best to send you away, if only for a little while."

Samantha's face paled. "Have I angered you and Mother that much?" she questioned, feeling queasy again.

"I am not angry at you, child. However, I do believe that you and Mother need to have some time apart from each other. I am well aware of the fact that you two do not see eye to eye on most matters. Perhaps if you were to join the other royals on this tournament circuit, with Talia of course, you might meet some . . . new friends."

Samantha searched her father's eyes. "And by friends, you mean a husband?"

Bennett cleared his throat. "Er, yes. That is, if you want to find one. But friends are good, too." He paused a moment, looking at her. "Sam, dear, I do not want to be harsh but . . . Do you have any friends? Friends that are not fairies or squires, that is?"

Samantha frowned, deep in thought. *Of course I have friends. There's . . . No, I can't count any of the knights, either.* She sighed and looked up at her father. "I must confess I do not have any friends who are ladies. All of my cousins from Harak are silly girls who I cannot stand. No one here in Mittra understands me. Most people are afraid of me! And today didn't do anything to improve their thinking, I'm sure."

Bennett snapped his fingers. "I've got it! Prince Linden has cousins who are princesses. The tournament circuit is traveling all the way to Synterius, so you will have an opportunity to meet them. There has to be at least one sensible girl in the bunch."

Samantha smiled. "I do remember the prince asking last night if he could introduce me to his cousin, but I won't get my hopes up just yet. When are we to leave?"

"In two days time. Have Talia and Bergette pack your clothing for you. They will have a better idea of what will be proper for a trip such as this. Balls and feasts are sure to happen as you travel to these tournaments, and I'm sure you will be something of a novelty on your first excursion around the continent. Now, Sam, do not give me that look. Maybe you've been too comfortable here in Mittra. I had agreed with your mother to keep tournaments away for as long as I could, but I think it's time to let you have a bit of freedom. Just keep up with all of your lessons as your mother would have you do." He folded her into his arms.

Samantha squeezed him back. "I will do just as you say, Father," she whispered before she left the tent.

"Well, Osric?" Bennett called out.

Osric wore a sheepish smile as he entered the tent. "Excuse me your majesty. I just wanted to be able to give you proper counsel on this matter with the princess. As a matter of state, who the princess chooses to marry can carry heavy consequences."

Bennett exhaled noisily. "I do know that, old friend. Tell me more about this Prince Linden. Is he one to watch out for?"

Osric rolled his eyes. "A young braggart, that one. He claims to be a dragon hunter, but no one has actually seen him kill one of the beasts. He just appears with the carcass and collects payment from the dragon-plagued country. But he is handsome and may eventually inherit the Synterius throne, since King Aspen only has daughters."

Bennett frowned and began to pace back and forth. "Aspen did tell me about his nephews. How old is the other boy?"

Osric glanced down at his sheaf of parchment. "Hawthorn is just fourteen years old. The brother of King Aspen, Prince Alder and his wife, Princess Acacia, both died seven years ago from the bilious fever that swept through Synterius. The king took in his nephews and established the eldest, Linden, as his heir apparent. Popular opinion is that he is young and reckless but can be groomed into a reputable ruler." Osric looked up at Bennett. "And he does seem quite taken with our princess."

Bennett ceased his pacing and gave Osric an odd look. "Indeed. That is one of the reasons I am sending her out on this circuit. Time will tell if the two should indeed wed. If only . . . No, no. That would be too much to hope for . . ."

"May I ask what that would be, sire?" Osric questioned with a smile. "Something involving the heir to Lagola?"

Bennett shook his head. "I had hopes for Edric and Samantha when they were younger. They are always friendly to one another, but even I can see she does not *shine* with any one the way she does with his brother. They pretend to hate each other but . . . never mind, Osric. Just the ramblings of a father." He clapped his hands together. "Call King Elden and Prince Edric in, Osric. My plan needs a little help."

‡

Edric sat back from the table, eyes and mouth open wide in astonishment. "You want *me* to monitor Samantha on her husband hunt?"

Bennett's face colored. "Now, I did not expressly say a 'husband hunt,' as you called it—"

"Edric, we can call it a wife hunt for you boys, but we must have a little more respect for the princess," Elden interrupted.

Edric stood up and looked at Bennett. "Sir, I am sorry if I offended you. I suppose I was taken off guard by the request. I will certainly watch out for Sam like she was my own sister."

Catching the look that passed between the two kings, Edric groaned. "I do not have romantic feelings toward Samantha!"

Elden raised his eyebrows. "Yet you said you proposed to her?"

Edric blushed and stammered, "Y-Yes. But it was a joke! Not that marriage proposals are a joke . . . Oh brother . . ."

Bennett and Elden both began to laugh as Edric covered his face with his hands.

"All I ask is that you keep her safe. I don't like the idea of Nolan and that prince from Synterius fighting over her," Bennett spoke soberly.

Edric nodded in agreement. "They are both competitive, and I'm afraid that Sam is the object they both want at the moment. Who knows? A few weeks together might cool their fire. We'll be meeting plenty of girls on the, er, 'goodwill tour.' Another girl might come along and turn their heads."

‡
‡

Samantha took a last look around her bedroom, checking to make sure she had all of her personal things put away before leaving. *Who knows how long this trip will take?* She wandered over to her dressing table, touching the various bottles and combs set out on the surface. She saw a piece of parchment sticking up out of the drawer and felt her cheeks burn. *The letters! I should hide those better.*

She had just removed the letters from the drawer when her mother entered her room. Samantha thrust them into the pocket of her skirt and held her hands behind her back, unsure of what to say.

Adelaide stood in front of her daughter for several long moments, looking at her face. She sighed and turned toward the tapestry hanging on the wall. "Do you remember how much you hated this tapestry when you were young?" she asked quietly. "That seems so long ago . . ."

"I remember I stayed up late at night thinking of ways to 'accidentally' destroy it." Samantha's laughter died out at the sadness in her mother's eyes. "Mother, I didn't actually *do* anything to it. It seemed to symbolize everything that was wrong with me. All of the things you wanted me to be, and I just . . . couldn't be those things. I understand why you are sending me away." She turned away so the tears streaming down her face could not be seen.

Adelaide clutched her chest and choked back a sob. "I'm not sending you away, Samantha. You must think I'm some kind of monster." She took a ragged breath and crossed the room to where Samantha stood, taking both of her hands.

"I have never thought you were a monster." Samantha threw her arms around her mother, feeling her sobs echoing through her body.

After a few minutes, Samantha pulled away and gave her mother a watery smile. "I'm so sorry about what happened on the field today. I was thinking about honoring you and then when those two boys started fighting, all I could think about was stopping them. Why are boys so stupid?"

Adelaide gave a little laugh as she led her daughter into the sitting room, guiding her onto the couch. "Don't be so harsh on them, Samantha. They were doing what men do—fighting over a beautiful woman. Did I shock you, my dear? Again, I must apologize for my lack of motherly affection. Not that I don't love you . . . How do I explain this?"

Samantha shook her head. "Mother, I've always known you loved me. What mother doesn't love her daughter?"

The queen sighed. "Unfortunately, I learned that from my own mother. She was raised very formally, and my siblings and I were raised in the same manner. It's odd, but I don't remember her hugging me or ever saying she loved me." She paused. "Do not look so sad, my dear! I suppose we can all learn new things. You are a shining example of that." Her eyes took on a luminous glow as she smiled at Samantha. "You have so much to be proud of. I am sorry that I never told you that before. Your father and I talked . . . argued, really. I must admit I am rather stubborn. I know you have the fairy gift of determination, but some of that might be old-fashioned inherited stubbornness!"

Samantha laughed with her mother this time. "Mother, I can't remember ever laughing with you before. It's too bad that I'm leaving now that we have an understanding. But I should go out and meet new people, as Father said. Mittra doesn't get many visitors, and I came to the sad realization that I don't have any girl friends besides Talia!"

Adelaide wore a look of chagrin. "It's my fault for not encouraging friendships for you. I thought that if you were around your Harakian cousins, you would eventually become more like them. As you can see, I didn't fully understand how fairy gifts work and the power they hold. And do not breathe a word of this to Elan or Osric, but I do rather like your gifts now."

Samantha's jaw dropped. "What? You like . . . *What?*"

Adelaide patted her daughter's hand and leaned in closer. "I wish I had your fire and spirit. You have so much . . . I don't know…a glow about you at times. I can only imagine that is the Queen Einara in you. If this country is to have a queen, it must have one who has all of the gifts you've been given. Giggling and growing long fingernails are not important aspects to ruling a country." She paused and looked into her daughter's eyes. "Be true to who *you* are, Samantha. In your friendships, in politics, and in . . . love. Oh, I see the way Nolan was looking at you at the ball. I do not suppose you find him to be a 'horrid, stupid boy' anymore?" She laughed at the blush on Samantha's cheeks. "Just be careful as you begin your journey. There are many pitfalls along the way."

A knock sounded on the door and Talia peeked her head into the room. She looked relieved when she saw the queen and her daughter sitting there. "I apologize for the interruption but the carriage is ready, Sammy. Do you have any last minute things to pack?"

Samantha shook her head as she stood. "No, I believe I am ready as I'll ever be. Goodbye, Mother!" she cried, wrapping her arms around Adelaide once more.

Adelaide felt the tears sting her eyes once again. "Write to me when you arrive at your first stop. I want to know everything. Well, probably *not* everything." She smiled at Samantha and Talia. "Just gossipy sorts of things. Preferably not fighting or fountain drenching or things of such a nature."

Samantha winked at her mother as she left the room. "I always try to be good, Mother. Bad things just seem to happen to me . . . ."

‡

"Sammy, dear. Wake up," Talia nudged the princess, who was sleeping on the carriage seat next to her. "We are here."

Samantha slowly opened her eyes while, stretching in the limited confines of the carriage. "Finally! We've been traveling forever. Well, five days isn't forever, but it still is a long time." She peered out the window of the carriage. *All of the buildings are so close together. In Mittra, there is so much open space. Here, people must have to fight to get fresh air to breathe. There are so many wagons on the road and horses and . . . people.*

"Harak is . . . different."

Talia laughed. "I appreciate your diplomacy, Sam. I know your mother was very shocked when she left Harak for Mittra. Here you are coming from Mittra and seeing Harak for the first time. "

Samantha sat back against the seat. "No wonder Mother didn't return here. It must have been suffocating."

Talia fixed a stern look on her young charge. "Those words need to stay in this carriage, Samantha. I do understand what you are saying, but the people of Harak are not so easygoing. You must remember all of the 'lessons' your mother taught you over the years. From my conversations with your mother, Harak was not a comfortable place to live. Years of tradition combined with a small country in need of good marriages seemed to place much emphasis on a certain standard of behavior."

Samantha shifted in her seat. "I wish Mother had told me about this years ago. *" I wonder how much my grandparents know about me. Many of my cousins have come to visit over the years, but my grandparents have never met me before. I'm sure they have been filled with horror stories about the odd princess from Mittra. I'll show them I am not a backwards 'country cousin' who has no knowledge of courtly manners and all of those things that are so important to Lacene and the rest of those girls.*

She peeked out the window again as the carriage slowed to a stop. "Taley, look at that!"

The palace in Tallinn, Harak's capital city, was something out of those fairy tales Talia used to tell her when she was young. The white sandstone castle seemed to gleam in the light of the setting sun while the sharp wind caused the Harakian standards to snap and unfurl from the turrets on the four corners of the castle. Though a stone gate surrounded the palace, there was no moat or any other defensible space around the castle.

The door to the carriage opened and Edric stuck his head in with a smile. "May I escort you ladies into the mouth of the lion?"

Samantha grinned at him while Talia shook her finger in a disciplinary fashion. "Edric, I am surprised at you. You are supposed to encourage Samantha, not encourage any bad behavior here in her mother's hometown."

Edric held out his hand and aided them out of the carriage. "Miss Talia, you know where my intentions lie. If this journey has taught me anything so far, it is best to be honest with Sam. Give her the bare facts and then let her draw her own conclusions."

Samantha raised her eyebrows at her friend. "And 'the mouth of the lion' is just the bare facts?"

The prince colored slightly. "Speaking from my own experience with Lacene," he mumbled as they approached the large entrance doors.

"Speak of the devil," Samantha whispered under her breath. Her cousin swept out of the castle, appearing to be floating rather than walking in her voluminous gown. She caught Samantha's eye, and a brilliant smile plastered her face.

"Samantha, darling cousin! So good to see you again," Lacene cooed as she swooped in to give an air kiss to both of Samantha's cheeks. "So many handsome men you've brought with you," she whispered in her cousin's ear. "Thank you."

The princess of Mittra stood rigidly still while she clenched her teeth together. *Don't speak. She's just trying to bait you. Refuse to give in. You can play this game.*

"Of course, Lacene," Samantha replied in an airy voice. "You may take your pick. I know you like a variety of suitors." A wicked thought came into her mind, and she smiled slyly. "Just stay away from Nolan, prince of Lagola. Oh, and Linden, prince of Synterius. They both seem to be awfully fond of me."

Lacene's eyes lit up with a spark of interest. "Of course, cousin! I wouldn't *dream* of coming between you and your suitors. So . . . would you point them out to me? Just so I know who to avoid?"

Oh, Lacene, I can see right through you. This week will be one of the longest of my life . . .

✝

"Brother, stop pacing. You're making me sick," Edric complained to Nolan the next evening. He watched as Nolan paced back and forth in the room they were sharing.

Nolan stopped, clenching and unclenching his fists. "I'm sorry. I just keep thinking about that stupid tournament and that brainless Synterius. It's not over yet." He paused, glancing his brother. "What does she even see in him? She's way too good for him."

Edric smirked at his brother. "So . . . is she too good for you?"

Nolan threw his hands up in frustration. "I don't know. I can't even talk to her without arguing, it seems. She's driving me crazy! I thought if I ignored her, she'd come back around to me."

"Is that how it's working out with Lacene?" Edric asked while checking his clothes in front of the mirror.

"She's an entirely different story. I can't shake that girl. Sure, she's beautiful, and she agrees with whatever I say. But . . . there's something missing," Nolan frowned at his reflection in the mirror.

Edric caught his brother's gaze. "She's not Sam," he said quietly.

Nolan shook his head. "I know she's not Sam. Sam is . . . ugh! Frustrating and stubborn and—"

"Beautiful?"

"Of course she's beautiful. Why else is Linden after her?" Nolan retorted, feeling his face redden when he realized what he'd said.

Edric threw Nolan's coat at him. "Well, finish dressing and we'll head down. But you must promise not to fight him tonight."

Nolan snorted. "I don't go out looking for a fight. These things just seem to find me."

The brothers started to leave the room when Nolan suddenly grabbed Edric's arm. "Do you get a headache when you talk to Samantha?"

Edric laughed loudly at his brother. "No! What, is your gift backfiring on you? Can't charm the ladies anymore?"

A brooding look settled on Nolan's face. "Well, I have no problem with Lacene. You've seen the way she's thrown herself at me since we arrived yesterday."

"And your problem with that is . . . ?" Edric teased as they continued down the hall.

Nolan shook his head. "I don't know. It seems like since I met Sam—I mean, since we were reintroduced—You know what I mean! Not that other girls don't matter or I don't notice them . . . I mean, how can you *not* notice Lacene?"

Edric nudged him as they approached the staircase that led to the main floor of the castle. "The girl you are trying to not notice is standing right there, or are you trying to notice her? Is she available or not?"

Lacene stopped them before Nolan could reply. "Good evening Prince Edric. Prince Nolan," she murmured coyly, delicately fluttering her eyelashes while reaching to take Nolan's arm.

Edric stifled a laugh, remembering what Samantha had said on the evening of her birthday ball. *Girls really do learn how to do that? Ridiculous waste of time. Or maybe not . . .* he reflected when he saw the half admiring, half bewildered expression on his brother's face.

"I'll leave you now," Edric said, bowing. "I must find my escort for the evening." His eyes searched the room for Samantha's golden head, but he failed to see it. He caught sight of a purple shimmer near the entrance to the ballroom and moved in that direction.

Edric found Linden, a blonde girl on his arm, bowing to Samantha and Talia. *I got here just in time.* "Samantha!" he called out, causing Linden to frown as he turned toward him. His face cleared when he saw it was Edric. *He must have thought I was Nolan at first,* Edric laughed to himself as he approached the small group.

Samantha watched Edric's face as he joined them, wondering what he would think of the beautiful girl with Linden. "Prince Edric, may I introduce Princess Chrysanthemum of Synterius to you?" she spoke formally, a smile lurking on her lips.

Edric bowed as he took the princess's hand. "I am very pleased to make your acquaintance," he answered automatically.

He straightened, looking at her face for the first time. He froze, staring at her heart shaped face, creamy skin, and large cerulean eyes. *She's gorgeous. Okay, stop staring. Don't drool.* "Do you like to dance? I mean, can you dance? Er, may I *have* a dance?" he stammered out, feeling sweat collect on his forehead.

The princess laughed, sounding like a tinkling of little bells. She smiled up at Edric, her light blue eyes filled with delight. "Yes, yes, and yes. I believe that answers all of your questions. I am free for the second dance, sir." She frowned slightly as Linden applied a slight pressure to her arm. "Unless my cousin has an objection to that?"

Samantha cut in. "I am sure that Prince Linden has no objection, since he is dancing the second dance with me. Isn't that right?" she asked, fluttering her eyelashes at him.

Edric stared at his friend. *What have I walked into tonight? I didn't misspeak when I told King Bennett this was a husband hunt.* He glanced over at Talia with a questioning look in his eyes. She nodded, winking at him. He instantly relaxed. *Sam is learning to play the game. This should be interesting.*

He turned his attention back to his future dance partner. "Thank you for the acceptance of my offer. I will return soon." He bowed again as she curtsied, and then he walked away from the group.

"Princess Chrysanth—" Samantha began.

"Please, please don't call me that," the petite girl begged with a smile. "Only my parents call me that and only when they are terribly annoyed at me. I go by Chrissy. Don't scowl so, Linden. You'll give yourself premature wrinkles." She rolled her eyes at him. "He is practicing being the king, you know. He goes about with very serious expressions, formal speech, and an accusation for anyone who challenges his authority."

Samantha looked over to see Linden's scowl deepen into a frown, fury written in his eyes. "I think you've angered him," she whispered loudly, winking at Chrissy. "How should we proceed now?"

"We'll just tease him a bit more," Chrissy whispered back. "What's the worst he can do? Not dance with us? Fail to escort us to dinner?"

Samantha remembered Nolan and Linden's previous fight, and knew that Chrissy had not truly seen what her cousin was capable of. "Perhaps we should get some punch?" Samantha offered, wanting to talk more with Chrissy without Linden around.

Linden released his cousin but stepped in front of Samantha, blocking her way with a tight smile. "You will dance with me, will you not? Or are you already promised to Lagola tonight?"

His eyes bore into hers, making her shiver. "If you are speaking of *Prince Nolan* of Lagola, then no, he has not claimed any dances from me. Edric, as you know, is my escort and will dance the first dance with me." She paused, unsure of what else to say.

He leaned closer and murmured, "As long as he releases you to me, I shall be a happy man."

Upon seeing the uncomfortable look on Samantha's face, Chrissy blurted, "Oh look, Linden, your friend! The prince of . . . that place we visited . . . last summer was it?"

While Linden turned around in confusion, Chrissy grabbed Samantha's hand and pulled her away to the adjoining sitting room.

"I must apologize for my cousin. He can be a bit intense around ladies he likes," Chrissy explained as they sat together on a small settee near the doorway.

Samantha nodded. "Yes, intense is one word for it." *Though I can think of several more. Scary, demanding, controlling.* . . . "Are you close to your cousin?"

Chrissy shook her head, a slight frown on her pretty face. "Not very. I only arrived in Harak two days ago to join the circuit with Linden as my escort. He's been away on his dragon hunting expedition for the last three years. This tournament circuit will be the most time we've spent together recently. Mother doesn't really care for the hunting, so he decided to go off on his own."

"Whose idea was it that you came along on the circuit?"

"Mine, actually. Does that surprise you? It shocked my mother. You would not believe the argument we had over it."

"You might be surprised . . ." Samantha smiled in remembrance.

"My seventeenth birthday is next month, and my mother was incredibly anxious that I had not accepted any marriage proposals. The only two men who were serious about marriage were completely ridiculous. Sir Bertrand is old enough to be my grandfather, and Prince Wilmur is cross-eyed, rude, and compared me to his brood mare!"

Samantha laughed at the fire in her new friend's eye. "You might not believe this, but I believe your mother and mine have so much in common! This is the first time I've been out of Mittra and away from my mother's all-seeing eye. Most of my growing up involved practicing being a perfect princess." She shut her mouth quickly, hoping she had not said too much. *Did I give anything away? Chrissy is just so easy to talk to. I need to remember to use discernment.*

Chrissy's mouth eased into a sly smile. "Which one of your gifts do you dislike the most?" The surprise on Samantha's face set off Chrissy's tinkling laughter. "So you know what I'm talking about. I brought this up to Lacene, the princess over there hanging on Nolan's arm, and she stared at me like I had a third eye!"

Samantha snorted. "Lacene doesn't have any fairy gifts. Harak, I'm sorry to say, forbade any fairies from settling here after the Fairy Rebellion and the fall of Sansevierra. The fairies responded by not bestowing any gifts on any Harakian children." She glanced over toward her cousin. "I am also sorry to say that Lacene is my cousin." Chrissy opened her mouth to interrupt, but Samantha held up her hand. "No, don't apologize. I can't stand her. She uses people for her own purposes. It looks like Nolan has fallen into her trap."

She turned back to Chrissy, who was looking at her closely. "You're jealous of the attention Nolan is showing Lacene?"

"*Jealous*? No. Oh no. I've known Nolan forever, and I don't have any feelings for him. At least, not any *romantic* feelings."

"And my cousin?" Chrissy questioned.

Samantha paused, hesitant to answer the question. "Linden is . . . persistent. It's rather confusing. Chrissy, to be perfectly honest with you, I'd rather your cousin give me some room. I know my parents want me to find someone to marry, but I'm working some things out. I just need time. Please don't hate me."

Chrissy laughed, patting Samantha's hand. "I could not hate you, especially when you tell me the truth as you just did. Do you know how different it is to have someone speak honestly? Look around the room. I've gotten to know all of these ladies over the years. I don't respect a single one of them. They will lie to you and tell you how beautiful your gown is and how lovely your hair is. Then they turn around, spreading rumors so fast you won't know what hit you. I've seen them do it over and over again."

"I wouldn't put it past them," Samantha murmured. *I need to make sure I don't give them any reason to start anything about me.* "We've talked about me enough. How about you? Do you have any suitors in mind? Obviously ones that aren't ancient or into bloodlines."

Chrissy laughed with her. "No one stands out . . ." she said, but Samantha caught her looking across the room at Edric.

Edric? Yes, that would be perfect! He asked me to help him find a wife. How do I do this? She had warned Edric that she was terrible at matchmaking and that was not a lie. She remembered how she told Elan that he should marry Talia when she was just twelve years old. *It would not have been so bad if it hadn't been right in front of everyone at the dinner table. Mother made sure I learned my lesson from that! After writing, "I will not be a busybody" five hundred times, it certainly sank in.*

"Well," Samantha said casually, "If you change your mind, let me know."

She stood up and Chrissy followed suit. "I see my grandparents entered the room. I must pay my respects to them, or my grandmother will send a detailed letter to my mother about how she failed to raise a proper princess. She'll compare me to Lacene, her *perfect* granddaughter." Samantha sighed dramatically. "At least I know I have a friend who shares my pain."

Chrissy laughed and waved as Samantha crossed the room towards the formidable King and Queen of Harak. King Pentral nodded to his major domo, who tapped his cane on the tiled floor. All eyes turned, focusing on him.

"Thank you for joining us tonight," King Pentral called out in his deep, somber voice. "We are pleased to announce that our eldest son, Prince Jonathan, has accepted a marriage proposal on behalf of his daughter, Princess Lacene. Lacene? Will you please come over?"

Samantha tried to keep the disgust off her face as Lacene removed her hand from Nolan's arm, giving him a sickly sweet smile before she glided over to her grandfather. *Her dress is ridiculous,* Samantha snorted to herself, staring at the yards of pink tulle crisscrossed with ribbons and sparkly jewels. *Why would Nolan offer to marry her? She's a big ball of fluff. I doubt she can ride a galloping horse, let alone defend herself.* Even though she wished to leave, her years of training made her stay and watch the unfolding drama.

"My beautiful eldest granddaughter, Lacene," King Pentral gave her a slight smile before turning back to the crowd. "And will her betrothed come forward?"

Samantha stared at Nolan's profile, waiting for him to move forward. *I thought better of you, Nolan. You seemed to have more sense than that. Wait, why isn't he moving?*

A sudden movement caught Samantha's eye, and she looked back at her cousin. Lacene was staring in horror at the man standing next to her, gazing proudly at his fiancé. Chrissy bumped Samantha's arm lightly and whispered, "Remember I told you about Prince Wilmur? I guess he found a new brood mare!"

Samantha quickly turned her laugh into a cough, which made Nolan turn to stare at her. Blushing, she searched for a way out the hall, but the excited crowd blocked every available path. Samantha groaned. *If I can't leave, I'll have some fun.* She lifted her eyes to Nolan's and mimicked wiping her forehead with the back of her hand in a gesture of relief.

A light jumped into Nolan's eyes and he struggled to keep his laugh concealed as well. *I'm going to get you,* he mouthed to her.

Ha! It's the same as when we were kids. We couldn't laugh during dinner, or we would get in trouble. Samantha wrinkled her nose at him, giggling. Chrissy bumped Samantha again and raised her eyebrows.

"It's nothing. I've just know him a long time," Samantha murmured, keeping her head down. She was relieved when her grandfather excused everyone to go into dinner.

✢

After dinner, Edric claimed Samantha for the first dance of the evening, noticing the perplexed look on her face.

"Trouble with your suitor?" he teased as they spun around the room, expecting her to laugh.

Instead, she frowned. "You could say that . . ." she replied slowly. "I was thinking that Nolan would be the one to propose to Lacene. But since it wasn't him, I was thinking about something that Linden said to me. And your brother as well. Do you remember the day of the tournament back in Mittra?"

Edric nodded. "Of course I do. Nolan was just talking about that earlier tonight." He shook his head and rolled his eyes. "I probably shouldn't have said that," he muttered when he saw the gleam in her eye.

"What did he say?"

Edric refused to look at her, focusing on his feet. "Er, nothing important. Oh, he said he gets a headache whenever he talks to you."

Samantha huffed. "He told me the same thing when he saw me down by the tents. I don't give *you* a headache, do I?"

Edric smiled kindly down at her. "No, I think this is only between you and my brother." Glancing over at another couple, he spoke in a whisper, "Your cousin doesn't seem to have a problem with him."

Samantha glared at Lacene and Nolan as they crossed the dance floor. "That girl makes me so mad I want to spit. Preferably at her. She's engaged now! Why do girls throw themselves at men? It makes me sick."

Edric laughed. "They were already committed to the dance before the announcement. Some men love it when women go after them. Perhaps men like Linden?"

"I wouldn't know. I've been trying to avoid him. He may be handsome, but he makes me uneasy. Chrissy, on the other hand, is a very sweet girl. I am glad you will be dancing with her next."

"Whoa, how did we jump from Nolan's headaches to my dance partner?"

"It's the female brain, old friend. Don't try to understand it."

The song came to an end, and Edric bowed to her curtsey. "Linden is coming over here," he told her. "I'll get out of his way and find my own partner. Save another dance for me later this evening, if you can."

Once Edric left, Linden bowed quickly, capturing her hand in his own. He pulled her close. "Together again," he murmured into her ear.

Samantha took a step back, resisting his strong arm. She enjoyed the look of uncertainty in his icy blue eyes and the falter in his dance step.

I may be a female, but that does not make me weak. She allowed him to lead her in the dance, but kept him at a distance. *I'm not playing hard to get, Linden,* she wished to say. *I really do want some space. I wish I hadn't agreed to dance with you, but it was the only way Edric and Chrissy could dance without your interference.*

"You seem to be thinking awfully hard," he stated, looking straight at her.

"I have never understood what it means to 'think hard.' Is it possible to think soft?"

Linden's eyes searched hers. "I don't quite know what you mean."

"Are you unused to being around a woman who thinks?"

"Are you trying to tease me, Princess? I admit that I am unaccustomed to Mittran ways. Are women educated to think for themselves?" Linden laughed derisively.

Samantha tried to avoid clenching her teeth. "Women are well educated in all matters. Languages, politics, literature, mathematics, history." She paused. "Warfare."

Linden laughed even louder, drawing attention to those around him. "You are most entertaining, Princess. Or may I call you Samantha?"

"No, you may not!" Samantha stopped dancing and stomped her foot. "Are you even listening to me? Are you listening to yourself? Do you have any idea how utterly—"

From out of nowhere, Nolan swooped in, seized her elbow, and pulled her away from Linden. "You'll thank me later," he muttered as he steered her out of the ballroom.

"Why is this so familiar?" Samantha asked sarcastically as they entered a room across the great hall. "Oh yes. You did the same thing at my birthday ball."

Nolan released her arm, slamming the door. He took a step closer to her. "Not exactly the same, Sam. Then I was saving you from Synterius. Now, I am saving you from yourself."

She took a step towards him. "What do you mean from myself?"

"Do you have any idea what you are doing when you speak your mind out on the dance floor? Other people are listening, people who do not care for Mittra. People who would love to see you, the crown princess of Mittra, fall on your face, both politically and physically. Don't roll your eyes at me. This is your first season out in this society. I've seen a lot more than you," he replied confidently, inching closer to her.

Samantha's eyes burned with green fire. "So I should trust you, Prince Nolan? Oh, you are so much older and wiser than me. Teach me what I don't know." She started to turn away, avoiding the gleam in his eye.

"You asked for it."

Suddenly Samantha felt herself being spun around. Nolan's strong arms surrounded her, his face inches from her own. He looked into her eyes for a moment and then pressed his lips to hers in a hard kiss. She tried to turn her head away, but his lips became more persistent, his arms drawing her closer. Unconsciously, she reached up and pulled his head down, deepening the kiss.

He suddenly stepped back, pushing her away. He was breathing hard, his dark eyes full of amazement. Samantha struggled to catch her breath, touching her fingers to her traitorous lips. Nolan looked like he was about to speak, but then turned and wrenched the door open, slamming it on his way out.

My first kiss. Not at all what I expected, she thought as she sank down into a chair, one lone tear running down her cheek. *Nolan. Nolan, of all people, was my first kiss. What am I going to do now?*

CHAPTER SEVEN

July 24

I'm using the charmed quill Talia gave me for my birthday for the first time. Oh, it's actually working! It is rather strange to see my words being written down without my hand writing them. I don't think I can erase any mistakes, so I should be careful about what I say. I need to ask Talia for a fairy charm that will keep my journal locked. That way, I can be honest without fear that anyone else will read it.

My grandmother finally told me I could return to my room after an hour of chastisement about my "unseemly" behavior. I know I sometimes thought my mother was bad, but I take it all back now! Grandmother is infinitely worse in the guilt department. She forbade me from speaking in my own defense. I even offered to bring Talia in as a character witness, but Grandmother informed me that I was not on trial. I know it was an unofficial trial, though. My only crime was speaking for myself and not bowing to Harakian tradition, where women only simper and compliment with empty heads and predatory skills. I know that Lacene has never had to go through that before. I know I shouldn't hate my cousin, but she makes it awfully hard to like her.

If Mother is so embarrassed that I am not married at eighteen, I wonder why Lacene is almost twenty years old and has only now accepted a marriage proposal? She desperately wants to be married. Does she not have a sizeable dowry? My uncle stands to inherit the throne, so he should be able to give his daughters something. But do I really want to enter into the gossip of Harak when we will be leaving so soon? I think I'll just leave it alone.

I have to say this or I might think it was a dream. Nolan kissed me. NOLAN. Kissed. ME. In the library, after he thoroughly embarrassed me in front of the entire assembly at the ball. I know he said he only removed me to keep me from embarrassing myself and Mittra, but I really think he likes to infuriate me. If I make his head hurt, why would he bother kissing me? He could simply leave me be. I was handling Linden and his pigheaded ways just fine on my own.

Linden. Ugh, I don't know how else to tell him to leave me alone. Grandmother advised me that he is the crown prince of Synterius, and I should not think of throwing away such an opportunity to marry a man in his position.

I hope Talia returns soon. The tournament is in two days, and I need to talk to her about it. Could we train Dawes to compete in two days time? If it's found out that I'm impersonating Palmer, Harak will not forgive that breach of etiquette. I still don't know how Nolan was able to see through the fairy mist. I need to tell Talia about that as well. The candle is getting low, so I should get ready for bed soon. What will I say to Nolan when I see him? Could I be fortunate enough to avoid him? Did I like the kiss? Oh, I wish I could erase that!

July 29

I competed for Palmer again. I told Dawes that I wanted him to enter as his brother. All of this training has worn him down so much that he began to cry. Yes, he actually cried! I was so shocked to see him carrying on in the training yard that I agreed to compete again. Talia tried to dissuade me, but I have to go along with the plan to help Dawes' family. Palmer had to stay behind in Mittra, so Dawes has been posing as his brother, which has been rather funny to see. He has avoided all of the banquets, hiding out in the tents near the tournament field. I heard some of the girls whispering about the knights, and they brought up "Sir Palmer." He is rumored to have been incredibly handsome but had a horrible accident, which left his face scarred. That is supposedly why he always keeps his visor down. All the ladies want to know if the scar is as bad as everyone says. I almost burst out into laughter right in front of them. I even told Dawes about his poor disfigured face. He didn't find it as funny as I did.

Dawes served as my squire, or rather as "Sir Palmer's" squire, at the tournament. Talia was on hand again to provide the haze over my face. I avoided Nolan, keeping my helmet on whenever I was on the tournament grounds behind the castle. It's been rather easy to avoid him, since he seems to avoiding me as well. I've been taking my meals in my room, which suits Grandmother because she doesn't have to apologize for the behavior of her "odd granddaughter from that wild land of Mittra." She said that in front of me to her ladies-in-waiting! Thankfully Talia was there to keep me from showing her how wild we Mittrans can be. I am so glad we're leaving tomorrow, even if it is at dawn, for Zynachnea. I only wish I didn't have to ride in the carriage.

Dawes explained the schedule to me after I complained about how fast we have to move. The tournament season schedule is established far in advance. It began in Lagola on a certain day and then moved to Mittra, which was the tournament that took place the day after my birthday. Some knights only compete in their own country, while those with more money and skill journey to each country on the tournament circuit. Palmer's family only had enough money to pay the entrance fee in Mittra. They were relying on him to win enough money to continue on the circuit.

Which brings me to the joust. I took second! I gave the winnings to Dawes and he said there was enough to enter two more tournaments. Nolan took first today. Linden actually didn't even enter. I wanted to ask Chrissy about it, but I didn't want her to think I was interested in Linden. Because I'm not. He's been avoiding me since the ball. It's so confusing! Linden seems like he's interested, but then he insults my intelligence. Nolan can't stand me, but then he kissed me! Why are men so frustrating?

August 2

We're leaving tomorrow for Personti. Zynachnea has been rather boring. The banquet was dull. There weren't any musicians or jugglers— just bland food and boring dinner companions. I was assigned to a different table than Chrissy, but Talia sat with me. Fairies are not very common here, so people kept staring at Talia and whispering. She handled it much better than I would have in her position. The tournament was, I regret to say, not profitable for "Sir Palmer." I only came in sixth position. I don't know if I'm tired or unfocused or if everyone is so much better than me. Dawes punched me when I started to cry while I was apologizing for losing. I punched him back and started to yell at him. He just laughed! I asked what was so funny and demanded to know why he hit me. He said he'd rather have me yell at him than cry at him.

I haven't been able to talk to Chrissy much lately. The queen of Zynachnea latched onto her the first day we arrived, intent on making Chrissy the next princess of Zynachnea. Ha! The prince is only thirteen *years old! Poor Chrissy told me that she had to refuse her third marriage proposal. Prince Wyler proposed to her IN FRONT OF HIS MOTHER! Chrissy alternated between laughter and tears as she told me. I assured her that her Prince Charming would come along soon. I just need to find a way for her and Edric to get together . . .*

August 4

We spent last night at an inn just inside the border of Personti. We had planned to travel all the way to Yikshel, the capital city, but we got word that the tournament that was scheduled for tomorrow was suddenly cancelled. Edric and Nolan decided to rest the horses before we set out again. Not everyone stopped, though. Linden insisted on traveling through, which meant that Chrissy and her chaperone were forced to travel as well. The timing was unfortunate, since I had been hoping to find a way for Edric to meet up with her again.

I need to stop writing and get ready for the day. Dawes and I are going to find somewhere to practice. After my poor showing in the last tournament, I'm going to need it. Talia just reminded me that I also have to practice my "princess lessons" so that I may write truthfully to my mother today. I haven't written since we arrived in Harak, but I'm sure my grandmother already sent her a letter. Time for me to do what I can to correct the situation. I only hope Father can calm her down.

CHAPTER EIGHT

Edric approached the wide plank table in the dining room of the inn where Nolan sat with a mug of ale. "Are things that bad, brother?" Edric asked with a smile, settling onto the bench opposite Nolan.

Nolan scowled. "You don't have anything better to do?"

"Oooh, touchy today. More problems with the ladies? Is the serving wench not talking to you?" Edric teased, trying to make Nolan smile.

"The wench? No, Edric, it's not about her." Nolan leaned forward, locking eyes with his brother. "Can you keep a secret?"

"Most of the time. Depends on what it is and who will be hurt by not knowing."

Nolan turned to stare at the fire burning in the nearby fireplace. "I kissed Samantha."

Edric lurched forward, his mouth open. "Are you joking? You *kissed* her? When? Where?"

Nolan turned away, frowning. "You sound like a woman! Yes, I kissed her. In Harak, the night of the ball. Do you remember when Synterius was making an ass of himself on the dance floor, and I escorted her out?"

"And by escorted her out, you mean you took her to a quiet place and told her how much you love and admire her?" Edric asked, his eyes gleaming with mischief.

"*No!*" Nolan pounded the table with his fist, causing his mug to spill ale over the edge. He could see other guests turn to look at him, so he lowered his voice. "No, I took her out so she wouldn't embarrass herself, but I only ended up embarrassing myself."

Edric studied his face. "How? Are you that bad a kisser?"

His brother narrowed his eyes at him. "She seemed to enjoy it. I think she even kissed me back. But then I realized what I was doing and I ... left."

"Wait. Are you telling me you pulled Sam out of the room, yelled at her, kissed her, and then walked away without saying anything? Did you apologize or do I need to make you? I told her father I would watch out for her! I was only thinking of Linden, not my own brother!"

"Calm down, Edric. I will apologize. I just haven't done so yet. What, do I simply walk up to her and say, 'Hey, Princess Samantha. Remember that night when I kissed you? I'm sorry I did it but not really.'" Nolan's face flushed.

"Mmm, the truth comes out! You like her, but you're afraid to tell her. Do you think she'll tell you off?" He smirked. "Only one way to find out . . ."

The innkeeper walked up to the table with a letter in his hand. "Someone said you are the Prince of Lagola. Is that right?"

Edric and Nolan both nodded and then laughed. "I'm the eldest, so I'll take it," Edric offered, giving the man a gold coin.

"Who is it from?"

"It's from Father and it's for both of us," Edric broke the seal and began to read the letter. "Hmm, do you remember Father talking about 'The Evil of the East' or some such rumor about a year ago? It seems he's recently heard from guards near the edge of the Sansevierra Desert, who also reported strange things happening in the east, far across the desert."

"Strange in what way?" Nolan asked, eyebrows lowered in concentration.

"Odd weather patterns, flashes in the sky—those sorts of things. He asked us to keep an ear out, and wanted you to use your gift as needed for more information. Whatever we can gather should be sent back to him immediately." Edric frowned. "What's beyond the Sansevierra Desert?"

Nolan shook his head. "I've only heard of a few explorers who have journeyed into the Sansevierra Forest, north of Synterius. They reached the Mountains of Desolation and turned around. There was hardly any game for food, little water, and the trees were all dead near the base of the mountains."

Both brothers shivered as if a sudden chill came upon the room.

"Do you remember that history book you gave me? Back in Mittra? I started reading it, and it mentioned something about the east. I'll have to go back and read that portion again. It's a really fascinating history about the Fairy Rebellion. It also talked about how this crazy Lord Oblex attacked the fairy king and queen using forces from Synterius. Not that King Aspen or the rest of Synterius is involved with anything like that now. Some sort of mind control or magic . . . "

"Let me know if there's anything I need to know," Nolan nodded at his brother, taking a sip of his ale.

"Do you still have your amulet?"

Nolan pulled it out of his pocket and handed it to his brother. "Maybe you should use it for awhile. It's supposed to see through magical disguises, finding the truth in a situation, but it doesn't seem to work for me."

"Since when?" A pout formed on Edric's lips. "I paid a goodly sum for that for your last birthday! I wonder if that merchant accepts returns?"

"Since the day of the tournament in Mittra. I saw Samantha down on the field, dressed as a knight, if you can believe that! She said that her father knew she was there, but her mother didn't. No one else noticed her but me."

A thoughtful look appeared on Edric's face as he held the amulet. "Interesting. I'll keep this for now. You should go get some sleep. We're training tomorrow, right?"

Nolan smiled. "If you really want to, yes, let's work off some of this rich food and ale. Got to stay in shape for the tournaments, you know."

✝

Samantha met Dawes behind the inn's stable the next morning. She smiled when she saw her friend wearing her helmet, even though no one else was around.

"Keeping 'Sir Palmer's' identity a well guarded secret, are we?" she teased as she entered the corral. "Didn't Talia place a mist charm on the helmet?"

Dawes lifted up the visor, looked around, and then removed it from his head. "Yes, she did, but I still keep the visor down just in case. Ugh, it gets so hot and stuffy in there! I don't know how you can stand it during competition. I don't see anyone else, and I didn't hear anyone mention they'd be out here practicing so early. Remind me again why we are out here at the crack of dawn?"

Samantha stuck her out her tongue. "We're out here for precisely that reason. No one else is up! I don't know how we'd explain it if someone came looking for Princess Samantha, and here I am in full armor. We'll do it this way until we can't. Agreed?"

Dawes sighed. "Agreed. It's hard to argue when you make so much sense. But you have to bring me some food next time. And hot coffee. It's hard to get good food when you're living in a tent with a bunch of men," he grumbled.

Samantha smiled as she held up her hands. "Fresh bread, apples, and a mug of coffee. It was hot when I left the kitchen a few minutes ago. You eat while I get dressed in my armor."

‡

Edric stretched as he passed the stable, feeling the tightness of his muscles. *I hate sleeping in an inn! The beds are always lumpy. It's too bad we couldn't go on to Yikshel. I know the beds in the castle would have been more comfortable, but who wants to take the chance of contracting bilious fever?*

He saw two figures already practicing in the small corral. *Someone is up earlier than me? It's not Nolan. He was still snoring when I went downstairs to eat. That armor looks familiar . . .*

The taller figure suddenly struck down his opponent with his wooden practice sword, lifted up his visor, and grinned.

"*Samantha?*" Edric yelped.

The knight turned sharply, pulled the visor back down, and lurched away in the opposite direction.

Edric ran into the corral, ignoring the other knight, who was struggling to stand up. He reached his hand out, grabbed Samantha's upper arm, and pulled her towards him. He flipped up the visor on the helmet and stared at her face.

"What do you think you're *doing?*" he asked, the disbelief clear in his hazel eyes. "And dressed up as a . . . *knight?* What is going on?"

Samantha sighed at the hurt, confused look on Edric's face. She lifted off the helmet, feeling her hair tumble down around her shoulders. "I'll answer all of your questions, but I have one for you first. How did you know it was me?"

Edric shrugged. "I could see your face."

"You could see? Do you have a fairy gift of seeing past magic or something?" Samantha asked, mystified.

"No, but I do have this." Samantha watched as he pulled Nolan's amulet out of his pocket. "It's supposed to see through magic, forcing someone to be honest. Nolan said it doesn't work, though. I'm going to try to get my money back."

"This is Nolan's? Did he have it in Mittra? At the tournament?" Edric nodded, and Samantha began to laugh. "I think I understand. Dawes!"

Dawes approached, and Samantha handed him her helmet. "Put this on and raise the visor." He did as he was told. "Okay, Edric. Who do you see?"

"Sam, I already know it's your friend," Edric stated, looking at her strangely.

"Would you just look?"

Rolling his eyes, Edric sighed but still looked. "Yes, like I said, it's Dawes."

Samantha held out her hand. "Hand me the amulet. Now look."

"I already told you it doesn't work . . . Hey! What's wrong with my eyes? No, I can see you, Sam. *Oh.* There's a charm or something on the helmet, right? Talia's work?"

"You know she's the best!" She gave the amulet to Edric and began to remove her armor. "Dawes, you can take the helmet off now. I think we're done for today. If Edric's here, Nolan's sure to follow. Let's try again tomorrow."

As Dawes left with Samantha's armor, Edric stared at her until she began to laugh uncomfortably.

"What?"

"I see my friend, my friend who is a *princess,* outside wearing custom fitted armor, practicing sword fighting, and you ask me 'what'?" Samantha was shaken to see the hurt, anger, and confusion swirling across Edric's face.

Samantha left the corral and started to walk toward the stable. "I don't know if you'd believe me if I told you the truth."

Edric jogged after her, following her into Windstorm's stall. "I do have the amulet, you know. Don't make me use it."

She picked up a brush and began to groom her horse. "Where do I start?" she murmured. *What would Talia tell me to do? I don't know if anyone else is around here, so I really can't tell him everything. He might tell Nolan! But he's my friend. If I can't trust him, who can I trust?*

"Start at the beginning."

Samantha glanced up to see Edric's face relaxing into his familiar smile. His eyes crinkled at the corners as he added, "I have to tell you . . . .You're really skilled! When did you start your training?"

Samantha spoke in a low voice. "Elan and Sir Cabot taught me after that last summer in Conti Wayo. My father thought it would be good for me to learn some leadership skills, so I did. I actually took the test to be a squire and passed. Elan was training me to test for knighthood just before my birthday. Obviously, other plans came up . . . ."

"But, you're still in training?" Edric asked, his eyes dim with confusion before suddenly lighting up. "I know why that armor looked familiar! Sir Palmer was wearing that in the tournament. Wait, that was *you!*"

Samantha gazed up at him. "Please don't tell anyone, Edric. Not even Nolan!"

"But, Sam, it's dangerous! Why in the world would you ever do such a thing? And who is Sir Palmer anyway?"

"Sir Palmer is Dawes' brother. He really is a knight, but he broke his leg right before the tournament in Mittra and I had—I felt I *should* help if I could." Seeing the look on his face, she pleaded, "Their family needs the money, Edric. Please don't tell."

Closing his eyes, Edric sighed. *What's the worst that could happen if I keep this a secret? Well, your friend could die! But she hasn't yet, and she does seem to be rather good.*

He opened his eyes and gave Samantha a small smile. "I'll keep your secret. Unless I feel it's in your best interest not to. Understand?"

Samantha ran around Windstorm and threw her arms around him. "Thank you! You're amazing, you know."

"Don't mind me," Nolan snapped as he stiffly approached the stall, crossing his arms in front of his chest.

Samantha felt her cheeks get hot as she stepped away from Edric. She refused to meet Nolan's eyes. *I have nothing to apologize for. He's the one who kissed me and then ignored me for days and days. He's mad if he thinks I'm going to talk to him!*

She finally looked at him, shocked to see the anger in his eyes and felt her own bubble to the surface. "This is none of your concern, Nolan," she retorted, assuming a position similar to his.

"What happens to my brother *is* my concern. So, what, Synterius takes off and you jump to the next available man around?"

Samantha's hand lashed out, slapping Nolan across the face. She heard it echo through the stable. Shaking with hot rage, she balled her fist, her head buzzing. She was ready to strike again when she felt Edric's hand on her shoulder.

"Go inside, Sam. I'll deal with this," Edric's voice was as hard as flint as he stared at his brother.

She cast one last angry glare at Nolan before she stalked away from the stable.

"Nolan," Edric began in a low voice. "Sam and I are just friends. You will *never* make such an accusation against her, or you will answer to me. You're not too old to be taught a lesson, you know."

"What was I supposed to think?" Nolan demanded as Edric passed him.

"Not that! Do you think after what you told me last night that I would swoop in and take your girl? Oh, wait, she's not your girl. I don't even think she's your *friend* anymore," Edric shot back, leaving Nolan in the stable alone.

"What is going on today?" Nolan yelled, making the horses near him shuffle restlessly and snort their disapproval. "Shut up!" he muttered as he stomped out in the yard, yearning to take his aggression out on the quintain.

CHAPTER NINE

August 8

This tournament circuit is getting rather tedious. It seems we see the same people over and over again and have the same conversations over and over again. I made this remark to Chrissy and, thankfully, she understood what I was saying!

Rothan is a pretty enough country, especially after being in Personti for four long days. Talia thought it was wise to stay another night in the first inn, and Edric agreed with her. The next day was spent traveling to another inn, where we again stayed two nights. I stayed in my room until Talia threatened to have Edric carry me out. I only found out after we left for Rothan that Nolan was sleeping out in "tent city," as the squires and knights call it.

Rigan, the capital of Rothan, is near the coast of the Zuiden Sea and there are fresh breezes that smell so sweet. It reminds me of summers in Conti Wayo. Ugh. Conti Wayo. Why does it seem that every time I try to forget Nolan, something comes up to make me think of him? I'm not sure what Edric said to him back at the inn, but it must have been serious because he hasn't been around me at all. Not that I care! Well, I do care. He should apologize for what he said.

I agreed to meet Chrissy downstairs at the ball this evening, so I should go get ready.

August 11

We're now in Calaway, the capital of Isonox. It is nothing like Rothan! The people here are rude and pushy. The roads were bumpy and muddy. Last night's inn was filthy. I am doing my best not to have a princess attitude, but this is rather much. At least here in the castle the bed is clean and the plates look like they have been washed. Talia says that I just need to relax, but if I stop entering competitions, I'm sure I would be a better traveling companion. I don't want to annoy her. I thought my attitude would be better after the last tournament. I knocked Nolan out of third place, and he ended up with fourth. The win didn't feel as good as I thought it would.

Linden came in first. Again. I really hate the way he looks down on everyone like they are all dirt under his boots. It's very time consuming to avoid two different men, especially when they are both at all the same balls, tournaments, and banquets.

There is yet another ball tomorrow night. I need to figure out a way to fill up my dance card so that I have an excuse not to dance with Linden. He is awfully persistent. I would have thought that my outspokenness would have cooled him off. But no. It's too bad that Chrissy is his cousin. I want to be able to talk to her and spend more time talking about interesting things, but when he's her escort, it's rather difficult. At the tournaments, I have to pretend that I'm allergic to the horses, the hay, or the grass just to get out of being present in the royal box. I think Nolan suspects something, but he hasn't said anything. Yet.

August 13

I am so ashamed when I read my previous entry. No wonder Talia was sick of me. I'm sick of myself!

But, good news: I came in first in the tournament today! Dawes was beside himself when I gave him the prize money. I do believe he cries more than me. I never knew that first place took DOUBLE what second place did. No wonder all of these men go on the tournament circuit. Dawes tried to make me take some of the money, but I told him to keep it and continue to pay for the entrance fee for each competition.

I heard a few of the other knights talking about the final events in Synterius. They called all of these other tournaments "practice" for the final events. One was even excited at the thought we might fight 'til the death. Barbarians! If it comes to that, I will have to bow out. I know that Talia would never approve, and Edric would not hesitate to reveal who I was. NOT that I want to fight to the death. There are quite a few things I want to do before I die.

There's a banquet tomorrow night, and we leave the day after that for Synterius. I hope I'll be able to see Chrissy more once we're in her home. I need to find a clever way for her and Edric to see more of each other. I would love to have a good soak in the tub—if I can convince some of the servants to fill one for me, that is. Maybe I should have kept some of the prize money for bribes . . . .

CHAPTER TEN

"Sam, you have to come down to the banquet. What will our hosts think?" Talia asked her charge, a slight frown on her pretty face.

"Taley, I need a night away. Please? I promised Mother in my last letter that I would continue practicing my lessons. Dawes promised to help me learn the dances that are popular in Synterius right now."

"And how does Dawes know the dances?" Talia asked, raising her eyebrows.

Samantha smiled impishly. "He has a crush on one of the ladies-in-waiting. She was more than willing to teach him how to dance, so I suppose the feeling is mutual. I need to see if he was really paying attention or not."

Talia sighed as she gazed at Samantha. *She really is growing up. She doesn't complain as much about the traveling and the tournaments. Well, except for when we were in Rothan. Something happened with her and Nolan, I am sure of it. I don't want to pry. Maybe some time away will be good for her.*

"Yes, you may stay behind and practice. I want you to be able to honestly answer your mother when you write to her. Be sure to stay away from the common areas of the castle. Perhaps near the library? You know as well as I do that not many people go there," Talia winked, her shimmer glinting in the candlelight.

"You're certainly right about that. Every castle that we've been to has a thick layer of dust on their books. Osric would die of apoplexy, I'm sure. If you see Dawes, will you ask him to meet me in the library, please? Thank you, Taley!"

‡

Nolan was standing near the broad staircase, slightly hidden by the heavy draperies hanging in the doorway, as the footman called out that the dining hall was now open for dinner. He glanced once again around the foyer, carefully searching each knot of guests for Samantha. *Where can she be? She's not with that princess Edric is so enamored with, and she's not with Synterius either.*

He spotted Talia coming down the stairs alone. *I'll have to ask Miss Talia. This has gone on long enough. But where is she going?*

He watched as Talia headed toward a man with brown hair standing near a small hallway. The man nodded his head, looked around the room, and walked toward one of the footmen standing against a wall. He said a few words to the footman, who pointed upstairs while holding up three fingers. The brown haired man nodded at the footman and turned back towards Talia. He spoke a few words, bowed, and began to walk up the stairs.

Speak to Talia or follow him? Just as Nolan made the decision to follow the man, Edric walked up to him.

"Nolan, I've just received a letter from Father. He believes that the true reason the tournament in Rigan was cancelled was not because of an outbreak of the bilious fever, as we were told. One of the castle guards wrote a short note to his cousin, who is one of the guards in Lagola. That guard told his superior—"

"I understand! Go on with it," Nolan said, anxiously looking up the stairs.

"Fine. The guard said that a cloaked visitor had arrived at the castle and met with the king and queen of Rothan. Shortly after that, they became horribly ill, but no one else in the castle was affected. The fairies who attended to them on their sickbeds had only seen this kind of illness back in Sansevierra many, many years before."

Nolan's eyebrows lowered in thought. "So, it's a magical illness? I mean, brought on by a charm of some sort?"

Edric shrugged. "That's what it seems to be, but the most interesting part is that the cloaked man came from the east."

Nolan locked eyes with his brother. "The Evil of the East, perhaps?"

"Father seems to think so. He wants us to be extremely careful, especially as we travel closer to the east. Once we reach Synterius, I am to alert King Aspen about the potential dangers Father foresees."

One of the footmen approached and bowed. "Excuse me, my lords. Dinner is being served in the dining hall."

Edric nodded his thanks and turned to enter the hall. "Aren't you coming?" he asked Nolan, who continued to stand near the staircase.

"No, I have other matters to . . . attend to at the moment. I'll see you in our room later."

Without waiting for his brother's response, Nolan quickly climbed the stairs to the third floor. *What did Talia tell that man? Why did he want the third floor? Could it have something to do with Samantha? If not, I'll return to the dining hall and speak to Talia. I must talk to Samantha about whatever this is between us. I never should have kissed her. No, I never should have accused her and Edric of impropriety. No wonder she's avoiding me.*

Seeing a footman walking past him, Nolan asked, "What is here on the third floor?"

Bowing, the footman answered, "Guest rooms mainly. Oh, and the library. But hardly anyone goes there, my lord."

"And where is the library?"

Following the simple directions, he arrived at the double door. He placed his ear against the door, listening for voices. After a moment, he heard a low rumble of a man's voice and the higher voice of a woman, Nolan smiled. *Found her!*

He pushed the door open and found himself staring at the whirling figures of Samantha and Dawes, executing an elaborate dance routine.

"Oh!" Dawes exclaimed, dropping his hands. Samantha stumbled, catching her foot on the hem of her dress. He heard the rip of fabric as she fell to the carpeted floor.

Both Nolan and Dawes rushed to where the princess fell, but Nolan knelt first, offering his hand.

"Dawes, please wait outside," Samantha said in a low voice, glaring up at Nolan. "Prince Nolan and I have some business to attend to."

Dawes glanced from one face to the other, unsure of what to do. "Do as the lady said," Nolan instructed. Dawes turned without another word and exited the room, closing the door.

"Can I help you up?" Nolan asked in a tight voice.

"No, I really don't need your kind of help." Samantha struggled to her feet. She glanced down at her dress and then fixed her eyes on him. "You made me rip my dress, and this is one of the few dresses I like."

He stood directly in front of her. "Why are you up here instead of down at dinner?"

"Why do you care?" Samantha retorted, folding her arms.

Of course. I knew that was coming. He sighed and sat in one of the high-backed chairs pushed back against the wall. "Why don't you want to be around me?"

Samantha gaped at him. "You need me to tell you *why?* Where should I start? Embarrassing me in front of my grandparents in Harak? Or maybe that scene in the stable while we were in Personti? Or—" she broke off, a blush rising to her cheeks.

Or when I kissed her. He pushed himself up out of the chair and ambled over to a nearby bookshelf. "Would you believe me if I said I was sorry? For all of that?" He turned toward the books, not wanting to see the look of loathing on her face.

"Can I ask *you* a question? Why aren't you at dinner? Who told you I was up here?"

"I saw . . . Dawes, is it? I watched Talia speak to him, and I didn't see you, so I followed him up here. I wanted to check on you. What were you two doing, anyway?"

"If you must know, we were dancing."

Nolan laughed. "Dancing? In the library? They do have a ballroom here, you know."

Samantha blushed again. "Dawes was teaching me some of the new dances from Synterius. I wanted to get them right before we got there."

"But isn't the gift of dance one of your fairy gifts?" he questioned, feeling his own cheeks get hot.

"You memorized my gifts?" Samantha tilted her head toward him.

"No! I mean, yes. Sort of. My father had me read all of the dossiers of the royals who we would meet on our goodwill tour. That way I could use *my* gift appropriately. I know that sounds horrible, but I was only doing what my father requested," Nolan finished quickly.

Samantha sighed. "Oh, I understand parental requests very well. It doesn't sound horrible. All I can tell you is that some of my fairy gifts are unusual in the way they . . . um, are displayed. Haven't you heard that some gifts take a stronger hold than others?" She searched his eyes. "I can't tell you more than that."

Nolan eased his lips into a smoldering smile, his eyes lighting up in anticipation. "Can't tell me more or *won't* tell me more? If you let me get to know you better—ahhh!" *What is happening? My head is killing me! Why does this happen when I talk to her? But it didn't happen earlier . . .*

He looked up to see Samantha gazing at him with a concerned look on her face. "Another headache? Have you seen a doctor about this? It could be something serious."

"No, I'm fine now. But, as I was saying, we should talk—"

"I'm leaving now. If this is only about adding one more girl to your list of conquests, no thank you."

"Samantha, please. You don't understand." He reached out to grab her wrist, but suddenly, he felt a vice-like grip on his own wrist. His legs were swept out from beneath him. He stared up at the ceiling, gasping for breath, unable to make a coherent thought.

Samantha stood over him, a look of horror on her face. "I didn't mean . . . I'm so . . ." she stammered, backing away from his prostrate form.

Dawes ran into the room without knocking. "I heard a thump! Are you—? Oh, forgive the intrusion, sir," he said, bowing to Nolan.

Samantha fled the room as Dawes helped Nolan to his feet.

"Dawes, tell me honestly. What kind of 'princess practice' is Samantha actually doing?"

Dawes gave Nolan a nervous laugh and bowed. "Prince Nolan, you'd have to ask Sam—er, the princess about that. I can't say anymore about it."

Nolan nodded at Dawes in dismissal and shuffled over to the same high-backed chair, gingerly lowered himself into it. *She practices dancing and self-defense,* he mused. *Samantha of Mittra, warrior princess? Edric needs to hear about this!*

CHAPTER ELEVEN

"Samantha!"

The princess turned from her carriage to see Chrissy. She was waving from the large main door of the castle of King Aspen in Synterius' capital city of Arbre. Samantha sighed with envy as she saw Chrissy's spotless blue gown, knowing without looking down that her traveling outfit was wrinkled and dusty. *These things shouldn't matter, but I would like to make a good first impression on Chrissy's parents.*

"Hello!" she called back, walking quickly toward her friend. Talia followed behind her.

Chrissy held out her hands, squeezing Samantha's as she grinned at her. "Finally! I feel like I haven't seen you in weeks. I know it's only been, what, five days? I begged Linden to stay in Calaway for a few more days, but he was insistent that we leave directly after the tournament." She leaned in and whispered, "I think he only wanted to leave because he lost to Sir Palmer. He did not appreciate my speech about being a sore loser. It probably made things worse." Chrissy looked over and suddenly exclaimed, "Oh! You must meet my mother and father. I've told them so much about you. My father was sure I was stretching the truth about finding another princess who dislikes princessy things as much as me!"

Samantha smiled warily. "I hope they don't have the wrong impression of me."

Linden suddenly appeared at her side. "I am certain they do not. I also gave them a report about how beautiful and . . . interesting women of Mittra are." His voice lowered as he murmured in her ear, "I also told them we would soon be announcing a momentous occasion."

Seeing the bright shimmer of Talia from the corner of her eye, Samantha nodded and turned to smile sweetly at Linden. "I do not know what you mean, Prince Linden. *I* am certain that you could not have spoken to *my* father about any momentous occasion, or he would have written and warned me about it. Perhaps you should keep your announcements to yourself."

Linden gave a little jerk and opened his mouth as if to protest, but no sound came out. Samantha gave him another wide smile and then turned back to Chrissy.

"Tell me what to do to stay on Miss Talia's good side," Chrissy whispered in an awed voice, a bit of fear lurking in her eyes.

Samantha laughed as she put her arm through Chrissy's. "You have nothing to worry about, my friend. I only hope your cousin has learned his lesson."

‡

"Do you like your room?" Chrissy asked as she stood in the doorway of the guest room Samantha was staying in.

"I love it! The bed is really comfortable, and the morning light will come right through this window and wake me up. And the little passage way to Talia's room is perfect. Thank you!" Samantha crossed the room to her friend.

"Would you like to go for a walk before dinner?" Chrissy asked with a smile. "I know you said that you wanted to see the stables."

"Yes! My poor horse is missing me, I'm sure. And hopefully no one would be looking for me," Samantha murmured as they walked down the corridor to the stairwell.

Chrissy laughed. "I don't think Linden will be looking for you anytime soon, but maybe another prince will be?"

Samantha blushed and concentrated on walking down the curving staircase. "I don't know any other prince who is interested in me, Chrissy. If you haven't noticed, I'm not the most popular girl on the circuit."

"I hate to disagree with you, but you can't tell me you haven't noticed Prince Nolan watching you whenever we are at a banquet. Or at a ball. Or when you arrived here," Chrissy teased as they stepped outside into the fading light of the afternoon.

"No, he must have been looking at someone else," Samantha protested, shaking her head. "Nolan hates me. He's been avoiding me since . . . Well, for a while," she finished weakly.

Chrissy turned toward the stables behind the castle. "Why would he be avoiding you?"

"I don't think you'd believe me." Samantha kicked a pebble on the dirt path.

"*Samantha.*" Chrissy stopped in the middle of the path. "You're the first person I've met who actually talks to me about real things. I've been honest with you. You can trust me to keep a secret."

Sighing, Samantha sat down on a large, flat rock that bordered the path. "Nolan hates me because I knocked him down."

Seeing the astonished look on Chrissy's face, she hurried to explain. "I was practicing dancing with Dawes, my friend. I'm sure you've seen him around. Anyway, Nolan walked in and saw us dancing. When Dawes left, Nolan and I had an argument. He grabbed my wrist, my training kicked in, and . . . I knocked him down."

Chrissy slowly sat down next to Samantha and began to giggle. "*You* knocked down a man? A *prince*? Oh, Samantha . . . ." She held her sides as she started to laugh harder. "I would have loved to see that!"

"It's not that funny! He hasn't spoken to me since that night, and I can't simply walk up to him and apologize. That would not go over well," Samantha muttered as she rose to her feet and continued toward the stable.

"When you said that your training kicked in, what did you mean?" Chrissy asked as she ran after her friend.

Samantha shrugged. "My father felt that a woman should be trained to protect herself, and I had Queen Einara as my model. She led her people into battle, and they respected her. She never married and . . . well, I don't see any men lining up for me."

Chrissy placed her hand on Samantha's arm. "Could you teach me?"

"*Teach* you? To defend yourself? What would your parents say? What would Linden say?" *When did I turn into my mother?*

"They wouldn't have to know. I won't even tell my sisters. We can ask Talia to do some kind of charm so no one knows who we are. I know that fairies have different powers, and Talia is the most powerful fairy I've ever met. Please, please say yes, Samantha!"

Samantha sighed, glancing at the pleading look on her friend's face. Then she smiled. "Okay, I will train you. But here are the rules. First, you cannot tell *anyone*. Talia can know because we need her for the charm. Second, you have to call me Sam. All my close friends do."

Chrissy threw her arms around Samantha and began to jump up and down. "This will be so much fun!"

"It's not all fun," Samantha cautioned, stepping back. "It can be dangerous. I must tell you that you'll have a wide assortment of bruises and scrapes that you'll have to explain. But hopefully you'll be able to fight off an attacker or come to someone's aid when it's needed. Those were the basics Elan and Sir Cabot first taught me. After that, I began the training to be a squire." Samantha clapped her hand over her mouth, groaning.

Chrissy's eyes widened. "A squire? To become a knight? You really are like Queen Einara! Can you teach me that as well? I *promise* I will not tell. This is the most exciting thing to ever happen in my life, and I don't want to ruin it."

"I believe you, Chrissy, I really do. But training as a knight is even more grueling. You won't like me anymore. You're going to be extremely tired, and you won't want to dance at the balls—especially when I know Edric will be there."

Chrissy's cheeks grew pink. "Prince Edric doesn't take any notice of me."

"Ha! Haven't you noticed that he can't keep his eyes off of you? He always asks you to dance multiple times and waits to escort you to dinner."

"I suppose I don't notice him the way you don't notice Nolan watching you," Chrissy shot back with a smile, seeing her friend's flush.

"Fine, we're even," Samantha declared. "Now to start your training. Do you think you can borrow some of your cousin's old clothes?"

✝

Samantha spent a week introducing Chrissy to the basics of self-defense. Chrissy begged her to start training for jousting but Samantha managed to put her off, promising they would cover that in the future.

"You two have worn yourselves out, haven't you?" Talia asked one afternoon. Samantha had just completed a training session with Chrissy and was soaking in the bath. "There's a ball tonight. Shouldn't you give Princess Chrissy a break?"

Samantha laughed. "It's me who needs a break, Taley! She has so

142

much energy and willpower. I can't hold her back. I almost suspect she has some latent fairy gifts."

She raised her eyebrows at Talia, who shook her head with a smile. "I have no way of knowing about that. Keeping track of *you* has kept me busy these last eighteen years." She stared out the window and sighed. "Did you know that Osric and Elan visited this castle many years ago? It was shortly before the Rebellion and the fall of Sansevierra. If you look far enough, you can see where Synterius' greenery ends at the Sansevierra Desert. Did Osric teach you about all of this?"

Samantha nodded as she stepped from the tub, wrapping herself in a robe. "I studied what you wrote about the Fairy Rebellion. Is it hard to come here, knowing that King Aspen's father was involved in something that killed so many fairies?"

"It *is* hard to be here, but not for the reason you think. King Aspen is a good man. He was not present when Lord Oblex deceitfully led the Synterius army into Alvan. Aspen has been most kind and has apologized to fairies by a decree, offering shelter to them after he ascended to the throne. That is why your friend, Chrissy, has fairy gifts. Not all children in Synterius do. There are many fairies that still hold a grudge and have been unwilling to bless those whom they feel as undeserving. The most difficult thing about returning here is knowing that my birthplace is forever gone, removed from the memory of most. My father died in that place, serving his king and queen. His sacrifice saved the life of his wife and daughter. I hope I can honor his memory by serving you and your family, Samantha," Talia answered quietly, tears streaming from her luminous eyes.

Samantha hugged the small fairy, feeling her own tears starting. "I'm so sorry. Oh, Taley! I appreciate that you're here with me. I'm the one who should be honoring you. You give me something to aspire to."

Talia reached up and brushed the tears off the princess's face. "Stop crying, Sammy. You need to look beautiful for the ball tonight, don't you? Now, you must tell me, if Linden is out . . . then who is in?"

Samantha turned toward her wardrobe, staring at the dresses inside. "Chrissy has been asking me the same thing. I suppose you think Nolan has been watching me as well?"

The fairy nodded as she helped Samantha step into her dress. "Every night since we've been here, he has been standing off to the side, observing you. Have you not noticed him?"

"I've been trying so hard to avoid both him and Linden that I haven't even seen him. I only know he's here because Edric tells me when we go out for a ride. Edric never asked me about what happened in the library, so I suppose Nolan didn't tell him."

Talia put her hands on Samantha's shoulders and smiled at her in the mirror. "Look for him tonight, Sam. Maybe he's been waiting for a sign from you. He might also not want to get flipped on his back again."

Samantha rolled her eyes as Talia went to fetch the maid. "Fine. I'll at least *look* at him tonight. Maybe I'll say hello, but I'm not making any promises."

‡

Nolan had been watching the doorway for the last fifteen minutes. He knew the second Samantha stepped into the room. He felt his breath catch in his throat as he took in her deep green dress that seemed to make her eyes shine like emeralds dug from the richest mines in Lagola. He took a step back into the shadows of the corner, content to simply watch her. Nolan saw her slowly scan the room as if she was looking for someone in particular.

Nolan's eyes narrowed as he watched Linden approach Samantha from behind, placing a hand on her shoulder. He scowled when he saw Samantha turn with an eager smile that slid into a frown as she faced the prince of Synterius.

Nolan's eyebrows shot up in surprise. *She doesn't care for Synterius? Then why was he bragging down at the training field yesterday that there would soon be an announcement of engagement?*

He watched as Linden held out his hand to Samantha, who shook her head in refusal. Linden's face was stormy as he spoke to the princess, but still she would not take his hand. Nolan heard the musicians begin to play the first song to open the ball and he turned to look for Edric.

Come on, Edric. You're her escort. I don't want to make a scene and embarrass her again.

He sighed with relief as his brother approached the couple. Edric bowed to Samantha, completely ignoring Linden as he took her hand and spun her away. Nolan caught a glimpse of the hatred burning in Linden's eyes. *He really needs to work on that jealousy issue,* Nolan thought with a smile, turning toward the dance floor.

Suddenly, Samantha was in front of him. Edric placed her hand in Nolan's. "Take care of her for me, brother. I need to attend to other matters." Edric winked as he walked across the ballroom.

Nolan looked into Samantha's eyes, sure that the surprise he saw in them was mirrored in his own. "May I?" he asked gruffly, gesturing toward her waist with his left hand.

Samantha nodded, her cheeks turning pink. Her front teeth lightly bit her lower lip.

Nolan led her out onto the dance floor, carefully holding her at arms length. He worried that he would scare her away if he held her any closer.

"Samantha," he murmured, a thrill shooting through him when she gazed up at him. Her eyes sparkled in the light of the ballroom. "I need to apologize to you about interrupting you and your friend back in Isonox."

"No," Samantha protested, "I must apologize to you. Knocking you down was inexcusable. You are completely justified in hating me."

Nolan came to a stop momentarily as he stared at her. "I do *not* hate you." He quickly looked around, spotting the open doors that led to the main courtyard of the castle. He spun her around, aiming for the doorway. "Can we continue this outside?"

Samantha nodded and then looked down again, biting her lip. *What is she thinking? I want to ask, but I don't want to start an argument again. Or get another headache.*

Once they were in the courtyard, Nolan released her, but immediately wished he had not. Samantha began to walk down the path leading to a large grove of trees. Nolan silently followed her to the center of the grove, where two marble benches faced each other. She glanced back at him and then sat on the bench facing away from the castle.

He sat on the bench opposite her, placing his elbows on his knees and leaning forward. "I want to talk to you. Not argue with you," he began, catching Samantha's eye. "I don't know what else to do. I've tried avoiding you, letting Synterius have—"

"Synterius? You mean *Linden*?" Samantha's nose wrinkled in distaste. "There is *nothing* between Linden and me. Well, not on my side, anyway. I've been trying to avoid him, actually. And avoid—" She stopped talking and stared down at her hands curled up in her lap.

"Me?" At her nod, he stood up and sat next to her. "Samantha—"

"You can call me Sam. You've known me long enough," she interrupted quietly, her eyes still cast down.

Nolan's face brightened as he leaned toward her. "Sam, I don't want us to avoid each other. We're going to be in Synterius for the next month or so, and we'll be at all the same events. I don't want things to be awkward."

Samantha raised her eyes. "I agree with you." She paused. "Speaking of awkward, can I ask you a question?"

Nolan nodded with a wry smile. "I think I know what you're going to ask, and I think I should have an apology ready for that as well."

"Why did you run away after you kissed me?" Samantha's voice was so faint that Nolan almost missed the question.

"Oh, I thought you were going to ask *why* I kissed you." He sighed and ran his hand through his hair. "I wasn't trying to run." He stood and began to pace back and forth. *How do I explain it to her?*

"Was the kiss that bad?"

He stopped pacing and stared directly at her. "That bad?" he repeated, grabbing her hands and pulling her up.

She stood before him, the question still in her eyes. Nolan softly placed his palm against her smooth cheek, and she raised her lips to meet his. He felt her soft lips tremble beneath his as he put his other hand on her waist, pulling her closer. Her arms wrapped around his neck and Nolan felt her fingers moving through his hair. He pressed his lips harder against hers and moved his hand to the back of her head, feeling her hair fall down from the pins that held it up.

His heart was beating so loud that he was sure she could hear it as he slowly pulled away. Wrapping both arms around her waist, he stared down at her. The blush on her cheeks brought on his smoldering smile.

"Did that answer your question?" he asked as she laid her head against his shoulder.

"I don't remember my question."

"Won't Synterius be jealous," Nolan said to himself, but Samantha sprang back from him. Her mouth crumpled into an angry slash against her pale face.

"*What* did you say?" she demanded, her green eyes glinting dangerously.

Nolan groaned and tried to pull her back to him. "I didn't mean it like that. I was only thinking—"

"You think rather loudly!" Samantha cut him off, swatting his hands away. "Is this just a game to you? Do you and Linden have a competition going on? Who can kiss the princess from Mittra first?"

"No!" Nolan yelled, feeling his frustration rise. "It's not like that, Sam!" He took a step closer to her, but she held up both of her hands.

"You know what, Nolan? I don't want to know what it's like. I understand now. Woo me, steal some kisses, and add me to your list of conquests. What do they say? 'Fool me once, shame on you. Fool me twice, shame on me.' Well, shame on me for believing you." Tears streamed down her face, and she hurried down the path toward the courtyard.

"Samantha, please believe me. Listen to me!" he called, running after her.

She spun around, a fierce look on her face. Balling her hand into a fist, she hissed, "If you come any closer, so help me, I will punch you in the face!"

Nolan stopped so fast that he stumbled on the gravel path. Samantha automatically threw her arm out, catching him. He recovered quickly, standing up while still keeping his hold on her arm.

"How did you get so strong?" he questioned, eyebrows raised. "I thought you were going down with me."

"Will you let me go?" Samantha huffed, trying to pull her arm away.

"If you really want me to, then I will. But I would *really* like to talk to you before you run away." He stared down into her eyes, willing her to stay.

Samantha sighed, frowning at him. "You have one minute to convince me you're not pond scum." She paused. "No, I won't insult pond scum that way."

Nolan threw his head back and laughed. "You are the most original girl I have ever met in my life. You run fast, you can climb trees, you threaten to punch princes in the face, and you are an amazingly good kisser." He smiled when he saw the blush creep onto her cheeks again.

"I don't threaten *all* princes," she muttered, pulling her arm away from him. "Only those ones who kiss and tell."

"I haven't told anyone but Edric," Nolan said quietly, stepping toward her. "And I don't know what I have to do to convince you that

I'm not scum. I can promise you that Linden and I do not have a bet, a competition, or any such thing going on. I simply hate the man. I hate it when his slimy hands touch you. I hate the way he looks at you."

Samantha's eyes filled with surprise, and then she smiled slyly. "So, you've been watching me?"

Nolan could feel his own face grow hot. "Not watching in a disturbing way. More like in a brotherly way." Seeing the knowing look in her eyes, he shook his head and stepped closer. "No, that's a lie. I don't feel brotherly towards you. Ever since I first kissed you, I've only been thinking about you. It's been killing me to see you with him. I want him to stay away from you. I don't trust him."

"Why don't you trust him?" She moved away, placing her hands on her hips. "Do you not think I can take care of myself?"

"You managed to flip me on my back, so I know you *can* take care of yourself," Nolan smiled, reaching his hand out to her. "But you shouldn't *have* to."

Samantha stared at his hand, hesitating for a moment. She started to reach her hand out, but someone suddenly shouted for her.

"Princess Samantha!"

She shook her head, flashed Nolan a weak smile, and turned to go back up the path. "I'm out here!"

Samantha was half way up the path when she glanced back to see Nolan standing there, watching her. "Remember what I said," he called as she turned back to enter the courtyard.

How could I be so stupid? I had her here, and she actually kissed me back. I had to ruin the moment by mentioning that idiot, Linden! Did she actually forgive me? Could talk to her? Maybe I can catch up to her.

‡

"Hello, I'm Princess Samantha. Someone was calling for me?" Samantha said to the young footman, who was standing at the door that led to the ballroom.

He stared at her for a moment, and then shook his head. "Prince Linden was looking for you quite insistently, Princess. He is in the ballroom at the present time."

Samantha nodded her thanks to the servant. Before she could leave, he hissed at her.

"Excuse me?" she said, slightly offended.

"Beg your pardon, princess, but you might want to er . . . look in the mirror," he whispered, pointing at his own head.

Samantha's eyes grew wide. *My hair must look affright after that kiss with Nolan!* "Thank you! I was taking a walk outside and it got caught in . . . something," she finished weakly, strolling down the hallway to the ladies chamber. *That something being Nolan's fingers!*

Samantha gasped at her reflection, looking into the mirror on the wall near a table that held brushes and combs. *Nolan certainly made a mess! How am I ever going to fix this?*

At that moment, the door opened and Chrissy walked in. "Sam, there you are! What in the world . . ." her voice trailed off as she looked at her friend's hair.

"Oh, Chrissy, I'm so thankful it's you! Can you please do something with this?"

Chrissy laughed her tinkling laugh and picked up a comb from the table. "How many guesses do I get?"

Samantha looked at her friend's reflection in the mirror. "Guesses for what?"

"To guess which prince managed to do this to your hair?" Chrissy's eyes shone with mischief as she pulled pins out of Samantha's ruined hairdo.

"One," Samantha answered, watching her cheeks grow rosy. *Why do*

I have to blush so much? It always gives me away.

"Well, seeing as my cousin was stomping about looking for you, I can safely assume it wasn't him. Since Prince Edric was in attendance tonight, but was dancing with me, that leaves . . . Prince Nolan?" Chrissy glanced down at her friend.

"You are an awfully good guesser, Chris. Yes, it was Nolan," Samantha admitted with a sigh. "But you can't tell anyone! Please." She turned on the stool and grabbed Chrissy's hand.

"Who will I tell, Sam? Really. One of those venomous princesses just waiting for the next piece of juicy gossip? My *cousin?*" Chrissy smiled and patted Samantha's hand. "Don't worry. Your secret is safe with me. Now, let's finish your hair and get back out there."

Samantha grinned, letting Chrissy comb out of the tangles of her matted hair. Once she was done, they both headed towards the ballroom.

"Do you know why your cousin was looking for me?" Samantha whispered as they stood in the doorway, watching couples pair up.

"No, but he looked really upset," Chrissy whispered back with a frown. "He was asking everyone he saw where you were. I know you would have told me, but you're not interested in Linden, right?"

"No! I'm sorry to say this about your own family member, but he is too demanding. He scares me." She looked around the room, hoping to steer clear of Linden.

Suddenly, a hand gripped her upper arm tightly and pulled her back against a solid object. "There you are," Linden murmured huskily in her ear, holding her against his chest. "I have been looking for you, Princess. Did you not hear?"

Samantha shivered as his breath tickled her neck. "Excuse me, Prince Linden. Your cousin and I were in the middle of a conversation—" She tried to pull away from his firm grasp.

"You'll excuse us, Cousin Chrysanthemum," Linden drawled out, backing out of the room. "The princess and I have some matters to discuss. Privately. In a spot she is acquainted with."

Chrissy's eyes were filled with panic, and she began to wring her hands. *What do I do?* she mouthed to Samantha.

Nothing. I'm fine! She tried to put on a smile.

When they were in the hallway, Samantha attempted to remove his hand from her arm once more. "This behavior is not very becoming. What would your aunt say?" Samantha scolded him, forcing down the panic that was threatening to take over.

"My aunt is in the ballroom, along with most of the other guests. No one will have much of anything to say," Linden spoke in a monotone as he practically dragged her outside into the courtyard.

Remember your training. Make a plan, Sam. Focus on the problem at hand. She remembered her birthday evening in the garden with Nolan, planning out how to humiliate him. *But this is so much worse. Nolan was right about staying away from Linden and needing his help. But I told Chrissy I don't need any help. Can I run away fast enough? Should I play along? I don't want to play along!*

"There is a charming area just ahead, Princess Samantha. I believe you know it well," Linden snarled into her ear. He shoved her ahead of him, strolling along the path she had walked with Nolan earlier.

What is wrong with him? How does he know I know this spot?

"Oh no," she cried, struggling harder against his hold on her. He brought his other hand down on her shoulder, forcing her to sit on the marble bench facing the castle.

"Oh yes. I saw you out here with him. Prince *Nolan*," Linden sneered, his face twisting with hatred. "Here you've been stringing me along, playing your little flirtation game, and making me think you wanted *me*. Only to see you kissing him! What am I supposed to think about that?" He grabbed her wrists and pulled her up against him savagely.

"You are mad! I have never played any sort of game with you. I have been avoiding you as much as I can," Samantha yelled at him, trying to push away from his body. "Let me go! I will scream if I have to!"

His cold laugh sent chills down her spine. "I will refute whatever you say. My uncle and the rest of the court will believe me. Who would believe a *woman*? Listen to me now, Princess. You will marry me. *I* will have you, *not* Lagola. If you do not agree, I will ruin your name, and then where do you stand?"

Samantha could not believe what she was hearing. *He is truly insane! How am I going to fight him? I don't even have a weapon on me.* Something caught her eye, and she quickly formed a plan. *I hope this works.*

"How could you? Oh, I feel faint," Samantha's voice faded as she rolled her eyes back in her head, forcing her body to go limp. She could hear Linden grunt with surprise as he took her body in his arms.

"What do I do now?" he muttered as he lowered her body to the bench.

As soon as she was free of his arms, she reached down and pulled a sheathed dagger from his boot. *I've never actually used a dagger before,* she thought for a moment. Suddenly, her hand somehow knew what to do. *Elan's gift! Thank you!*

Crouching down in a defensive position, Samantha unsheathed the short blade and brandished it before Linden.

He approached her, hands out. "You don't even know what you're doing," he sneered.

Samantha's arm flicked out and nicked his hands several times before he stepped back in shock. "What *are* you?" he bellowed before he charged her again.

She managed to slice his arm as she dodged him, but she was thrown off balance. She fell to the ground, the dagger clattering away under the bench.

Linden grabbed her by the hair, his face dark with rage. He jerked her up, ignoring her screams of pain. "Enough!" he shouted as he slapped her across the face. "You are mine!"

Samantha looked through her swollen eyes to see his lips coming down toward hers. "Nolan!" she screamed as loud as she could.

‡

"Prince Nolan?" Chrissy's voice was very high as she interrupted Edric and Nolan's conversation in the drawing room. "Could you please come with me?"

Edric came to Chrissy's side and took her hand. "May I be of assistance to you, Princess?"

She flushed, shaking her head. "No, just Prince Nolan. Unless . . . yes, fine. Just come now!" she said in urgency.

She led them through the passageways quickly, glancing down various hallways with an anxious look on her pale face.

"Princess, could you please tell us what this is about?" Nolan asked as he followed her, giving Edric an inquiring look.

"My cousin Linden and your . . . um, Samantha," she answered over her shoulder.

Your Samantha? Edric mouthed to him with a wide smile.

"What about your cousin and Samantha?" Nolan demanded, touching Chrissy's arm. "Where are they? Is she in danger?"

Tears filled Chrissy's eyes as she shook her head. "I don't know. He came into the ballroom and made her leave with him. They could be anywhere!"

Nolan could hear the blood roaring in his ears, but he made himself focus on the girl in front of him. "What exactly did he say?"

Chrissy twisted her hands together as tears ran down her cheeks. "He said they had private matters to discuss in a spot that she was acquainted with. But that could be anywhere!"

The grove. He must have seen us there. Nolan's eyes were furious as they turned toward Edric. "Gather whatever men you can and meet me outside by the little grove of trees. The princess knows," he nodded at Chrissy. "Get there before I kill someone."

Nolan barely registered Chrissy's gasp as he ran through the hallway and out into the courtyard. He could see a shadowy figure out in the grove and he sprinted as fast as he could. *Let her be okay! I'm going to kill that swine if he's hurt her!*

His stomach twisted as he saw Linden strike Samantha across the face and then force his lips towards hers.

"Nolan!" Samantha screamed. It shook him to his core, causing him to see red.

He ran, pushing Linden down in a flying tackle. He rolled onto the ground with him and came up on top. Nolan fisted his hand and drove it into Linden's mouth.

"Don't you dare kiss her!" he cried as he punched him again, smashing Linden's front tooth. "Don't even touch her!"

Nolan felt hands pulling him off, but he continued to kick and punch as he was dragged away.

Linden slowly raised himself from the ground, holding his bleeding arm. He turned his swollen face toward the silently watching crowd.

Nolan shrugged off Edric's hands, ignoring everyone else. He dropped to his knees where Samantha sat huddled next to Chrissy. "Where did he hurt you?" he demanded, looking deeply into her eyes. "Is it just your face? Samantha!"

She only shook her head, staring up at him as if she had never seen him before. Something under the bench caught his eye and he moved towards it. "Whose dagger is this?" Nolan questioned as he lifted it up.

Chrissy gasped. "My father gave that to Linden last Christmas."

"What is the meaning of this?" King Aspen's booming voice was heard throughout the grove, and the crowd parted for him.

Nolan bowed his head at the king, offering him the dagger. "Your majesty, your daughter brought word to my brother and me that your nephew took this young lady, Princess Samantha, against her will. I arrived to see *him*," Nolan paused, glaring at Linden. "Strike her across her face and then attempted to force her to kiss him. I . . . er, intervened."

King Aspen gave both Linden and Nolan an apprising look. "I can see that. And the cuts on my nephew?"

"That was me," a shaky voice sounded. Samantha stood up with Chrissy's help and stared at the king. "He didn't understand me when I said no, so I had to show him."

The king gazed at her. "Do they train all women in Mittra the art of self-defense?" He didn't wait for an answer. "We will discuss that later. Linden, come forward!"

All eyes turned toward the Prince of Synterius as he limped towards his uncle.

"What have you to say, boy?" King Aspen spoke sternly.

"It wasn't my fault, uncle. That *wench* tempted me." Linden turned toward Samantha. "You should have just said yes and married me! Do you see the trouble you've caused? You—"

"Enough! Linden, this will be brought before the high court. They will have no trouble determining that there will be a new heir to the throne. This behavior is unseemly for anyone, especially for a prince. You are officially discharged from the role of my heir."

Linden charged for Samantha. "I'll kill you for ruining me!" he screamed. He never got close enough to make good on his threat. Edric and Nolan both stepped forward, creating a wall in front of Linden. He crashed into the men, staggering back from the impact.

Edric caught Nolan's arm as he prepared to strike Linden. "My turn, brother. Samantha is like a sister to me, and we take care of our family, don't we?" Edric grinned.

Nolan stepped back and Edric quickly put Linden in a chokehold. "Your majesty, perhaps some of your men could bring some rope to tie his hands?" Edric called out, just as Linden passed out.

CHAPTER TWELVE

"What do you think, Taley? Have they faded enough to go out today?" Samantha asked as she looked at her face in the mirror. It had been two days since Linden's attack and she missed being out in the sunshine.

Talia's smiling face appeared in the mirror behind Samantha, carefully searching the features so familiar to her. "Sammy, dear, your face looks . . . dreadful. I think you should stay in again today."

Samantha gave a little laugh. "I appreciate your honesty most days. When you're talking about my face, 'dreadful' is not on my list of favorite words."

Sighing, she rose from the padded seat and walked over to the arched window that looked out to the east of Synterius. The sun was only beginning to rise, and the surrounding countryside was lit with golden rays, making the grass shimmer and glow. *I want to be out there! I am so tired of staying inside my room. I didn't do anything wrong. I want to ride Windstorm. I want to practice for the tournament. I want to go walking with Chrissy.*

Samantha glanced down at her hands, noting the scrapes that were starting to heal. *Why did I have to fall down on that path? Why couldn't I have beaten Linden on my own?* The night was still a blur to her.

"What are you thinking about?" Talia quietly asked, joining her at the window.

"How I could have done something different with Linden. I should have been able to do it on my own. Why did Nolan have to interfere?" she cried, slapping her palm against the wall. "Ouch," she whimpered, cradling her sore hand, which had begun to bleed again.

"Samantha." Talia's stern voice caught her attention. "You need to stop this attitude. *I* am thankful Nolan was there. What might have happened if he hadn't gotten there when he did? What if King Aspen hadn't believed you?"

The princess hung her head. "I hadn't thought about all of that. I've been mad at Linden for what he did and frustrated at Nolan for not believing I could take care of myself."

Talia shook her head as she led Samantha to a chair. She began to wrap a bandage around the bleeding hand. "I have spoken to Nolan, and I was surprised to hear him say something about that night. You didn't tell me about this, so I do not know if it did, in fact, happen."

"What did Nolan say? I haven't been trying to keep anything from you, Taley. I promise," Samantha said earnestly, looking up at her.

"Nolan said that after Linden hit you, you screamed his name." Talia waited for Samantha's reaction.

"Why would I yell Linden's name?" Her eyes slid shut as she tried to think, and then they suddenly snapped back open. "Oh! I yelled Nolan's name. Why did I do that?" She stood and began to pace back and forth rapidly. *He's going to think I wanted him to save me. And after I told him that I didn't need his help. Does he think I owe him something now?*

"Sammy, you're going to wear a hole in the floor with all that pacing," Talia smiled. "I think you said Nolan's name because you knew he would help you. Did you two work things out?"

"You could say that." She sighed and began to straighten the various bottles on her vanity table. "We were able to talk. And argue. And then talk again."

Talia's eyes twinkled. "*And?*"

"And he kissed me. Oh, Taley, I kissed him back! What must he think of me? He saw me out there with Linden shortly after I was out there with him. I can't face him right now."

A knock sounded on the door, and Samantha hurried to answer it. A servant stood there with an envelope in his hand.

"Thank you." She took the letter and closed the door. "Look, a letter addressed to you and me."

Talia sat down with her embroidery. "What does it say?"

"We are specially invited to sit in King Aspen's box during the amateur tournament in two days time." She paused and lightly tapped the folded letter against her open palm. "I suppose we can go. 'Sir Palmer' can't enter the amateur events. He's already been paid for winning. I believe Edric said he wanted to enter this tournament, just to see if he has the skill to do it. Nolan would probably be down on the field with Edric, so I won't have to see him." She paused, thinking. "Yes, that would work. Taley, would you like to attend the tournament with me? I seem to have gotten over my allergies to horses, grass, and whatever else I've said in the last two months."

"Of course. It would be nice to see the tournament from a different perspective for once." Talia smiled. "And, of course, we won't have to be fearful that 'Sir Palmer' would be exposed for who *she* really is."

‡

"Have you seen Chrissy anywhere?" Samantha whispered to Talia. They were in the royal box, ready to watch the amateur tournament. "She said she would be here."

"No, I have not," Talia whispered back as she scanned the crowd. "Have you asked her mother?"

"I didn't want to worry her, but I suppose I should say something," She rose and walked down the riser to the front row where King Aspen and Queen Laurel sat in comfortable chairs. "Excuse me, your highness," Samantha began, looking at Chrissy's mother. "Have you seen your daughter anywhere?"

Queen Laurel's heart shaped face and wide blue eyes were obviously handed down to her daughter. Her honey blonde hair was beginning to show streaks of grey, but her face was unlined by wrinkles. Her lips parted in a smile as she leaned toward Samantha. "Princess Samantha, how good to see you! Which daughter did you mean? I believe Chamomile is sitting with Magnolia over to the far right of the box. Lilac is . . . oh, she's down there near that knight from Lagola. Prince Edric, is it? As for Chrysanthemum, I have not seen her all day." A faint frown creased the queen's face. "She did say she would be here."

King Aspen patted his wife's hand. "Chrissy will come, my dear. Do not fret." He turned his eyes toward Samantha, gesturing for her to come closer. "I am very happy to see you looking so well," he said quietly, a serious look on his face. "I must again apologize for my nephew's appalling actions against you. He has been taken care of."

Samantha's face paled. "You didn't execute him, did you?"

"No! Oh, perish the thought. We simply exiled him forever. He's now a man without a country. Once word gets out what he did, no one will take him in." Aspen's eyes were hard. "My younger nephew, Hawthorn, is now my heir apparent. I will be more involved with his training to make sure he does not come out like his brother."

Samantha nodded, unsure of what to say. She saw movement on the field and turned to see what it was. *Edric is entering! Let's see how good he is,* she thought with a smile.

"Ah, Prince Edric of Lagola, is it?" King Aspen asked. "He seems to be an honorable man. Your opinion, Princess Samantha?"

"Edric is the very best of men. I spent many years of my childhood with the princes of Lagola." Noticing Aspen's raised eyebrows, she hurried on. "We have no romantic interest in each other, King Aspen. Edric is like a brother to me."

"I see. Well, in that case, how do you think he would suit my Chrissy?" Aspen asked, looking down at the man in question.

Samantha began to laugh. "I think he would suit Chrissy very well. I've been trying to find a way to get the two of them together, but I'm not the best matchmaker."

Aspen joined in her laughter. "You are quite honest, princess. I see why my daughter values your friendship so much. Oh, they are starting with a joust! That is rather surprising for an amateur competition."

Hawthorne leaned forward from his seat in the second row. "Uncle, it's not a *real* joust. They don't have to knock each other off the horse. The lances have blunt tips with colored chalk on the end. Whoever manages to mark the other the most after three runs is the winner."

"And how do you know this?" Queen Laurel asked her nephew. "Did you sneak down to the training ground when you should have been with your tutor?"

"Excuse me," Samantha said, eager to avoid a family confrontation. She returned to her seat next to Talia. "Any sign of her?" she whispered.

"No, but I believe Dawes has entered this competition. Isn't that your armor?" Talia pointed to the field. Samantha saw the armored figure astride a dark brown horse with white stockings.

Samantha looked at the knight that was getting ready to ride against Edric. She frowned. "It is my armor, but that's not my horse. It looks like . . . ." She squinted. "Oh no. Talia, we must do something!"

She jumped up and started down the steps at the back of the royal box. Talia ran after her, calling out, "Sam, wait! Who is it?"

Samantha ran as fast as she could, ignoring the glances and murmurs of those she passed as she made her way to the field. "Excuse me, please move!" she exclaimed as she pushed her way through the crowd.

A path opened in the crowd, and Samantha somehow knew it was Talia's doing. She pushed her way to the front and then came to a halt, her face frozen in horror.

The knight on the brown horse was already charging down the field, the lance held tight against his body, hooked into place. Edric's mount began to run as well. Samantha desperately thought of what she could do. *Could Talia help? What spell or charm would work so fast? Think, Samantha!*

She ran out onto the field, waving her arms to get the riders' attention. Edric was aiming his lance at his opponent's right shoulder. He turned his head toward Samantha, failing to notice that his lance was aimed at the other knight's head.

"Stop, Edric!" Samantha yelled, waving her arms. "You cannot—"

The two riders hit each other at the same time, but Edric's blow was harder, causing the smaller knight to slide from his saddle.

Edric threw up his visor and looked over at Samantha. "What?" he cried as he pulled his horse to a halt. She noticed a wild look of panic in his eyes.

Samantha ignored him. She darted toward the unmoving figure lying on the grass. After carefully removing the silver helmet, she stared down into Chrissy's pale face. She distantly heard the crowd cry out. She felt Talia sink down beside her as she patted Chrissy's cold cheek.

"Wake up, Chris. Please wake up!" Samantha urged, tears in her eyes. "I am so, so sorry. This is all my fault."

Talia reached into the pouch that hung from her side and removed a small bottle. She uncorked it and spilled a few drops out onto Chrissy's chalk white lips. The color slowly returned to Chrissy's face, but her eyes did not open.

"What's happening?" Samantha asked, but Talia just shook her head. "Edric!"

Samantha turned to see Nolan shouting and standing over his brother's body. *What happened to Edric?*

Talia stood and hurried over to Edric. "Nolan, what is wrong?" she asked, kneeling down.

"He threw himself off his horse to get over to Princess Chrissy, I suppose. But he stumbled and his horse kicked him." He turned to Talia, his dark eyes filled with despair. He grasped the fairy's hand. "Can you help him?"

Talia frowned. "We need to move him off the field and see how extensive his injuries are. Can you call for a stretcher?"

Nolan glanced over at Chrissy and then hurried away, bringing back four squires and two stretchers. He approached Samantha and Chrissy, directing the squires to carefully move her body.

"Nolan." Samantha's eyes were dulled of their normal vibrancy, and her bottom lip quivered. "Will they be okay?" She reached out, clinging to his arm.

He stared down at her, and she could see the intensity of his feelings in his eyes. "Did you know about this? That Chrissy would be competing today, I mean?"

"No! Nolan, believe me, I would *never* have encouraged her to do this. Would I want my friend to be hurt?" Before he could respond, she ran off the field, following the stretchers.

Chrissy, why would you go into a competition so early in your training? This is all my fault! If Edric is seriously injured, I will never forgive myself. Nolan will never forgive me. This is a nightmare.

Samantha entered the medic tent, Nolan right behind her. Her eyes slowly became accustomed to the cool darkness. She moved toward Chrissy's bed at the right side of the tent.

She picked up her friend's cold, limp hand and began to cry. "Chrissy,

I am so sorry! You have to wake up." She laid her head down on the bed and sobbed.

A hand rested on her shoulder, and Samantha glanced up to see King Aspen standing above her. His handsome face had turned a pallid grey.

"How did this happen?" he asked as Samantha stood up.

"Chrissy wanted me to train her in self-defense. We also did some work on the quintain. I am so sorry, your majesty. If I had known she would enter—"

"Will she live?" Aspen directed his question to Talia, his features strained.

Talia glanced up at the king before evaluating Chrissy. Gradually, her tense expression eased into a small smile. "She will live. I believe she might have a concussion, either from the lance or hitting the ground. It is difficult to say which one it was. I will be better able to appraise her condition when she regains consciousness."

Samantha watched the king take a deep breath as he closed his eyes. "Thank you, Miss Talia."

"Please, your majesty. I am so very sorry—"

Aspen held up his hand. "Don't apologize for my daughter's actions. She is responsible for her choices. I appreciate that you taught her the basics." He turned to Talia. "Will she wake soon?"

Talia administered a few more drops from her little bottle. After a moment, Chrissy's eyes slowly fluttered open. She stared up at the roof of the tent, blinking in confusion.

"How did I get here?" she murmured, turning towards her father. "Father, my head hurts so much. What happened?"

Aspen knelt beside the bed, taking his daughter's hand. "You do not remember entering the tournament?"

Chrissy gave a little gasp. "You knew it was me? All I remember is riding Brownie and seeing Edric's colors."

"I hit you in the head and knocked you off your horse," Edric's hoarse voice called out from the other side of the tent. Everyone rotated toward him. "Please forgive me, Princess. King Aspen, I will leave as soon as I can mount my horse. I have disgraced myself and my family's name."

"You will do nothing of the sort!" Aspen boomed. "This is *my* fault for not knowing what is going on in my own family. You must stay and convalesce until you are completely healed." The king glowered down at his daughter. "And you, young lady, are on restriction for scaring your mother and me half to death. We will discuss your punishment in full later."

Samantha walked toward Edric's bed, picking up his hand. She shook her head, her eyes brimming with tears. "I'm sorry for distracting you. I realized it was Chrissy and I wanted to warn you off."

Talia came over to examine Edric's body and shooed Samantha away. "Please wait outside the curtain, Sam. I'll let you know when I'm done. Nolan, you can stay if you like."

Samantha left the tent and stood in the shade behind it, noting that no one else was around. She wrapped her arms around herself, feeling the tears stream down her face. *How foolish can I be? How could I think that I could train someone? Once Elan and Sir Cabot hear, they'll take away my title of squire and I'll never test to be a knight. What will I do then?*

She didn't hear Nolan step up behind her until he cleared his throat. Samantha jumped and gave a little scream. He held up his hands, wearing a wary expression on his face.

"I'm not going to hurt you, Sam. I only came out here to talk to you," he said, glancing at her.

She shook her head, touching her forehead. "I'm sorry, Nolan. After everything with Linden, I'm just a little on edge."

Nolan tentatively moved closer, touching her elbow. "Your face looks a little better. Are you feeling well?"

Samantha ducked her head. "Thank you, I'm fine. Although my hair needs to grow back in a few places."

"Are you scared of me?" Nolan asked quietly, stepping back from her.

She shivered, thinking of the hateful rage on his face when he was punching Linden. "I've never seen you like that before. It was a little … disturbing."

Nolan crossed his arms over his chest, frowning. "He was attacking you. What did you expect me to do? And when you called—"

Samantha felt her face flush. "I wasn't *trying* to call out for you. I didn't even remember doing it until Talia reminded me. I thought I was able to handle it on my own." She wrapped her arms around herself again and faced away from him.

She felt Nolan's hand on her shoulder and she spun around, staring fearfully up at him. He gently gathered her into his arms, rocking her back and forth. "I'm not going to kiss you, so don't be afraid," he whispered. "I only want you to feel safe with me. Do you remember what I said? You shouldn't have to go at it alone. Whenever you call for me, I'll be there."

Samantha pulled away, wiping her eyes on her sleeve. "As my friend, Nolan?"

He dropped his arms to his sides. "If that's what you want."

Is that what I want? It would be so easy to just fall into him and let him solve everything. A sudden thought shook her. *What would Queen Einara do? Would she leave it to a man or would she try to work things out herself? If Linden ever comes back, I need to be ready to fight him. Nolan might promise he'll be there, but he really can't keep that promise. I need to be able to focus on other things. Chrissy needs to get better, Linden will need to be dealt with, and I need to train for the last tournament before going home.*

"That's what I want," she whispered brokenly.

Then, she darted away toward the castle, missing the look of disappointment flash over Nolan's face.

CHAPTER THIRTEEN

"*H*ave you noticed a change in your brother?" Chrissy glanced over at Edric. He sat on the couch opposite from her, and a low table loaded with books stood between them.

Edric glanced over at the elderly lady-in-waiting in the corner of the room. She was snoring softly with her eyes tightly closed and her chin was almost touching her chest.

Chrissy laughed. "Don't worry about Lady Louisa. She is quite old and mostly deaf. Mother wanted us to have a chaperone." Her cheeks flushed, but Edric smiled at her.

I wonder if she knows how adorable she looks. He took in her blonde hair, simply braided down her back. A few curls had escaped to frame her face. Her blue eyes danced merrily, while her lips . . . *Stop staring at her lips, Edric!* he admonished himself.

"Your mother doesn't trust a man with broken ribs and a broken hand to keep himself away from her daughter?" Edric asked, eyebrows raised.

"No, it was my father that had the issue. He said he remembers the goodwill tour he was on. A few broken bones wouldn't have kept him away from a pretty girl. Oh, dear. I shouldn't have said that." She opened up a book and held it in front of her face.

"You can't hide from me. I can see your cheeks glowing from here," Edric teased. "You and Sam have the same tell, you know. Whenever you are too honest, you blush. Or when you are given a compliment."

"And how would you know about me blushing from a compliment?" She lowered the book, a mischievous look on her face.

"You have the most beautiful laugh I have ever heard in my life. When I hear it, I want to laugh along." He paused. "What? No blush?"

"That's not exactly a blush inducing compliment! Maybe Nolan can teach you a few things. He's the one with the power to charm a girl, isn't he? Which brings me to my original question. Does he seem different to you?" Chrissy leaned forward, waiting for his answer.

Edric thought for a moment. "He's a bit more serious, I suppose. There aren't as many girls following him around. He doesn't dance as much at the balls and doesn't seem to flirt anymore." He paused. "Oh no, what's wrong with my brother?"

"The only thing 'wrong' with him is that he's in love." Chrissy grinned. "Isn't it obvious? He's not encouraging other girls. He's only dancing with *one* girl lately. We know he was in the garden with—"

Samantha swung open the door to the drawing room, startling the occupants inside. "Am I interrupting?"

The two invalids looked up at her with guilty expressions shining on their faces. Lady Louisa snorted in her sleep. Samantha nodded towards her. Chrissy held a finger up to her lips.

"How are your ribs, Edric?" Samantha asked, taking a seat on Chrissy's couch.

He winced as he touched his side. "They still feel broken, even with Talia's tonic. She said that healing bones is quite tricky, so I only have her tonic to work on my other injuries. I know it's only been four days, but I wish I was fully healed now. Ugh. This wouldn't have happened if Midnight hadn't stepped on me. I should sell the stupid animal. Can't even keep him from stepping on his master."

Chrissy and Samantha laughed at Edric's look of disgust. "Now, Edric, you know you love Midnight," Samantha admonished gently. "Do you think he *tried* to kick you in the ribs? Or step on your hand? Give the poor thing a little slack."

Edric held up his bandaged hand. "How am I supposed to fight with this?"

"It's a good thing you're a peace-maker, isn't it?" Samantha teased.

"If you're a peace-maker, how were you able to do what you did to Linden?" Chrissy asked, her voice low.

Edric looked directly at her. "Just because I have the fairy gift of peace-making doesn't mean that I let evil men hurt my friends or my family. I protect those I care for."

Samantha watched as Chrissy's cheeks turned pink. Edric continued to hold her gaze. *Ha! These two are finally able to talk,* Samantha thought. *Looks like Edric has someone else to care for now.*

Samantha cleared her throat. "I don't want to stay long, but I wanted to ask if you wanted to go for a ride next week, Chrissy. You told me about the Vexwalden Forest, and I'd hate to go home without seeing it. I wanted to plan ahead because next week will be busy with the final tournament and banquets."

A sudden loud snort caused them all to turn and look towards the corner where Lady Louisa had awoken.

"Princess Chrysanthemum, will you excuse me, please?" the lady asked in a wheezing voice. Chrissy nodded, and she slowly left the room.

Chrissy glanced up at Sam. "I would love to go for a ride in the forest! The doctor ordered me to stay inside for a few more days, just until my concussion is fully healed. My ankle is still rather sore, and the doctor said to stay off of it for a bit longer. I'm thankful that the fall didn't break it."

"The final tournament is next Thursday, eight days from now. Maybe we can ride on Wednesday?" Samantha proposed. Chrissy nodded in approval.

Edric fixed his gaze on Samantha. "I hope you learned something from Chrissy's incident, Sam. Maybe you can pass the word on to Sir Palmer?"

Samantha felt her smile falter. "What word might that be, Edric?"

"Tournaments are dangerous. He should consider avoiding the final one," Edric clenched his teeth. "I'm sure Chrissy would be happy to tell him the same thing. Broken ribs and a broken hand are hard enough to heal. A concussion could be life threatening, as *Sir Palmer* well knows."

"I am sure that *Sir Palmer* is already aware. He has been very careful in his training." Samantha plastered a fake smile on her face. "He would appreciate your concern, but would say it is unnecessary."

Edric's face showed his anger and frustration. "Do I need to get Nolan involved in this?" he demanded.

"No, I can take care of it," Samantha answered harshly. "Sir Palmer will not be entering the competition if it bothers you that much. I would ask you not to speak about this conversation with your brother. He takes on enough as it is."

"What is going on?" Chrissy's eyes were wide with disbelief. "I thought you two were friends. What does Sir Palmer have to do with this?"

"Princess, you have no idea what this is about," Edric warned, keeping his eyes glued to Samantha. "I do not think Samantha wants me to say anything more."

"More secrets, Sam?" Chrissy asked quietly, her mouth turned down.

Samantha sighed. "Fine." She stomped over to the door and swung it shut. "Chrissy, I was not fully honest with you. I told you I was in training to be a knight. That was true. What I didn't tell you was I've assumed the identity of Dawes' brother, Sir Palmer, a knight back in Mittra. He needed to enter the tournaments to make money for his family. He was injured and I took his place."

Chrissy's mouth hung open in disbelief. "I don't believe it. You are the most amazing princess I have ever met!" She clapped her hands, a grin spreading on her face.

Samantha glanced at Edric, noting his surprise. "Then you're not mad at me?"

"How could I be mad? You do things other people only dream about. Here I am, doing my embroidery, painting landscapes, and learning to dance. But you're winning competitions to help your friend! You really are like Queen Einara," Chrissy said softly.

Suddenly, the door swung open. Nolan stood in the doorway, a bouquet of flowers in one hand and a chessboard tucked under his arm. "Here you all are!"

Samantha held her breath as he walked by her. She had not seen him since that day outside the tent. When he passed her, he just smiled and nodded politely. *Treating me just like a friend*, she acknowledged with a pain in her chest. *Just like I asked.*

Nolan could hardly believe his luck. He had come to visit his brother and Chrissy, but Samantha happened to be there as well. He felt his heart skip a beat as he glanced at her, noting that the bruises had completely faded and the bandages had been removed from her hands. *She really doesn't know how beautiful she is. How was she able to fight off Linden for as long as she had?* Nolan knew personally how strong an adversary Linden was, and he was surprised that Samantha could fight back as hard as she did.

Nolan saw his brother glance at Samantha and then back to him. Edric raised his eyebrows and then winked at him. He narrowed his eyes at his brother's insinuation. "I've come to play chess with you and keep you from boring this poor girl to death," he said as he started setting up the chess set.

"He doesn't bore me!" Chrissy laughed. "We were just discussing ... um, current events."

Nolan could see Edric smirk from his couch. He quirked an eyebrow at his brother, and Edric smiled blankly back at him. *What were they really discussing?*

"Oh, and the history of Sansevierra," Chrissy added as Edric nodded enthusiastically.

"I need to teach my brother how to talk to women," Nolan joked, avoiding looking at Samantha's face. "History? Come on, Edric."

"Actually, Nolan, there's something very interesting in this book," Edric said, his voice low. He pushed a thick, leather bound book toward his brother. "The book from Mittra was actually written by Miss Talia. This one is similar and it has a little more information on the man who led the troops from Synterius into Sansevierra."

Nolan opened the book where a ribbon marked the page. His eyes widened. "The Evil of the East?"

Chrissy nodded. "Yes, that's what they called it when a man named Lord Oblex was appointed as the head of my grandfather's advisory committee many years ago. Oblex is the one who instigated the war against the fairies. My father was out on a dragon hunt at the time and had no knowledge of it until after the massacre. The soldiers who returned from the attack on Alvan said they did not know what they were doing. My father believes that Oblex used some sort of dark magic on them. The soldiers claim Oblex ran away to the far east of the continent. Shortly after that, the trees began to die in the northern part of the Vexwalden Forest. The Aretes, the mountain range at the far end of the forest, was given a new name: The Mountains of Desolation. Only a few men were brave enough to travel that far. They brought back word of rotting dragon carcasses and strange smoke beyond the mountains."

The Evil of the East might be this Oblex fellow, but that had to be more than fifty years ago. He wouldn't still be alive. Maybe it's one of his followers. Nolan looked over at Edric and saw the spark of understanding in his eyes.

"Interesting story, Chrissy," Nolan smiled, hiding the anxiety he felt. "Let's hope the 'Evil of the East' stays in the east, hmm?"

Edric turned carefully toward the chessboard. "*I'm* hoping it stays away."

"Why don't you read it to us?" Samantha insisted, staring at Nolan. "I haven't read Talia's account in years. It would be good to hear it again."

Chrissy turned questioning eyes toward Samantha, who lowered her eyebrows and frowned.

Samantha knows something is not right. We can't put anything past that girl. Never could, Nolan reflected while he pretended to study the chessboard.

Edric sighed, opening the book from Mittra. "We can take turns reading. It's rather long. I suppose I'll start. Let's see . . . '*Back when the Sansevierra Desert was not yet a desert, good fairies ruled the country of Sansevierra in the beautiful capital city of Alvan for three hundred years of relative peace. Everything changed after the last fairy king created the Academy for Magical Abilities. Fairy males and females, rich and poor, were invited to study at the Academy, provided they met the necessary requirement of significant magical ability. One of these male fairies was recognized as having a truly amazing amount of latent ability. He was admitted, and the professors made every endeavor to give him opportunities to be the best fairy he could be.*

"'*However, this fairy forgot the promise he made to the school. It was the same promise that was on the Academy's crest. "Agnitio, Robur, Potentia," in the Ancient tongue. "Knowledge, Strength, Power" became Dagan's personal creed, but not simply in his Academy studies. He strove to overpower the other students. He flaunted his prowess in magical abilities. He frequently voiced his resentment of the female fairies educated at the Academy. Dagan was prevented from physically assaulting one female in particular, his so-called nemesis. The woman was a female fairy, two years younger than himself, and her name was Tatiana. A military senior officer, Elan, son of Soren, was present at the event and attempted to intercede on Dagan's behalf, showing the young fairy other positive avenues to work out his anger.'"*

"That sounds familiar!" Samantha remarked but then fell silent when all eyes turned to her.

"'*After graduation from the Academy, Tatiana was offered a position on Queen Fee's council and married a junior advisor, Nilvan. Dagan, too, sought employment with the royal family. The first year after graduation, every application submitted by the proud Dagan was denied. The king was aware of Dagan's past history based on reports from his advisors, Soren, and Osric. He also held the accounts of Elan and Tatiana.*

"'*Later, Nilvan and Tatiana welcomed a daughter into the world and named her Talia. Dagan eventually ceased submitting applications and began to work in a small bookshop in Alvan.*

"'*Word began to creep into the palace of a secret society. This society focused on something called "deeper magic." King Marchen placed spies around the city, hoping to gain a true picture of what this society practiced. It was reported that the members of the group attempted to raise a body from the dead as well as gain control over a fairy's speech and actions. A guard came to the king and reported that the followers of this deeper magic met in the back room of Dagan's bookshop. A group of soldiers, led by advisor Nilvan, stormed the meeting place and arrested those present. Dagan refused to come with them, leading the soldiers on a chase through Alvan. He slipped off the Feldian Bridge and fell into the freezing water below, never resurfacing.'"*

Chrissy pulled her blanket tighter around her shoulders. "That's a horrible way to die."

Nolan took the book from Edric and began to read as Samantha poured cups of tea for everyone.

"*'Nilvan brought word of Dagan's death to the king. The followers of the deeper magic were publicly admonished and cast out of Sansevierra. The bookshop was cleaned out, and every scroll and book dealing with the dark magic was burned in a giant bonfire. Everyone felt the country was safe once more.*

"*'King Marchen fell ill in early summer, four years after Dagan's death. Every fairy with healing ability tried to make the king well once more. The king recovered some of his strength in the following months. News of border disputes with Synterius, their southern neighbor, came to the ears of Marchen and his advisors. The king sent Osric, his newly established ambassador, and Elan, his chief military advisor, to journey to Synterius and speak with King Hawthorn about the border issues.'*"

"That's interesting," Samantha stated. "Osric and Elan work in the same basic capacity for my father now. Osric is the secretary of state, and Elan is in charge of the armies and training of future knights, like—" Edric caught her eye and Samantha stopped talking. *Don't give too much away, Sam! You can't say, "Knights like me!"*

"*'A journey of this magnitude usually takes months to prepare for. The representatives were able to leave within three weeks, due to the constant vigilance and planning of Osric and Elan. Two months passed before they reached the capital city of Synterius, Arbre. King Hawthorn was distressed and did not want to have a conversation with them. He insisted that he was relying on advice from Lord Oblex, his new advisor. He did not know of any border issues and refused to believe such a thing was possible. Osric asked to speak to the king's eldest son, Prince Aspen. It was explained that Aspen had been sent away by Oblex on a quest to kill a dragon that was nearby. Osric and Elan requested to speak with Lord Oblex. The fairies were turned away and told to leave Arbre immediately.'*"

Edric interrupted the reading. "Has your father ever spoken to you about this, Chrissy? Did he ever speak to your grandfather about these things when he returned?"

Chrissy shook her head sorrowfully, cradling her cup of tea in her hand. "Father avoids the subject unless someone asks him a specific question about it. No one asks."

Nolan continued reading after taking a sip of his tea.

"'Osric and Elan returned to Alvan, unsure of what to do about the situation with Synterius. The border crossing was uneventful, and both wondered if the journey had been a foolish errand. The following year, Synterius cut off trade relations with Sansevierra without explanation. Marchen never received answers to the messages sent to Hawthorn, Aspen, or Oblex. King Marchen never fully recovered from his previous illness and began to grow weaker each day.

"'Tatiana brought Talia to visit with Queen Fee and King Marchen during this difficult time. When Talia saw the king, she patted his hand, as a seven year old will do, and said, "Oh, King, feel better soon!" The queen and Tatiana watched in awe as Talia's faint shimmer gave a radiant pulse of light. The king's face lit up, and his own shimmer glowed faintly. Talia ran and hid behind her mother, while Fee helped the king sit down.

"'"Tatiana, your daughter is exceedingly powerful!" Marchen murmured as he felt the strength return to his gaunt body. "Perhaps the Academy . . . ?"

"'Tatiana laughed and said, "We will wait until she is twelve before we make that decision, your highness." Her mother could see that Talia was excited at what had just taken place.'"

"I remember Talia telling me about this," Samantha said. "I was rather young, but I had just read this portion of the history. I asked Talia to tell me more about it. All of those things she was feeling were similar to what I had been going through." Afraid she had said too much, she cast her eyes down.

Nolan glanced over at Samantha before continuing.

"*One year later, Synterius convinced several other countries to stop trading with Sansevierra as well. When the fairy council questioned Synterian representatives about this decision, no answers were given. Sansevierra was slowly cut off from buying necessities and trading their goods with the human countries. Many unhappy fairies moved out of Sansevierra and into Synterius. Sides were drawn and families were split.*

"*Finally, rumors came that the Synterian army was marching north. King Marchen appointed Elan as commander over the fairy army. Elan and his troops met the Synterian army just outside the gates of Alvan. No one could understand how the enemy reached the capital so quickly with little warning. The fairies with the greatest magical abilities were able to hold back most of the Synterian force, but one small regiment made it through the gates and into the castle.*

"*Elan, armed for battle, searched for the commander of the Synterian army. "Cut off the head of the army, and the troops will scatter," he thought.*

"*He heard a shriek from the king's study and ran toward it. Inside, he saw a man dressed in the uniform of a Synterian troop. The man was attempting to overpower King Marchen and Queen Fee with magic. 'Not a man, a fairy!' Elan thought, shocked for a moment into inaction. Marchen and Fee's combined ability could not hold back the fairy's malicious skill. Elan gripped his sword and silently approached the enemy fairy.*

"*The soldier turned toward Elan. He wore a twisted, insane smile. "Miss me?" Dagan asked.*

"*"Dagan!" Elan burst out.*

"*"No, it's Lord Oblex now," Dagan took a dagger from his belt. "Who did you think was able to create all of this mayhem?"*

"*Elan slashed his sword, cutting Dagan's right arm and upper chest. The dagger fell to the floor.*

""*"Fool! Do you think you can defeat me with a simple sword?"* *Dagan hissed as he backed away from Elan.*

"*'Dagan closed his eyes and began to chant. Elan, thinking on impulse, yelled a binding spell. Dagan froze, his counter spell effectively cut off as if he'd been frozen in a block of ice.*

""*"Yes, I do think I can defeat you. I taught you, after all,"* Elan told him. *"It didn't have to come to this. You could repent for your misdeeds and evil, Dagan. This is your chance."*

"*'Elan murmured the counter spell. Dagan's eyes came back into focus, and his lips began to twitch. The rest of his body remained motionless. His eyes were as black as coal, and his shimmer had turned a flat gray, pulsing in a disturbing manner.*

"*'Dagan hissed at Elan, "You have made the biggest mistake of your life."* He suddenly lifted his hand toward Elan, intent on murder, when an arrow struck his upper chest. Dagan fell backwards onto the king's desk, unmoving.*

"*'Elan turned to see Nilvan holding a bow and shaking wildly. "Did I hit him?"*

"*'Elan rushed over to King Marchen and Queen Fee, afraid of what evil Dagan had done to them. "Your majesties! Please, speak to me,"* Elan begged.*

"*'Fee's eyes fluttered open. "Elan . . . is he gone?"*

""*"Yes, my queen. He has been taken care of."*

""*"I will sleep now," Fee's eyes slid shut. Her shimmer dimmed until it was no longer visible. Elan choked back a sob and looked over at King Marchen's body. His shimmer too had disappeared.'"*

Nolan looked up, noticing Chrissy had started to cry. She choked back a sob. "Don't mind me," she sniffled. "I always get this way when I read an emotional story. Keep going, Nolan, if you please."

Nolan glanced over at Edric who gave him a smile that seemed to say, *Women! Who can understand them?*

"I'd like to read, if you'd like a break," Samantha offered. Nolan handed her the book. She began to read in a clear, strong voice.

"*'A series of crashes caused Elan to cut his mourning short. He rushed to the open doorway to see the Synterius army rushing through the gates of the castle. They began to burn everything in sight.*

"*'Nilvan awoke from his faint and yelled, "Elan! Get Tatiana and Talia out of here. I'm going to make sure Dagan is dead."*

"*'Elan rushed from the room, using the secret passageway behind the tapestry of the Vexwalden Forest. "Tatiana, Talia! You must go now!" Elan called into the family's suite of rooms.*

"*'Tatiana's pale face appeared at the door. "We are ready."*

"*'Osric appeared in the passageway. "I will take them, Elan. You take care of the king and queen."*

"*'Elan's eyes spoke of his grief. "They're dead. I need to take care of Dagan."*

"*'He rushed into the study only to find Nilvan's dead body on the floor. Dagan was nowhere to be seen.*

"*'"No!" Elan cried. He picked up his sword and ran out into the courtyard. He frantically slashed at the Synterian army surrounding him, searching for Dagan.*

"*'Sir," one of his men called. 'It's over.'"*

"*'Elan stopped swinging, gazing out over the innumerable slain bodies in the courtyard. He dropped to his knees. "Where is he?"*

"*'Osric led Tatiana and Talia through the twisted maze of secret passageways for what seemed like miles. They finally came to a thick wooden door with a rusted lock. Thin slivers of golden light shown through the cracks in the door.*

"*'"Stay back," Osric warned, unlocking the door with a large key. He slowly pulled it open. "Come now," Osric called. "It's safe here."*

"*'Tatiana and Talia emerged into a hidden wooded glen just as the sun was rising.*

"'"We are near the border of Mittra," Osric told them. "We shall see if King Braddon and Queen Culdania are sympathetic to our plight."

"'"What of Papa? And Sir Elan?" Talia quietly asked her mother.

"'"Hush now. They will find us when it is time," Tatiana assured her.

"'By noon, the three had arrived in Halat, Mittra's capital city, after receiving many stares from the Mittrans. The king and queen, horrified at what had occurred in Sansevierra, invited the three fairies to remain in Mittra. King Braddon sent troops to ascertain the damage done to Alvan. Within a week, many other fairies sought refuge in Mittra, as well as nearby Lagola and Rothan. Two weeks after the attack, Elan arrived in Halat. He brought a grim picture of what Sansevierra's future held, as well as the news that Nilvan was indeed dead. Talia vividly remembered her mother's shimmer fading before she fainted. She also remembered crying for days, wishing for her papa to return. She wanted to go after Dagan, who everyone whispered about when they thought she was not listening. Her greatest desire was to leave this strange place that was so different from Sansevierra—so different than her home.

"Talia has told me this story several times, but it never fails to make me cry for her and her mother," Samantha admitted, wiping her own tears. She cleared her throat and began again.

"'Gradually, the humans lost most of their fear of magic. The fairies showed their goodwill towards the people of Mittra by bestowing blessings for babies that were brought to them. After a while, humans tried to bribe the fairies to give their children more gifts. This news reached Tatiana, and she approached King Braddon and Queen Culdania with the proposal about the fairy blessings. A child would be given gifts based on the month he was born in. A child born in January would be given one, while a child born in December would be given twelve. The king and queen were delighted with this idea, and Tatiana was offered the newly created position of royal fairy liaison.'"

"So Dagan is Oblex?" Edric asked.

Nolan nodded. "What do we do with this information? Could he still be alive after living in that forest or mountains for so long? Chrissy, didn't you say that there's not much up there?"

"Yes, only a few dragons, if the reports are true. That's where Linden says he goes when he's brought home the carcasses. My father hasn't had any reports on this evil that you're speaking of. Should he know about this?"

Edric and Nolan looked at each other and shrugged. "It's probably someone else who is modeling himself after this evil Dagan fellow. We should probably let the king know," Nolan said to Edric. "And maybe Talia, too?"

"Yes, that's a wise idea," Samantha replied, looking thoughtful. "I'll talk to her. Maybe she has already heard something about it."

As soon as Samantha left the room, Chrissy turned to Nolan. "Why don't the three of us visit my father? He may know something of this account. There must be something we can do."

CHAPTER FOURTEEN

*S*amantha was in the barn with Windstorm the day before the final tournament. She was preparing for the ride with Chrissy later that morning. While brushing Windstorm's already glossy black coat, she noted that Nolan's horse, Blaze, stood in the stall adjacent to Windstorm's. *Did Nolan have him moved closer to Windstorm's stall?* Her cheeks flushed. *Goodness, Sam. Could you be more conceited? It's obvious he's not interested in you. But only because I told him to back off,* she argued, shaking her head.

"Talking to yourself, Sam?"

Samantha's head jerked up. She dropped the curry brush when she saw Nolan leaning casually against Blaze's stall door. He was twirling a piece of straw in his fingers, a lazy smile playing on his lips.

"Maybe. It's been known to happen." *He's here, and he's smiling at me! Calm down. Take a breath. He's just your friend.*

She turned towards Windstorm and began to braid his mane nervously, feeling Nolan's gaze upon her still.

"May I use your brush, please?" he asked, stepping into the stall.

"Sure," she answered. She knelt to retrieve it at the same time he did, narrowly missing a collision.

Nolan reached out a hand to help her up, but pulled it away quickly. *Don't scare her, stupid. She only wants to be your friend, remember?*

Samantha placed the brush into his hand. He felt a tingle run through him when her fingertips brushed his palm. Nolan took a step back and Samantha did the same, not meeting his eyes.

He slowly began to groom his red roan stallion when Samantha spoke, "Is your horse named for his color or his marking?"

"His color, though the blaze on his nose is a good guess. He was born at sunset. From the open barn door, I could see the setting sun. It made the fields look like they were ablaze with fire. I looked over to see this newly dropped colt with a coat that matched the blaze of color outside. My father agreed with me and gave him to me as a gift for my sixteenth birthday."

"That was kind of him. Windstorm is my second horse. I got him when I was—"

"Fourteen," Nolan interrupted.

There was a moment of silence before he turned to see Samantha in front of Blaze's stall.

"How did you know I was fourteen?" she asked, looking right at him.

Nolan felt his neck grow hot. He pulled at his collar with one hand while brushing Blaze distractedly with the other. "Uh, I heard it from …" He sighed, dropping his hands to his sides. "I might have read some of your letters to my brother." He nudged a pile of straw with the toe of his boot. Samantha just laughed, throwing her head back. "You're not mad?"

Samantha wiped her eyes and shook her head. "I think it's funny that a boy stole some letters written by a girl that he supposedly hated. Why'd you do it?"

"I wanted to know if *you* hated *me*," Nolan retorted, flashing a smile. "The truth is, I wanted to see if you mentioned the letters I wrote to you."

Samantha could see the flush creeping up his neck and decided to leave him alone. She walked back to Windstorm's stall, thinking about Nolan's confession. *Did I write anything about him in my letters? Where did I put them? I remember packing at home when Mother came in. I must have put them in my pocket. They're probably in the bottom of my trunk.*

"I didn't hate you," Nolan's deep voice traveled over the wall.

Samantha looked up, but Nolan remained in Blaze's stall.

"Then the worms and the crickets and the mud were—"

"Gifts from an admirer?" Nolan peeked into her stall.

Samantha choked back a laugh. "That's really smooth. I'm sure that's worked for you recently. 'Oh Princess Lacene, please enjoy these mud covered crickets. They're a delicacy in Lagola. I only give them to ladies I admire.'"

Nolan stuck his tongue out at her. She mimicked his gesture, and he burst out laughing.

"That's mature, Sam. I'm sure your mother would love that!"

She laughed. "You started it."

They smiled at each other, soaking in the comfortable silence.

"I've never given any gifts to Lacene," Nolan said suddenly. "I don't even like your cousin, truth be told."

Samantha raised her eyebrows. "Then why were you so chatty with her in Harak?"

"She was the one who followed *me* around. I was not using my gift to charm her. She only wants a husband, and I'm sure any man would do." Nolan glanced down. "I'm sorry, Samantha, I should not speak of a lady, especially your cousin, in such a way."

"You've said nothing that I haven't said myself," Samantha excused him with a smile.

"But you're right," Nolan said cautiously, taking a step closer to her. "About your admiration theory, I mean."

Samantha knew her cheeks were flaming red, so she retreated into the stall. "I didn't say that so you would compliment me."

"I wasn't just throwing out a compliment. I really meant it! How many girls could throw a punch like you? And when I kicked you in the mouth, you didn't fall on the ground in a screaming fit. You kept up with all of us boys every summer. Well, until you had to leave. No," he corrected, "Until I forced your mother to make you leave. Sam, I'd really like to apologize for everything I've ever said. Or done. Or even *thought* that was hateful toward you. I realize that's a very broad apology and I should have more concrete evidence, but I'd probably be here until winter if you made me list everything. Would you forgive me?"

Samantha looked up to see him petting Windstorm's neck, his eyes honest as he looked down at her. "I forgive you," she said quietly, clutching her hands together.

"Even for what I said to you and Edric in the barn in Isonox?"

"I was including that in your previous apology." Samantha smirked at him.

Nolan heaved a sigh of relief and reached out toward her. He quickly dropped his hand, smiling awkwardly. "Thanks, Sam. You're a great friend."

He left the stall and strode over to the wall where Blaze's tack hung, removing the leather bridle and returned to Blaze. He placed the bridle over the horse's nose and adjusted the bit between his teeth. As he retrieved the saddle and saddle blanket, he glanced over at Samantha. She was tacking up her horse.

He grinned. "Were you going to go for a ride by yourself, or do you want to ride with me?"

"'No' to the first question and 'that would be rather inappropriate' to the second," Samantha shot back, throwing him a smile over her shoulder while she worked. "I can't go riding with a man without a chaperone. My mother would have a fit! I'm meeting Chrissy here to take a ride into the forest."

Nolan's face darkened. "I don't think that's a good idea." He crossed his arms over his chest. "I've heard of awful things happening in that forest."

"We're not afraid of the boogey man, Nolan," Samantha laughed, tightening the girth on the saddle.

"I wasn't speaking of the 'boogey man.' More like a real man. There have been rumors that Linden escaped into the forest after his uncle exiled him. And what about the person we were speaking about last week? Dagan, Oblex, or whatever he calls himself? We can't be sure that he's dead. Sam, look at me," Nolan said sharply before feeling a searing pain in his head. He pressed his fingertips to his temples and groaned.

"Didn't I tell you to go to the doctor?" Samantha asked, her voice tight with anxiety as she approached him.

Nolan waved her away. "I don't want to have this conversation again. It's fine now. I think you just get me so . . . fired up when you refuse to listen to what I have to say about important issues. It makes my head hurt." He opened his eyes to see Samantha staring at him, worry lurking in her eyes. *She really does care! How can I make her see that I'm only thinking of her best interests?*

Edric staggered into the stable, holding his hand against his ribs. "Sam, just the princess I wanted to see. I have a message for you from Chrissy."

"Chrissy? Isn't it *Princess* Chrissy, brother?" Nolan teased, helping him sit down on a bale of hay.

"What I was saying," Edric continued, shooting a glare at Nolan, "Was that Chrissy is unable to ride today. The doctor wants her to rest her ankle for one more day."

"But tomorrow's the tournament!" Samantha protested. "There isn't any time to go for a ride."

"You could go shortly after dawn," Edric suggested, ignoring the look Nolan gave him. "Take one of the grooms with you for safety. You could come back in plenty of time before the tournament starts. Just watch the sun."

"Great idea, Edric!" Samantha smiled at Nolan. "See, we'll be safe. No boogey men or any other men will get us. And Talia said she didn't think Dagan could still be alive. King Aspen agreed with her. So we'll be okay when we do go." She glanced at the stall. "I guess I should unsaddle my horse."

"Unless you want to go for a ride now?" Nolan asked, the question lingering in the air.

Edric grunted and tried to stand. "That's my cue to exit," he muttered, his face paling. He tried to stand up and would have fallen if Nolan had not caught him. "Maybe I need a little help after all . . ." he gasped, holding his side again.

"I'll unsaddle Blaze for you, Nolan. Get him inside," Samantha instructed.

Nolan nodded as he secured his arm around his brother. "Up too soon, Edric. You can't push yourself so fast. You'll undo all of the healing and then where will you be? Oh, yes. Back in a cozy parlor with Chrissy. I can see why you walked all the way out here."

Nolan gave Samantha a wink and that lazy smile that made her heart race. She turned quickly to her task at hand to give her something to do other than swoon like a silly girl.

☩

"Sammy, stop pulling at your dress," Talia said as she stepped into the princess' room.

Samantha dropped her hands from the blue gown as she turned from the full-length mirror. "I'm sorry. I'm just nervous. This is the last ball of the tournament circuit and . . ." Her voice trailed off as a shadow crossed her face.

"Did you receive a letter from your mother?"

"Yes! She and Father are in Harak visiting my grandparents. Mother is helping with Lacene's wedding details. She hinted that she looks forward to planning *my* wedding soon. She put special emphasis on tonight because it's the final ball. I must 'remember to do my best not to offend any potential suitors.'" Samantha anxiously smoothed her dress again, checking her reflection in the mirror.

"Relax. If you happen to receive a proposal tonight, that is good. If you do not, all is not lost. Who knows how a man will act? Men and women do not think in the same manner! Timing to you may be different for . . . a certain young man."

"But, Taley, what do I do *tonight*?" Samantha's voice was full of anxiety.

Talia smiled, holding Samantha's hand. "You will go to the ball. You will dance and talk and enjoy yourself. And try not to antagonize poor Nolan. Talk to him as you would to Edric. As a friend."

A green flame rose up in Samantha's eyes. "I don't *try* to—"

She was cut off by Talia's laughter. "That's the Sam I wanted to see! Keep that spunk tonight and enjoy being with your *friend*."

‡

"Get out there before she forgets your name," Edric called out to Nolan from his bed.

"Samantha said it was acceptable for me to be her escort tonight?"

"Well, I said I *thought* she'd be okay with it. I can't dance, and I know she doesn't want to sit around all evening. You'll be a fine escort. Won't you?" Edric waggled his eyebrows at his brother playfully. "Treat

her how I would treat her. No kissing, no hand holding. Pretend that her
father is watching you," Edric's eyes twinkled.

"Mmmhmm . . . the way you act toward Chrissy?"

"I haven't kissed her yet! I'm waiting to propose before I do that!"

"Well, in the words of my brother, 'Get out there before she forgets
your name.'" Nolan threw over his shoulder as he left the room.

‡

King Aspen stood on the raised dais at the end of the ballroom, raising
his right arm for silence. "Thank you for attending tonight. We have a
custom here in Synterius. The evening before our final tournament, we
have a showcase of sorts. We invite those young people blessed with
musical abilities to perform for us. First, my daughter Chamomile.
Cammie, if you will?"

The petite princess approached the dais, a light pink blush on her
cheeks. Cammie sat down behind a harp near the musicians and began
to play a particularly difficult piece. The whole assembly swayed in time
with the music.

Samantha entered the ballroom with Talia in time to hear the end of
Cammie's song.

"What are they doing? I thought this was a ball?" Samantha whispered
to Talia as they edged closer to the dais.

"A talent showcase. The king enjoys hearing from those who have
been blessed musically."

The king called up several other musicians to play for the audience,
ending with Cammie playing the harp once more.

"On that note," King Aspen laughed at his own joke. "We will open
the floor for dancing."

Nolan tapped Samantha on the shoulder, bowing low. "Edric asked
that I escort you this evening. I had to pledge to treat you as he would

treat you."

Samantha put her hand in his, and they began to dance around the room. "So if you're treating me like Edric would treat me, does that mean no arguing? You'll get me dessert? And a glass of punch?"

"Edric waits on you hand and foot, does he? Funny, he didn't mention those things to me."

"What *did* he mention?" She grinned as Nolan's face turned red.

Nolan murmured something so low Samantha could not hear him. *Should I tease it out of him? Talia told me to be nice to him tonight. Perhaps I should save the questions for later.*

"Have you and your friend had more dancing lessons?" Nolan's eyes twinkled at her.

Samantha groaned inwardly. "That's not fair. You know some gifts take a strong hold and others need nurturing."

"Or lessons?" Nolan teased as he twirled her across the floor.

"I do believe you've had some lessons yourself. Who taught you? A lady-in-waiting? Did you have to use your gift to convince her?"

"Oh, you're very funny, princess. What, you don't think I have been blessed with the gift of dance?"

"You have the gift of convincing speech and thick hair." She looked up at his face when she heard him chuckle. "What's funny? What did I say? Oh . . ."

Nolan laughed harder at her furious blush and refusal to meet his eyes. "You were so offended by my 'file' on you. Now I find out that you have one on me?"

"Not a file, just a good memory," Samantha squeaked out. "Edric told me years ago that your Gift Givers wanted you to be a handsome ambassador."

"And you've remembered that all these years?" Nolan asked, surprised.

"Um . . ." Samantha stammered, looking anywhere but at his face.

"I'll give you a pass. You gave one to me earlier," Nolan said softly, causing her to look up at him.

Samantha became aware of the sound of laughter around them. "Why are they laughing? Did I miss a step?"

Nolan glanced around and then led her to the edge of the dance floor. "We both missed a step. No one else is dancing. The song is over."

"You're a good distraction," Samantha said with a shy smile. "I wasn't even thinking about dancing."

"At your service, miss," Nolan replied with a gallant bow. "Distractions come easily to me."

Samantha curtsied to him. "Tell Edric you conducted yourself quite admirably. He'll be proud of you."

"Will I see you tomorrow at the tournament?"

"Yes. Chrissy and I are riding out early and will be back hours before the tournament begins. I'll wave your colors, if you'd like," Samantha smiled back at him.

"You do me quite an honor, Princess," Nolan murmured formally before bowing again and walking away.

Samantha watched him go, feeling a strange sense of loss. A thought suddenly occurred to her. *He didn't get a headache when I spoke to him tonight! See, it's not my fault after all.*

CHAPTER FIFTEEN

*T*he sun was beginning to rise as Samantha and Chrissy set out on their long awaited ride. Windstorm and Brownie quietly nickered to each other as the girls took the well-worn path north of the castle.

"Do many people travel through the forest?" Samantha asked, pulling her cloak up higher around her neck.

Chrissy looked out from beneath her hood. "Many people hunt in the lower portion of the forest. The game is plentiful, and there is a stream that is usually teaming with fish in the spring and summer. Nobody usually travels to the upper portion."

Samantha glanced towards the north. She could see the distant mountain peaks and the low clouds surrounding them. "The Mountains of Desolation?"

"Yes, but don't worry. We're not riding that far. Those are about a five day journey if you're riding hard. I promised my father we'd stay close to the path in the lower forest, since he couldn't spare a groom from the tournament preparations today."

"Well, I'll tell Nolan we tried. At least now we can have girl talk without worrying about what a man is thinking! So tell me more about the forest, oh wise one."

Chrissy laughed. "I really only know what I've been told and what I've read. My father paid some adventurous knights to chart the Vexwalden Forest and the foothills of the mountains. He wanted to stake a claim on any valuable land on the outlying areas of Synterius."

Samantha reached for an apple in her saddlebag. "What did they find?"

"The further north they went, the more dismal the landscape became. They returned to tell my father it wasn't worth rewriting maps and claimed the land for Synterius." She glanced at Samantha. "Could you pass me an apple, please?"

"Of course! I'm glad you thought to have food brought to the stable for us."

"I wanted us to have a long ride. Turning back because we were hungry seemed ridiculous." Chrissy laughed before taking a bite, juice dripping from her chin.

Samantha handed her a handkerchief. "I come prepared, as you see."

Chrissy wiped her mouth and grimaced. "I should have packed one. My one useful gift has failed me."

"The first time we met, you asked me which of my fairy blessings I hated the most. You never told me yours," Samantha said as they entered the cool, dark forest.

"My favorite one is the gift of being sensible. An elderly male fairy gave me that gift. I wish he was alive to thank for that. My least favorite is a tie between feet that love to dance and long fingernails. I mean, only feet? What about the rest of my body?" Chrissy joked.

"I was given long fingernails, too!" Samantha exclaimed, pulling off her left glove and holding up her hand.

"How do you keep them long with all of the training you do?" Chrissy demanded, showing her own bare hand. Her nails were trimmed short. "I cut my nails down but don't tell my mother. All of my sisters have the same gift, but I'm the only one who has rebelled against it."

Samantha stopped her horse and waited for Chrissy to stop hers. "Chrissy, I'm going to tell you something that only few know. But you must not tell anyone else."

Chrissy's eyes grew wide. "I won't tell anyone."

Taking a deep breath, Samantha told her about her true blessings and the cover up that followed that fateful ceremony.

Chrissy burst out laughing. "They tried to bless you to be petite? Maybe it bounced off you and affected me!"

Samantha joined in Chrissy's laughter, starting to walk her horse forward again.

"What are your real blessings, then?"

Samantha quickly ticked the list off, smiling self-consciously. "Not what you'd expect from a princess, right?"

"You could say that. So, that's six blessings, isn't it? Weren't you born in July?"

"Yes, my seventh blessing is still a mystery to me. Even though Osric gifted me to learn languages, it was written in the tongue of the Ancients. I haven't yet found a book to translate all of the wording. All I could decipher was 'princess' and 'magic.'"

"And neither Osric nor Elan could remember what they said?" Chrissy asked as they arrived at a stream that flowed slowly towards the south.

"I never asked them," Samantha reflected as she dismounted, tying the reins to a nearby fallen log. "I should send a letter and ask if they can remember that far back. They're both getting rather old."

Chrissy tied Brownie near Windstorm and then knelt down by the water. She scooped some water into her hand and began to drink it. Brownie nickered at her, and Chrissy rifled through her saddlebag until she found another apple. "Here you go, girl," she murmured, petting Brownie's mane.

"You are spoiling that horse," Samantha remarked as she sat on a flat rock near the water's edge.

"Of course I do! Brownie has been with me since . . . well, forever! Father wanted me to get a new horse, but I was insistent that I would keep her. She's a good horse, aren't you, Brownie?" Chrissy rubbed the horse's neck gently.

"Windstorm needed this walk as much as I did." Samantha threw a pebble into the stream. "I talked to Nolan yesterday when I was waiting for you in the barn. He said he didn't hate me when we were little. Evidently, boys just *pretend* they hate the girls they really like and do hateful things, like kick them in the mouth and tease them incessantly."

Chrissy sat next to her, picking up her own pebble. "I remember when Linden liked a girl. He would chase her and pull her pigtails until Father ordered him to stop. I suppose all boys are alike."

"Not Edric," Samantha replied, giving Chrissy a sidelong look, "He was always the nice one. He never beat me up or teased me or threw mud at me. He was my best friend. And now my new best friend is in love with my old best friend."

Chrissy's cheeks turned pink as she tossed her pebble into the water. "Is it that obvious?"

"Only to those of us that have eyes."

"But he hasn't even said anything yet. He still needs to ask my father for my hand, and then my father needs to send him on a quest. And you are all planning on leaving tomorrow." Chrissy's blue eyes filled with tears. "There isn't any time."

"We can stay longer. You two were meant to be together. Edric is probably waiting for his ribs to heal before he goes out on a quest. He didn't look well yesterday."

Samantha glanced behind her and suddenly stood up. "Chrissy, where are the horses?"

Chrissy jumped up, slipping on the loose pebbles. Her leg shot out as she fell hard on the embankment. "Ouch! My ankle! I've wrenched it again." She held her leg while tears dripped down her cheeks.

Samantha wrapped her arm around Chrissy and helped her stand. *If her ankle is seriously injured, she can't possibly walk back to the castle. It must be ten miles!* Scanning the area, Samantha thought she saw something move behind a copse of trees.

She turned to Chrissy. "Can you stay here while I go find the horses? If they get back here before I do, try to catch them without hurting yourself."

Chrissy nodded and hobbled over to the fallen log. "I'll wait here."

Samantha strode deeper into the forest, only to find out that the movement was a doe. It leapt away after spotting her. Shaking her head, Samantha continued through a thicket of trees, calling for Windstorm and Brownie.

After a while, she made her way to a clearing and glanced up at the sky. *Oh my! I must have been searching longer than I thought. It's probably close to nine o'clock now. The tournament starts in an hour. I need to get back to Chrissy.*

A sudden thought hit her. "Everyone will be too busy with the tournament to notice we're gone. I need to find those horses." She glanced around. "Where am I?"

Samantha froze, looking around. *Which way did I come from? Listen for water. That will take you back to the stream.* She closed her eyes and strained to hear something besides her own heartbeat. A faint sound of running water came to her, so she began to walk in that direction.

When she finally emerged from the trees, the log where Chrissy was sitting was empty. "Chrissy! Where are you?" Samantha called, cupping her hands around her mouth. "Chrissy!" *Did the horses come back? Has she set off to find me?*

Windstorm suddenly emerged from the forest, blowing and nickering at her. Samantha grabbed his bridle and ran a soothing hand over his neck. "It's okay, boy. Where's Chrissy? Where's Brownie? Why am I talking to my horse?" she asked herself, rolling her eyes.

Using the log as a mounting block, Samantha climbed into the saddle. She held the reins in a tight grasp. "Let's go find them, boy."

After riding for hours on end, Samantha and Windstorm trudged into the large barn when the sun was at high noon. One lone groom was in the barn, mucking out the empty stalls. He looked up as Samantha dismounted and then hurried over to remove Windstorm's saddle.

He scratched Windstorm between the ears. "Looks like this fella needs a good rubdown and a bag of oats."

"That he does," Samantha agreed wearily. She emptied the saddlebag of the remains of a loaf of bread and empty water skin. "Has Princess Chrissy returned yet? We went for a ride and became separated. I was hoping to find her here."

"No, miss. I haven't seen the princess since this morning. Perhaps she got turned around and is making her way home." A consoling smile creased his dirty face. "I know that horse of hers knows the way. When she returns, I'll send word up to the castle for you, if you'd like, miss."

Samantha nodded and trudged toward the castle. She could hear the sounds of the tournament but could not work up her enthusiasm to go out and cheer for her favorites. *I need to keep away from the field. I made a promise to Edric but if I see Dawes and he asks me to help, I'd have to say yes. I better get ready to sit in the royal box with Chrissy. I'm sure she'll be here soon.*

Samantha asked a passing maid in the corridor if she would bring some warm water for washing up and then she pushed open the door to her room. Samantha laid out a simple gown on her bed and waited for the water to arrive.

After a minute of fidgeting, she crossed the room to her trunk and opened the heavy lid. Digging through the extra pairs of riding boots and gloves, she spotted the bundle of letters caught in the bottom corner of the trunk. Samantha lifted the seal of the envelope, noticing the childish writing scribbled on it.

Samantha,
Edric said I had to say I'm sorry.
Sorry.

Nolan, second prince of Lagola

Samantha laughed quietly at the stubborn, proud boy she could remember Nolan being at twelve years old. She imagined him being forced to write a letter to a girl. *Second prince of Lagola! I'll have to tease him about that,* she thought as she opened the next letter.

Princess Samantha, Edric said that the last letter was rude and I had to try again. So, I'm trying again. Sorry.
Please write to my brother and tell him that I sent you a letter.

Nolan, second prince of Lagola

"Well, it's a good thing I didn't read these when you sent them, Nolan. I would have written to Edric and asked him to punch you for me. What an insincere brat! Though I suppose I was a brat too. I didn't even read these letters until now, after all."

She rose from the floor with the handful of letters and sat on her bed. "Why is growing up so hard?" she muttered as she opened the next letter in the pile.

Princess Samantha,

It's been a year and you still haven't written back. Maybe the other letters got lost. Or maybe someone stole them from you. Anyway, I don't know why you haven't written back. Edric told me you have to take dance lessons. My mother is making me start them, too. I'd rather be outside on my horse or swimming or climbing trees. ~~Do you remember climbing trees with me and Edric?~~ Never mind that last sentence.

Write back. Please.

Nolan

"He was actually trying to be nice to me. Yes, I remember climbing trees with you two," she whispered, running her finger over the faded ink. "I guess you were telling me the truth yesterday. You really didn't hate me."

The ink was fresher on the final letter. As Samantha cracked the seal, she held her breath. *When did he send this one? Only a couple of years ago, I think.*

Dear Samantha,

Edric reminded me that today is your sixteenth birthday. I hope this year is a good one for you. Do you remember all of those letters I sent to you? I can hardly recall what I said in them, but I suppose they were so bad you never wrote back. So, I want to take the time to ask you, again, as an adult, to forgive me for all those hateful things I did when we were growing up. I can see now that I should have been nicer to you. You were a girl. I mean, you are still a girl. Or a lady now, I'd think. You know what I mean. I hope.

Please tell your mother sorry for me, too. I know our families haven't seen each other in the last few years because of us "wild Lagola boys," and I'm sorry for that. Acton and Ellery are wilder than Edric and I ever were, but don't tell her that. Well, happy birthday. I hope to hear from you.

Nolan

"I am so stupid for not reading this silly letter sooner." Samantha watched as teardrops hit the page, causing some of the ink to run. "Ugh. 'As an adult.' You were much more of an adult than me. I still wanted to smear mud in your face when I saw you." She gave a giggle as she wiped away her tears.

A knock sounded on the door, and Samantha hurried over to answer it. The maid stood there with a large pitcher of water. Three other maids were lined up behind her, all holding pitchers as well. A servant boy at the end of the line clutched a tray piled high with bread, cheese, and fruit.

"Please, miss, I thought you'd might like a bit more than a pitcher of water," the young maid said with a shy smile.

"I guess I look worse than I feel," Samantha declared with a grin, gesturing them to come inside.

They filled up a shallow tub and left Samantha to her bath. A while later she was clean, dressed, and waiting for Chrissy to arrive.

A sharp knock sounded on the door, and Samantha opened it with a flourish. "Finally! Where have you—"

"Excuse me, Princess Samantha," a young lady-in-waiting stammered. "There's a groom outside that insists to speak to you, but I told him it was inappropriate."

"Where is he?" Samantha felt her body tense with alarm. *It's probably nothing,* she thought as she followed the young lady down the stairwell.

She led her to the small side door and into the stable. The groom from the stable was pacing back and forth across the path. He rushed up to her when she emerged from the castle.

"Miss, er, I mean, *Princess* Samantha," he corrected, seeing the stern look on the lady-in-waiting's face.

"What is your name?" Samantha asked kindly, excusing the lady to leave them.

"Tobias. Toby, if you please, miss," Toby answered with a slight bow.

"No need for bows and such, Toby. What news do you have for me?" Samantha asked, trying to control her anxiety.

"You remember what I said about the princess' horse knowing her way home? Well, I was right. But the princess wasn't with her horse," Toby said in a low voice.

Samantha felt her knees shake. She closed her eyes to steady herself, breathing deeply. "Is there anything else?"

"This was on the saddle, miss," Toby answered, holding up a scrap of dark blue velvet.

Chrissy's cloak. What could have happened? Samantha looked into the groom's eyes. "Toby, can you keep a secret?" He nodded. "Okay, good. Please saddle my horse and pack extra rations for him. Full water skins would also be helpful. I need to return to my room for a moment."

Toby stared at her with something akin to horror. "But, miss, you're not thinking of going after Princess Chrysanthemum yourself, are you?"

"Who else will go? Everyone else is at the tournament. If I go out there, everyone will make a huge ruckus. I'm sure Chrissy is just wandering in the forest. I don't want to embarrass her. I believe I can find her and return before nightfall. Please, Toby, please keep this quiet. Do you promise?"

The young groom stared down at the ground. When he finally looked up, he said, "I promise to keep it quiet as long as I can. But, if someone comes and asks me for particulars, I'm going to have to tell them. I might be let go if I'm not honest with them. You do understand, don't you, miss?"

Samantha resisted the urge to hug him and grinned at him instead. "I completely understand. I will be back soon."

She ran up the back staircase and burst into her room, hurriedly casting off her dress. She pulled on her training shirt, trousers, and boots. *Do I wear my armor or not? I could use Chrissy's sensible gift right now! The sensible thing would not be to run off after her myself. But I must help her if I can! I'll take whatever will fit in the bag.*

She threw her gloves, charmed helmet, and short dagger into her canvas equipment bag and heaved it onto her shoulder. Stopping at the food tray the servant boy had brought, Samantha wrapped the loaf of bread in the cloth napkin. She laid it in the middle of a large handkerchief, surrounding it with the apples, pears and the hunk of cheese from the tray. She tied up the bundle and placed it inside her equipment bag. Samantha grabbed her heavy cloak from the wardrobe and then surveyed the room. Spying the letters from Nolan, she grabbed them and stuck them inside her bag. *I don't want anyone else to see those. I should leave a letter for someone so they don't panic about where I am. I know Talia would have someone go search for me immediately.*

She set down her bag, taking out a fresh piece of parchment. She readied her quill and ink, beginning to write.

Dear Nolan,

As you know, Chrissy and I went out on a ride this morning. We were separated, but do not fear. Sir Palmer is out searching for Chrissy at this time. He will return with her soon.

Samantha

"If I wear the helmet of Sir Palmer, am I really lying when I send this to Nolan?" Samantha sighed. "Yes, but I hope everyone will understand it's for a good reason."

She folded and sealed the letter and slipped it into the pocket of her trousers. Picking up her heavy bag, Samantha started down the stairs again.

She entered the stable where Windstorm stood waiting. "Thank you Toby! I wish I had a coin to give to you, but I'll be sure to reward you once I return with the princess later tonight," Samantha assured him with a smile.

Toby helped her fill up the other saddlebag with the items she brought down. "You don't have to do that, miss. I'm glad to help you. I just hope you come back with the princess by nightfall."

Samantha gave him a smile as she pulled the letter out of her pocket. "I plan to come back as soon as I can. Will you please give this letter to Prince Nolan of Lagola's squire at the tournament? I wanted to let someone else know what is happening."

Samantha felt a twinge of guilt at the look of relief on Toby's face. "I'll take it right over, miss!"

"No hurry," Samantha insisted as she mounted Windstorm. "As long as it gets to him in the next hour or so."

She set out on the path she and Chrissy had taken that morning. "See you soon!" she called.

I hope.

CHAPTER SIXTEEN

"*A*re you about ready, Clark?" Nolan called down to his squire who was polishing Blaze's front hooves. "I really don't think anyone will notice how shiny his hooves are."

Clark stood up and gave his knight a crooked smile. His freckles stood out on his pale face. "I'll notice, sir. Since this is the final tournament, all the lords and ladies will be looking at you. I want you both to look the best you can." He stepped back and smiled proudly at the warhorse. "He looks magnificent. I'm sure the ladies will be falling all over themselves when you come out, sir."

"I don't want all of the ladies noticing me," Nolan grunted as he shifted in his saddle. "Just one would be fine." The image of a tall blonde haired girl with sparkling green eyes rose in his mind. He unknowingly smiled.

"You've got a lady friend that you haven't told me about, sir?" Clark hooted with laughter, stopping when Nolan fixed a steely look at him. "No disrespect, sir."

"Never mind, Clark. It's not your fault I've got my head in the clouds. I'd like this tournament to finally begin. The amateurs have had their final showing this morning, and I thought the final rounds would have begun at noon," Nolan grumbled, his unease causing Blaze to stomp and blow in the corral.

Edric slowly approached the outside railing, his face showing the strain of the effort. "Little brother, I just wanted to come wish you good luck on your final tournament."

Nolan smiled. "Thanks Edric. It's good to see you looking a little better than yesterday. You're not as pale and worn. Are you sitting in the royal box with Chrissy?"

Edric shook his head with a frown. "No, she and Sam haven't arrived yet. They went for a ride this morning, but I'm sure they are getting ready."

Nolan laughed at Edric's frown. "They'll be here sooner or later. Just relax and enjoy the tournament."

Toby entered the corral and called out, "Is there a Prince Nolan of Lagola here?"

Nolan raised his hand and the groom hurried over to him. "A lady asked me to give this letter to you," Toby said, handing over the letter.

There was a sharp blast from the trumpet as Nolan handed the letter to Edric. "Open this for me, will you? If it's personal, stop reading it. If it's important, let me know. Right now I have to get out to the royal salute. Signal me over after I pay my respects to the king and queen."

Edric broke the seal as Nolan followed the other knights to the field. Edric quickly noted Samantha's handwriting and began to read the letter. His eyes flew open in panic. He walked as fast as he dared to the sidelines of the field, searching for Nolan.

The knights presented their colors and rode past the royal box, receiving a nod from King Aspen. Edric waved his arms to catch Nolan's attention.

205

Nolan cantered over, eyebrows raised. "What's the matter? Is it a letter from home?"

"Not from home, from Samantha," Edric answered, his eyes darkening. "Chrissy and Sam were separated, and she's gone to look for her—"

"*What?*" Nolan yelped, drawing looks from those around him. "Let me see the letter!"

Edric handed it up to him, all color disappearing from his face. "It says Sir Palmer but—"

"Why would Sir Palmer go look for Chrissy? You said Samantha went to look for her. This letter says—"

"First up for the joust . . . Sir Palmer of Mittra and Sir Octavian of Isonox!" the herald bellowed out.

Edric looked completely confused. "If Sir Palmer is in the tournament, how is she out looking for Chrissy?"

Nolan stared at his brother. "Did you get kicked in the head, too? You aren't making any sense! Sir Palmer is a *man*. He's right there." Nolan held out his gloved hand and pointed at the figure on the horse wearing Palmer's colors.

"I don't understand," Edric stammered, holding his head in his hands. "This is very confusing. Why would Samantha lie about this?"

"How is Samantha lying?" Nolan demanded. "Edric, do you need a medic?" He quickly re-read the letter. "Maybe she meant Sir Palmer would go after the tournament. I don't know why she wouldn't ask me. It's pretty obvious you can't get on a horse right now to search the forest. Edric, I'm next up for the joust. Just stay here. We'll figure this out when I'm done."

"She promised she wouldn't enter," he heard Edric mutter as he rode away. *I need to ask Talia to check him again,* Nolan thought. *He's not thinking straight!*

The tournament seemed to fly by in a flash of colors, explosion of noises, and heart pumping adrenaline. The final competition came down to Nolan versus Sir Palmer. *He's a worthy opponent*, Nolan thought as Clark helped him get ready for the final joust. *He's given a decent showing on this circuit. Let's see if he can beat me.*

The two knights lined up at their respective ends of the field, waiting for the flag to drop. There would be a series of three charges, each scored based on their hits. The highest scorer would be the winner of the tournament series.

The flag dropped and Nolan spurred Blaze into a run, hooking his lance into position on his saddle. Leveling it toward Palmer's shoulder, Nolan broke the tip of his lance on his target and felt the glancing blow of Palmer's lance skip off his own shoulder. *One for me*, Nolan thought with satisfaction, circling back to accept a new lance from Clark.

During the second charge, Palmer broke the tip of his lance on Nolan's shoulder while Nolan's lance barely hit Palmer's upper arm. *One for him*, Nolan grimaced while rotating his shoulder, still feeling the dull pain of the impact.

Nolan blocked out the sounds of the crowd and the waving of the flags from the stands, concentrating on breaking his lance on his opponent's shoulder. *That would make two for me and a large purse for a prize*, he thought as he waited for the flag to drop. *Enough for a bride price?* He shook his head to clear that thought away. *Don't think about Samantha. Think about this! She's not even interested.*

Nolan saw the flag and began to charge, struggling to get his lance into position. A frantic movement to the right caught his attention. He glanced over and saw Edric's waving arms but he turned back to the joust. He had just locked his lance into place when Palmer's lance shattered against his shoulder, throwing him back in his saddle.

Clark helped him dismount. As soon as Nolan removed his helmet, he began to yell at his brother. "What was that for? I was so close to winning! What is wrong with you?"

Edric motioned him over and pointed to Talia up in the stands. "Miss Talia told me that Samantha kept her promise and didn't enter. Sir Palmer's not Samantha!"

Nolan narrowed his eyes, frowning in disgust. "I know that already. We had this conversation. You seriously need to get your head checked." He looked over his shoulder. "I need to go to the awards ceremony. To receive *second* place."

Nolan watched as King Aspen and Queen Laurel, surrounded by their three younger daughters, smiled at the final three competitors.

"Sir Gilbert of Rothan, congratulations on your third place position. Here is your reward," King Aspen boomed out with a large smile. He gestured toward Princess Magnolia, who handed him the purse. She shyly dropped a kiss on the knight's cheek before running back to her sisters, giggling. Gilbert looked slightly dazed but grinned at her until Nolan elbowed him.

"Drool later at the ball," Nolan whispered drily, fixing his attention on King Aspen.

"Prince Nolan of Lagola, second place is awarded to you. Here is your reward. Only the purse, if you please, Lilac," King Aspen spoke to his third eldest daughter but looked at Maggie, who blushed. Nolan took the purse with a bow, smiling at Lilac who shyly refused to look him in the eye.

"And Sir Palmer of Mittra, our champion! You have had a wonderful run during this tournament circuit, I've been told. Would you care to remove your helmet and let us all see the face of our champion?" King Aspen stood there expectantly.

Slowly, the knight reached up and pulled off his helmet, revealing the face of Dawes.

"Dawes!" Nolan blurted out. Seeing the confusion on King Aspen's face, he continued. "I mean, does *Sir Palmer* get a kiss from one of the princesses?" He looked at the three girls. "I'm sure he's too shy to ask for one himself."

Cammie giggled as she stepped away from her sisters. She stood in front of Dawes. "I've been following your career, Sir Palmer. You are my champion." She kissed her handkerchief and handed it to him.

Dawes stared at the cloth and then at the girl, his eyes uncertain as what to do.

"Bow, stupid," Nolan muttered under his breath. "She's a princess."

Dawes gave a jerky bow and then stuffed the handkerchief in his glove.

"Thank you to all of our competitors," King Aspen called out. "Please be sure to join us tonight at the banquet and ball."

Nolan grabbed Dawes by the elbow and pushed him toward the tents on the side of the field. "I don't know what this is all about, but I do know you're not a knight." Nolan said. "Does Samantha know you're out here?"

Edric threw open the door to Nolan's tent and stared at Dawes. "*You* entered in the tournament?"

"Ignore him," Nolan muttered, letting go of Dawes' arm. "Start talking."

"Well, your brother knows most of it, actually," Dawes said nervously, glancing over at Edric.

"Knows what?" Nolan yelled, throwing his hands up in the air. "Somebody needs to start talking sense!"

Dawes took a deep breath and then rapidly told Nolan about Samantha secretly entering the tournaments as his brother.

Nolan stared at him incredulously. "Are you seriously telling me that Sam, *Princess Samantha*, has been entering these tournaments as a man? And you two didn't stop her?" He began to pace back and forth in the small tent. "I should punch you or something! Do you have any idea how dangerous this is?" He spun and faced Edric. "You knew better! Especially after what happened with you and Princess Chrissy. She could have died out there! Edric—"

"Stop it," Edric's voice rang out, his haggard face bristling with anger. "Just shut your mouth. I told Samantha that she could not enter today and she obviously didn't. You know how hard it is to make that girl do what you want her to do. Don't stand here self-righteously and tell us what we should have done differently. *This* is what is important now." He thrust the letter into Nolan's hands.

"If Sir Palmer, that is, if Dawes is here . . . *Samantha* is out there," Nolan said quietly, finally understanding. "I warned her about going out there alone. I told her that there are reports of bad things in the forest. Why didn't she listen to me? I have to go after her."

"I should be the one to go after Chrissy!" Edric insisted.

"You'd never make it. We both know that. Dawes, would you go ask my squire, Clark, if you can help him pack up what I'll need to go out in the forest?" Dawes nodded and hurried from the tent. Nolan turned to his brother. "Edric, you need to stay here and keep the peace. Make sure King Aspen and Queen Laurel don't panic. Keep the news from them, if you can. Assure them I will bring the girls back soon," Nolan instructed as he removed his heavy armor.

"I should tell Miss Talia what is happening right away. Maybe she can use some of her fairy powers to help. Nolan," Edric said, grabbing the front of his brother's shirt, "You *must* bring Chrissy back. And Sam, too. But Chrissy . . . I want to marry her, Nolan. And I haven't even told her yet."

"I'm sure she knows by the way you've been looking at her lately," Nolan assured his brother, pulling his hands away. "I'll bring them *both* back."

He started to leave, but Edric's voice stopped him. "What if 'The Evil of East' has something to do with this?"

"Then be sure to tell Talia as soon as you can," Nolan answered before walking quickly toward the corral.

✢

Samantha wrapped her heavy cloak tightly around herself, curling into a ball in the dirt of a small clearing. She scowled at the small pile of twigs and branches she had assembled in a hastily dug fire pit. *I should have thought to bring a flint. But, then again, I thought I would have found Chrissy already.* The moon was just rising, and the scuttling of clouds across it gave Samantha a chill. She startled when an owl hooted from the tree behind her. Windstorm shuffled about nervously.

"Shhh, that's a good boy," Samantha murmured, patting her horse to relieve his unease. *If anything, he's comforting me.*

A sudden, sharp breaking of branches sounded in the forest south of her. *It's probably a wild animal, like a rabbit or a deer. Or a bear!* She fumbled in her saddlebag for her dagger and held it tightly in her hand, waiting to see what would emerge from the trees.

To her surprise, Nolan burst into the clearing. He was holding Blaze's bridle, an angry scowl on his face.

"Nolan!" she exclaimed, relief coursing through her body as he crossed the clearing to her.

Nolan grabbed her by the shoulders and began to shake her. "*What were you thinking?*" he yelled, a violent shake accompanying each word. "Out here, alone, in the woods! By yourself!"

"I understand the meaning of *alone*, thank you," she snapped as she wriggled away from his grasp. "What are you doing here? Why didn't you stay at the castle and wait for me to get back?"

Nolan barked out a harsh laugh. "'Stay at the castle and wait'? I told you there are dangers out here in the forest. Did you think I was kidding?"

"No, I took your words to heart, which is why I'm out here trying to find my friend. It got dark and I had to stop. I can't even light a stupid fire." To her embarrassment, hot tears sprang to her eyes. She rushed to wipe them away.

Taking a deep breath, Nolan backed away. He glared at her, crossing his arms over his chest. "I'll start the fire for you. *I* came prepared. I didn't just fly out here without thinking things through."

"I had a plan to save my friend. Don't do me any favors, Nolan. I can survive without a fire. Just go away," Samantha yelled, stomping away from him.

A few minutes later, she sensed him kneeling down next to her. After listening to a faint scraping sound, a spark leaped out onto the dry twigs, eagerly devouring the small pile. Nolan fed a few small branches to the fire and then sat back, his arms circling his knees.

"I know about Sir Palmer. And Dawes. I don't know why you'd keep it a secret for so long," his voice was low as he stared into the flames.

"Edric told you?"

"Sort of. Actually, *Sir Palmer* entered the tournament. Did you know that?" Nolan turned to her.

"What? Oh, no. Dawes entered?" Samantha said, her eyes wide with horror. "Was he seriously injured? Why are you smiling?" She swatted his arm and he started to laugh.

"Take a breath! Yes, Dawes entered. He did quite well, actually. He beat me, in fact. First place." Nolan's lips pulled into a grin at Samantha's stunned smile.

"He could have done it all along. He just had to try a little harder, that's all. Good for you, Dawes," Samantha whispered into the night.

"So . . . why in the world did you become a knight?" Nolan asked, his gaze intense.

Samantha hoped the heat from the fire covered her flushed cheeks. "I'm not officially a knight, but I'm in training to be one. At least, I was. I don't know what will happen when I return home." She sighed and looked into the depths of the fire.

"Go on . . ."

"I don't know how much you already know. I don't want to give too much away."

"Come on, Sam, you can tell me," Nolan coaxed before his face creased with pain. He held his head between his hands. "How are you doing that?"

"I'm not doing anything. You're the one trying to use your stupid gift on me, trying to sweet talk me into answering you."

Nolan sat stock still, glaring at her. "I am not trying to 'sweet talk' you, *princess*. You know what? I'm tired of talking to you. At daybreak, I will make sure you return home." Samantha opened her mouth to protest. "Do not try to argue with me."

She watched as he stood up and strode back to his horse. The sounds of rustling filled the darkness. He returned to sit on the opposite side of the fire, pulling a thick blanket around his shoulders.

Samantha ignored him and covered her head with the hood of her cloak. *If you're going to insist I go back at first light, I'll just have to wake up before you.*

‡

Nolan woke as the sky was starting to turn pink. He had slumped over while he slept and ended up lying on the hard ground, stones beneath him. He groaned. *Not the most comfortable bed*, he thought ruefully, looking across the cold fire pit. After noting that there was no sign of Samantha or her horse, Nolan jumped to his feet in alarm.

"Idiot! Why did I have to tell her I would make her go back? Of course she'd take off." Mounting Blaze, he started searching for Samantha's trail.

Luckily for him, she was not skilled in covering her tracks. *Most likely, she knew I'd follow her. She didn't even try.*

213

After traveling for a while, he started to think about how much he would like a hot cup of coffee. Instead, Nolan took a bruised pear out of his saddlebag and ate it without enthusiasm. A moment later, he heard the jingling of Windstorm's bridle. Nolan urged Blaze to go faster. Spotting Samantha's cloaked figure, Nolan whistled loudly to alert her of his presence.

"I'm not going back now, Nolan!"

"I realized that when I woke up and you were gone!" he answered, riding up to her side. "You didn't have to go off on your own. Again."

"You know, that's funny. Just last night you told me you were going to send me back. *Alone*. It seems like your logic is a little off."

"Cool the hostility a minute, will you?" Nolan demanded, grabbing for her reins.

Samantha finally looked up at him. The weariness of his face combined with the smudge of dirt across his cheek lessened her frustration. "Why are you so mean to me?"

Nolan sighed. "I'm not being mean. I'm trying to keep you safe. That's why I wanted you to return to the castle. We don't know what could be out here."

Samantha tried to pull his hands off her reins. "Would you let *go*?"

"No! Not until you agree to go back." He grabbed his head with a moan. "Stay back! No, go back! Ahhh! I'll go back. No, that's not what I meant . . ."

"Are you okay?" Samantha stared at him with wide eyes. "You should stop and rest."

"No! I don't need to rest. You need to return to the castle," Nolan enunciated each word clearly. Suddenly, an intense grimace came over his face, and he moaned, "How do you do that? What kind of crazy fairy magic do you have?"

"I don't have any 'crazy magic.' I only have my gifts and those certainly won't affect you."

"Are you sure those are your real gifts?" Nolan demanded, fixing his pained eyes on her. "Giggling, and so forth? Were you secretly cursed to make those who want to help you have intense pain?"

"Secrets, yes. But cursed? No!" Samantha shouted at him. "Don't talk about things you don't even know." She pulled her reins free and began to ride through the trees.

"Samantha, wait!" Nolan called, but she refused to stop. "I don't understand." He shook his head, still dazed from the pain. "Come on, Blaze."

Nolan followed at a distance, but he kept Samantha in his sight the whole time. She finally stopped at a small stream and let Windstorm take a drink. The horse began to graze while she sat on a log, facing away from Nolan.

He approached the log. "Mind if my horse drinks the same water as your horse?"

"I have no problem with Blaze. It's his pigheaded owner I have a problem with," Samantha answered back sharply, keeping her eyes on the stream.

Nolan sat next to her, glancing at her profile. "You know you're beautiful when you're mad."

She turned toward him, her mouth open. "What? You insult me back there and now you—"

Nolan laughed. "I just wanted you to look at me. It worked."

She pushed him off the log. "If you're going to play that game—"

But before she could finish, Nolan grabbed her hand and pulled her down to the ground next to him. She froze for a minute and then laughed. "Boys never change. I thought after reading your letters that you were different. But now, I'm not sure . . ."

She started to rise when Nolan caught her hand again.

"You read my letters?" His voice was low, and he stared straight into Samantha's eyes.

"Yes, I did. I actually packed them on this journey." She blushed. "Not that I was trying to."

A smile grew on Nolan's face. "And?"

"And I'm sorry I was such a brat and never read them," she admitted. "But, to be fair, you were awfully bratty yourself!"

"I doubt I was as bad as you say." He stood up and offered her a hand.

Samantha looked at his outstretched hand and placed hers in it. He pulled her up and gazed into her eyes. Samantha flushed and pulled away, her heart racing.

"Um . . . well, if you need proof, I have the letters in my saddlebag," she turned to her horse.

"You brought them with you?" Nolan asked incredulously, following her.

"I didn't pack them because they were precious to me!" Samantha replied, feeling her blush spreading. "They were in my room. I didn't want to leave them lying around."

"You were protecting me."

Samantha removed the letters and handed them to Nolan. "I suppose so," she said quietly. "If you want to look at it that way."

Nolan returned to the log and began to read the letters. "Oh no! 'Second prince?' How proud was I?"

"I was going to use that one against you. How can I tease you now?"

"You weren't kidding. I was awful. It's probably good you didn't read these. You would have come after me with your intense knight skills and beaten me to a pulp!" Nolan chuckled.

"I was only a page at that time," she told him, smiling.

Nolan's face was suddenly serious. "Can I ask you a question?"

"You can ask. I can't say if I will answer."

"What did you mean when you said you had secret gifts?" Nolan watched her expression.

She sighed and picked up a leaf from the ground, spinning the stem between her fingers. "You know Elan and Osric, don't you? Well, they've always had a competitive thing between them. They began to boast about what gifts they would have given to a boy. I received all of those gifts. Mother didn't want anyone to find out, so it was kept quiet. Now you know why the Princess of Mittra is such a freak. Surely no one wants to marry someone like that." Samantha threw the leaf on the ground and walked over to the edge of the stream.

Nolan kept his seat and spoke to her back. "You're not a freak, Sam. I think all of those blessings are rather amazing. How awesome would it be to be superior at something that can help others? It is so much better than my gift of charming speech. We both know my gift fails. Well, only with you, that is."

Samantha turned back to him, her mouth gaping open in surprise. "Maybe I do have fairy magic after all!"

"What do you mean?"

Samantha told him her real gifts. "The last one is a mystery to me. At least, it always has been. I've never been charmed by your speech, right?"

"I don't think that's a gift, Sam," Nolan said drily.

"Just listen. Edric is a peacemaker. Did he ever get me to agree to make peace with you? No, he didn't. You and I fought all the time. I'm sure there are other instances, but the only thing I can think of is my seventh blessing. It's something to do with 'princess' and 'magic.' Maybe magic doesn't work on me? No, that can't be it. Talia has used magic on me before."

"But only when you let her, right? I mean, she always been nice to you. She doesn't make you do things you don't want to do."

"You're right." She stood up. "Well, we can think about this as we ride. Can't we?"

Nolan grumbled, helping her into her saddle. "Who is sweet talking who now?"

"Chrissy said the mountains were about five days away," Samantha told him. "Are you up to it?"

"I am if you are," Nolan answered as he urged Blaze into a canter away from the stream.

CHAPTER SEVENTEEN

*T*wo days later, Samantha and Nolan stood frozen at the base of the barren mountain, staring at the enormous corpse of a dragon. Samantha pinched her nose to try to block the stench. She clamped her mouth shut as she felt her stomach lurch. She glanced over to see Nolan doing the same thing. He motioned for her to lead her horse around the dragon and toward a fallen log several yards away.

"So it's true?" Samantha asked when she could finally breathe freely. "There are dragons in the forest? Who killed it?"

"My first guess would have been Linden, but I didn't see any obvious wounds to it. Maybe it died of disease or old age."

"Or magic?" Her eyes fixed on Nolan. "Lord Oblex?"

"We don't know for certain that Oblex is here in this forest. If he is alive, he'd be quite old. Even with magic, he would have a hard time climbing down."

"It only took us three days to reach the mountain. Why do you think the scouts gave a wrong report?"

"Maybe they arrived at the edge of the forest, saw dragon carcasses, and became afraid. Maybe to warn others off from journeying this direction. It doesn't matter. We're here now, and it will make it that much faster to return home," Nolan answered as he glanced back toward the forest of dead trees.

Samantha handed Windstorm's reins to Nolan and began to climb the fallen log. The blackened trees surrounding the base of the mountain filled the sky with wiry, brittle branches. The small amount of grass that grew was mottled yellow-green. Samantha could see several huge lumps in the distance that she now suspected were dragon carcasses. A cloud of flies buzzed around each mass. "It's like the life has been sucked out of these trees." She shaded her eyes and looked back at the mountain. "There!" she cried, rushing over to a long row of boulders at the base of the mountain.

Nolan ran after her. "Samantha!" he yelled, leading the horses toward the boulders. "Are you okay?"

Her head popped out from behind a boulder. A mischievous look played on her face. "I'm perfectly fine, but it's nice to know you were so worried about me. I've found a hidden trail back here."

Nolan tied the two horses to a branch and ducked behind the boulders where Samantha waited for him. He watched her crouch down in front of a small hole in the face of the mountain.

"If you look in, you can see that the hole widens quite a bit about ten feet in. It's dark further inside, but I think we can feel our way through." Samantha turned her face up to Nolan. "What should we do?"

Nolan thought quickly. "We'll have to let the horses go. We don't know how long we'll be gone and it's not fair to keep them tied up. We'll have to carry only the necessary items with us." He looked down into Samantha's eyes. "Are you scared? You can head back. No shame, no questions asked."

Samantha blew out her breath. "I intend to keep going. I've made it three days in the wilderness with you without crying. Well, without crying *much*, that is."

Nolan loved to see the spark of adventure in her eyes. "Let's go."

After removing the water skins and dried fruit from their saddle bags, they turned the horses loose.

"Let's hope they return to the stables. Actually, let's hope we find Chrissy quickly so we can get back out here and find the horses ourselves. I don't want to walk all the way back to the castle," Nolan said with a wink as they returned to the opening in the mountain.

Samantha flashed him a quick smile before dropping down to crawl into the hole. After about twelve feet, she was able to stand up, though slightly hunched over. Another ten feet allowed her to stand without hitting her head on the roof of the tunnel, but she was shrouded in complete darkness.

"Nolan?" Samantha called out, trying to keep the tremor out of her voice.

She felt a warm hand on her shoulder and was instantly comforted. He found her hand and began to lead her through the tunnel. "Not afraid of the dark, are you, Sam?"

A small pinprick of light slowly grew in size and brightness as they continued toward it. No sounds of alarm reached them in the tunnel. They cautiously crept on as the light grew stronger.

"Duck down and let me scout it out," Nolan whispered as they approached the end of the tunnel. He crawled on his hands and knees to the doorway cut into the rock, peeking out. "Come here, Sam. It's clear."

Samantha stood next to Nolan and looked into a small hut. "What is this?" she asked incredulously, turning around.

"The entrance to the tunnel is a secret. This hut keeps it hidden from those outside. Whoever created the tunnel didn't want others to find it and use it, apparently." Nolan walked to the wooden door. He peeked out of the slats for a long moment. "I don't see anyone moving outside. Let's see what else is out there."

The door creaked slightly as they swung it open. Samantha looked out to see a large castle carved out of black stone in the center of the depression in the mountain.

"Was this valley always here, or did someone dig into the mountain to create this?" she whispered to Nolan, unable to take her eyes away from the sharp peaks and crags of the castle. *Not a castle. A lair,* she thought with a shiver.

He shook his head and held his finger to his lips. "We'll find out later. Right now, let's find Chrissy."

They crept across the hard gray slate that made up the valley floor, searching for guards. Nolan pointed to a small door at the side of the stone castle, and Samantha nodded. Reaching the door without incident, Nolan pressed on it. It instantly gave away and they slipped inside. Before they could take another step, they froze.

In the hallway before them was a huge, green dragon. It was rearing up on its hind legs, snout open to breathe fire, claws fully extended. Nolan pushed Samantha behind him as he slipped his dagger from his belt.

"Nolan, it's not alive," Samantha whispered behind him. "It's stunned or something. Look, it's not moving."

Nolan exhaled noisily, sliding his dagger back into its sheath. "That was close. We must be prepared to meet something that means to do us harm. Keep your dagger close to you. As much as I don't want to leave you, I think we need to split up to find Chrissy. This place is huge. I'll take the lower level and see if there is a place to keep prisoners locked up. You take this level and scout it out. We'll both look on the upper level together, if we need to."

Samantha nodded. She started to walk down the hallway when she felt Nolan catch her hand.

His eyes searched her face. "Samantha, promise me you'll be safe."

She gave a hollow laugh. "I promise that I'll be safe. I can't guarantee what will happen to anyone I meet that keeps me from my friend."

She squeezed his hand and started to move away. Before she could think about what she was doing, she flung her arms around his neck. Her lips gently met his. Just as Nolan began to return the kiss, Samantha dropped her arms and ran down the hall.

"You be careful now," she called.

"That's my girl," he murmured while he watched her go. He clutched his dagger as he crept down the dark passage. He found a rocky ledge of stairs descending into the bowels of the castle. *I can feel the bad magic here,* Nolan thought as he cautiously stepped down into the darkness. *Edric, at least if I die, you'll know I died trying to save your true love.* Nolan shook his head. *Don't be so macabre. You'll find Chrissy, defeat whoever has her trapped here and . . . what? Head home. Right. And ask Samantha to marry me? No, stay focused!*

He reached the bottom of the stairs. A lantern hanging from the ceiling cast a sickly pale light on the dirty stone walls. The bars of the dungeon cells gleamed in the weak light. *Who purposely builds a large dungeon?* Nolan asked himself in disgust. *Only someone evil.*

The two rows of cells ran down the length of the room. Nolan glanced into each cell he passed. The first few held the bleached bones of skeletons. He turned his face away from a rat that was chewing on an arm bone of an unlucky former prisoner. A flash of movement in the sixth cell caught his attention. A body was curled up in the corner of the cell, rocking slowly. Nolan ran to the barred door.

"Chrissy?" Nolan asked in a quiet, forceful voice. "Are you well?"

Chrissy's panic-stricken eyes struggled to focus on Nolan's face. "Who's there? Oh, Edric, is that you? I knew you'd come for me. I told Linden you would. He didn't believe me, but I never lost hope . . ." Her voice trailed off as tears ran down her cheeks.

Nolan's heart constricted, and he had to clear his throat several times before he could speak. Chrissy's face was covered with dirt and bruises. He could see the dried blood at the corner of her mouth. Her hair was in tangles and her cheekbones stood out in sharp contrast, apparent signs that she had been starved down here.

"I will get you out," he pledged behind clenched teeth. "And whoever did this, so help me, I will beat him—"

"I seriously doubt that," a familiar voice echoed throughout the dark room. "It is I who owes *you* a beating, don't I, Lagola?"

Nolan turned to see Linden sneering at him from the base of the stairs. He was dressed completely in black. His hair, once fastidiously groomed, was cut so short that it stood out sharply from his scalp. He leaned lazily on the hilt of his sword, the tip of it resting on the stone floor.

"Why are you here, Linden?" Nolan's voice was harsh as he approached his enemy. "Why would you lock up your own cousin like this? She is a lady! I demand that you release her—"

"Or what? You'll challenge me to a duel? Have me kicked out of my country? Oh, wait, you already did that. Well, not alone, did you? You had help from that shrew, that hellion, *Samantha*." As he said her name, Linden's face turned in an ugly scowl. His eyes took on a shade of madness. "She was mine! And do you see what she did? She scarred my hand and my arm! But I will make her pay. My beloved cousin Chrysanthemum will be my negotiating tool. They will hand over Samantha, and I will give them back their precious princess."

"You're mad!" Nolan exclaimed. "Do you honestly think your uncle would release a guest of his house into your custody?" Nolan hoped Samantha would stay in the upper levels of the castle so he could deal with Linden.

"My uncle will do as I command when he discovers that I have magic." Nolan raised his eyebrows in disbelief. "That's right. He found me lost in the forest after my uncle cast me away. Away from my home and my birthright! He promised to care for me. He said he would make me king, and I *will* reign over the kingdom that is rightfully mine!" Linden's eyes seemed to sparkle in the lantern light.

Nolan swallowed, a twisting of fear in his belly. "Who is this *he* that you speak of? Only fairies can do magic, and everyone knows there aren't any fairies here."

Nolan was trying to stall for time. His eyes found an open cell tucked away to the right of the staircase that was being used as the armory. Bows, arrows, crossbows, swords, shields hung from pegs on the wall. Nolan slowly backed up. He hoped Linden would allow him space to run so he could find a weapon better suited to fight against Linden's broadsword.

"Don't try to be brave. I won't release my cousin until I deem it is time. Your silly dagger will never open the lock to her cell. It is held in place with magic. A magic you will never know," Linden called out in a mocking voice.

"Your master holds the secret?"

"He is *not* my master! I am the one in control!" Linden insisted shrilly. "He will teach me the magic he holds. He has promised it to me. Along with the kingdom of Synterius. Once I have that, who knows how far my power will take me? I may just rule all of Gymandrol one day. Everyone will bow down to King Linden."

Nolan glimpsed at something at the base of the stairs. He was determined to keep Linden from looking that direction. "And why would *your master* share his power with you? Wouldn't he keep it for himself? That would make him the Potentate Supreme or some such nonsense?"

"Shut up!" Linden screamed. "I do not obey him. He will do as *I* say. I will be the Supreme One!" Linden lifted his sword and began to charge at Nolan, his eyes shining with madness.

"Now!" Nolan cried.

A bolt from a crossbow flew across the room, sinking into Linden's right arm. He crashed down in front of Nolan, his sword flying from his hand and sliding across the floor. Samantha lowered the crossbow and gave Nolan a weak smile.

"I told you I can't guarantee what I'd do to someone who tries to hurt my friends," she said, rushing down the stairs.

"I'll kill you!" Linden screamed at Samantha, trying to grab her. Nolan kicked him in the back of the head, knocking him out.

Nolan cast a sheepish look at Samantha. "I'll find some rope and tie him up."

Samantha hurried over to Chrissy's cell, grabbing Chrissy's hand through the bars. "Chrissy, are you okay?"

Chrissy's eyes brightened at Samantha's voice. "Sam, are we going for our ride now? I wanted to go earlier, but Linden said I had to stay here. Where's my horse? Did you see Edric? He came for me."

Samantha began to cry softly and pull at the lock on the cell. "Help me, Nolan! How do we get her out?" *What did they do to her? Has she gone mad?*

Nolan finished tying up Linden and then shoved his body into a cell. He closed the door and tied it shut with a length of rope. "That won't keep him for long, but it's better than nothing. As for the lock, Linden said it was bound with magic. I don't know how to get past magical charms."

Samantha picked up Linden's sword and began to hack at the lock. "Open! Open for me! Please," she cried as she hit the lock with all of her strength. "Talia, I need you!"

Nolan carefully grabbed her upper arm and forced her to drop the sword. "We'll figure it out, Sam. We need to find the . . . magician, fairy, whatever he is and make him open it for us."

Samantha wiped the tears from her face, smearing dirt across her cheeks in the process. "Let's go then. Chrissy, we'll be right back, okay?"

"And then we'll take our ride?"

"Yes. A ride. We'll be back as soon as we can," Samantha replied in a broken voice before she turned to run up the stairs.

She could hear Nolan behind her, and she slowed down so he could catch up with her. "I didn't find anything on the first level and then I heard voices down here, so I came to investigate."

"I'm glad you did," Nolan replied, squeezing her hand and keeping it in his as they reached the first floor.

"We need to find whoever Linden was working with. Let's go up to the second level. I saw a staircase over this direction."

Samantha turned right and began to run down the hallway. "I don't think we have the element of surprise anymore."

"Let's try to be cautious," Nolan suggested as they reached the second level of the castle. They crept through the narrow doorway and peered into a large, dark room. Nolan placed his hand on her arm, motioning to the left side of the room. Samantha could see a dark, cloaked figure staring into a mirror on the wall.

"I finally meet the great Princess of Mittra," a low voice warbled toward them. "Linden, my apprentice, has told me all about you. Do you mind if I call you Samantha? I know we'll be good friends. You will have to rely on my hospitality to feed and shelter you. *And* your new husband."

Samantha forced herself from shuttering at the man's voice. "If your treatment of Chrissy is any indicator of your hospitality, I will pass, thank you."

"Princess Chrysanthemum was an unfortunate choice on Linden's part. I spotted both of you in the forest and told him to grab you. Unfortunately, he missed you. I had to settle for her as a ransom victim. But now that you've brought yourself here, we don't need her anymore. We can be rid of her anytime. That will be my next task after I kill your hero."

The cloaked figure turned from the mirror. Samantha gasped. *What kind of man is this? No, he's a fairy!* He was shorter than her, but tall by fairy standards. His hair was completely white and hung limply around his face in greasy strands. His face was pale and his skin hung loosely from the bones, as if he had recently healed from a long illness. Deep wrinkles surrounded his mouth and eyes, making his flat grey eyes stand out. Samantha was used to the silver eyes of Elan and Osric and the silver shimmer that shone from their foreheads. This fairy's eyes pulsed with madness. His shimmer was so bright that Samantha could not look at it directly. She struggled to remember why he looked familiar.

"Nolan, the history!" she gasped, clutching his hand. *The history of Sansevierra is true. Dagan is Oblex. Or rather, Oblex is Dagan.* She sensed Nolan stiffen next to her.

"Dagan, you must release Princess Chrissy immediately," Nolan spoke authoritatively to the fairy.

Dagan laughed hoarsely, clearly unused to doing such a thing. "You know who I am? Does my fame extend all the way to Lagola?" Nolan raised his eyebrows. "Yes, foolish boy, I know from where you come. I have watched your journey in my mirror. Quite admirable, I must say. You are the perfect gentleman to our Samantha here. And Samantha, you are very clever, finding my tunnel behind the boulders. I had cast a glimmer about them so my enemies could not find them, but here you are."

"Don't speak to her—"

Dagan held up his hand, cutting Nolan off. "I did not give you leave to speak, boy," he sneered. "Do they not teach manners where you come from? *I* was taught that ill-behaved boys are disciplined." A flick of his wrist sent Nolan careening into nearby shelves laden high with books and crockery. "And now you've broken some of my possessions. How shall I teach you a lesson?"

"Leave him alone!" Samantha shouted, pulling on Nolan's hand to help him stand. She winced when she saw blood trickling from a cut on his forehead.

"Sam, get out of here," Nolan urged.

Dagan flicked his hand to the side and Nolan's body flew across the room, slamming into a wall. He collapsed in a heap on the floor.

"There. Now we don't have anyone interrupting our conversation, do we?" Dagan asked. His rasping voice made the hair on her arms stand up. The fairy crossed the room and began to circle her, looking her up and down. "Maybe I'll tell Linden he can't have you after all. I shall take you for my wife."

"I'd rather die," Samantha shouted, grasping her dagger in her hand.

Dagan made a tisking noise with his tongue. "No need for histrionics, my dear. And no need for violence. Put away your dagger."

Samantha clasped the hilt tighter and unknowingly growled at him. "I will not put it away. You will release my friend and let us leave."

Dagan gave her a surprised look. "You dare refuse me? Do you not pity an old fairy that has such a small window to the world? Though I do love my portal to the outside world," Dagan murmured as he stroked the frame of the oversized mirror.

Samantha spat at his feet. "I do not pity one such as you. You murdered innocent people! You murdered your own king and queen! You deserve to die."

"I see someone has been teaching you history. Who was it?" Samantha refused to answer him. "Ah, it was that fool of a clerk, Osric, wasn't it? He tried to teach me at the Academy, but I knew so much more than he did. I destroyed Sansevierra using the simple minded soldiers of Synterius. I will use Synterius again, but this time, I will take over all of Gymandrol!"

"You think you're all powerful, but there is a fairy more powerful than you," Samantha retorted. "Talia has more power than you and she uses it for good."

"And where is Talia now? Clearly, she isn't here to help you. Talia

… Why does that sound familiar? Oh yes. I killed her father." Samantha gasped. "Oh, do not look so shocked, princess. One does what one must do to get ahead in this world. Talia's mother would be Tatiana, is that right?" Dagan's eyes shone brighter, and Samantha felt a thrill of fear. "Do you want to see what life was for me? Look into my mirror and you will see."

Samantha wanted to refuse, but she felt a tug of curiosity. Would she see Talia as a child? Would she see Sansevierra in its glory? She walked over to the mirror and saw only her own reflection. Her face was filthy with trail dust. Her hair hung in tangles with leaves and twigs caught in it. *You kissed Nolan looking like that?* she thought. She shook herself out of her thoughts and concentrated on the dim image of a room in the depths of the mirror.

She realized she was seeing Dagan's thoughts and memories. She wanted to turn away, but she kept her place. *I need to see more so that I understand how to defeat him.*

Suddenly, she saw a much younger Dagan enter his room, looking at himself in a mirror. She could see the same eyes and shimmer that he had now. The effect was just as disturbing when he was a youth. She was able to hear his thoughts, which frightened her, but she stayed rooted to her spot.

The young Dagan glanced at his reflection in the mirror, scowling at what he saw there. His hair was due for another cut, although it seemed like he had just cut it last week. No, that wasn't right. Last week was review for final examination week. Dagan sighed and turned from the mirror. I need to get it cut before they will let me into the final examination chamber this term, he thought to himself. He recalled with a slight smile last term's examination day. He had, once again, put off his haircut and was refused entrance into the chamber until he cut it. He borrowed a pair of scissors from a scribe sitting nearby and hacked at his hair in the hallway. The professor, Master Fredelpic, turned bright red while his shimmer sent silver sparks into the air.

"Good enough, Master?" Dagan asked in a faintly sarcastic tone.

Fredelpic could only nod. His mouth grimaced with displeasure at the upstart student who was determined to do things his own way. Dagan had gone on to pass the examination with the highest grade of the third year students, just as he had done the previous two years.

"But still they insist that I stay here for the entire four years!" Dagan muttered to himself as he stalked around his private bedchamber. He picked up study materials that had been tossed about during his late night study session the previous evening. He piled the scrolls on his already full desk, willing the heap of parchment to keep its balance. The stack seemed to freeze in mid-sway as he simply thought of the action. He smiled to himself.

He could never understand when other students' complained about thinking of an action and seeing it carried through. They thought it was more difficult than memorizing charms and spells. He, on the other hand, found spells tedious and thought charms were a waste of time.

"Leave those to the females," he spit out, his face twisting in malice.

He found the presence of female fairies to be a distraction to his brethren in the Academy. He had no interest in marrying anytime soon, so he paid no attention to girls.

Unless it was Tatiana.

He loathed Tatiana, a fellow fourth year student. She was always coming in right behind him in scores on both written and practical examinations. The most frustrating thing to Dagan was Tatiana's relentless enthusiasm and good sportsmanship after a "match," as he secretly called them. He knew he was better than her, but she was annoyingly humble about it.

As he left his chamber to go to the examination chamber, he reviewed the history of the Fairy-Human War. He was a bit shaky on the exact dates and names of the lesser commanders of the battles. He was concentrating so hard that he did not see who was standing in front of him, waiting to check in for the exam.

"Hi Dagan!" Tatiana exclaimed, turning toward him.

Dagan closed his eyes, trying to visualize the dates and names from his notes taken in class. He knew it was rude to ignore Tatiana, but he did not care. He was more concerned with taking first in this competition.

"Excuse me?" Tatiana demanded.

Dagan met her glowing purple eyes, which flickered with anger. "What?"

"Do you know what you just said to me? You think it's okay to be rude to me because you want to win this 'competition?' Is that what this is to you?" Tatiana looked ready to cry.

"I was only meaning to think that. Not say it out loud. I am sorry you heard it." Dagan could not meet her eyes.

He started to turn away but was jerked backwards from a sudden impact on his upper arm. "What was that?" Dagan roared, starting towards Tatiana.

He felt a pair of strong arms surround his torso from behind, holding him back. "Think before you act, young sir," a voice hissed into his ear. "Your actions may haunt you for years."

Dagan pulled away from the dark haired fairy holding him back and stepped across the hall. He glared with undisguised fury at Tatiana.

"Maybe you should give the female the same advice, sir," Dagan spit out, feeling his temper flare. He knew that his shimmer was glowing so bright that it could practically blind anyone looking directly at it.

"I have a name, you know," Tatiana shot back. "I hit you because you deserve to have some sense knocked into you. Some commonsense! I hope you think twice before you insult someone. Particularly someone who is just as smart as you."

Dagan narrowed his eyes menacingly at Tatiana before filling the hall with derisive, incredulous laughter. "Oh, please. You really think *you're as smart as me?" He continued to laugh, drawing a crowd of professors and students.*

Soren, the head administrator, pushed his way through the crowd. He stopped short at the sight of the Academy's two best students locked in a raging debate. He noticed the handsome, muscular fairy standing next to Tatiana and his frown deepened.

"Elan! Why are you simply standing there? Do something before someone is hurt," Soren admonished his former pupil.

The crowd began to murmur when they realized who was visiting their school. Elan grimaced at the attention his name received but advanced to stand between Dagan and Tatiana. He whispered a few words in the ancient tongue. Instantly, Dagan and Tatiana froze, unable to move but still able to hear. Elan nodded at Soren, who muttered a spell himself. The students turned from the scene between Dagan and Tatiana and started toward the examination room.

Elan stepped to the side as the fourth year students streamed into the chamber, oblivious of the two students frozen in the middle of the hallway. Soren saw the last student in, and then closed the door with a bit more force than necessary. He sighed at Dagan and Tatiana before turning to Elan. He raised his arm out in greeting and Elan did the same. Soren advanced and pulled Elan into a hug.

"Son! It has been too long since you have visited your old father," Soren admonished.

Elan smiled. "You're not old, Father. Just well aged."

"Do you actually have leave, Elan?" Soren questioned.

"Actually, I have been transferred back here to Alvan. I am training the king's personal guards." Elan worked hard to keep a humble look on his face.

Soren's eyes filled with tears. "My son is training the king's own guards? Oh, I am the proudest father in all of Sansevierra!" The feuding students caught Soren's eye. "I am pleased that the army has not lessened your skill with the language of the Ancients." He nodded toward the *frozen figures. "I am impressed you remembered that spell. Much power is found in the words of the Ancients. Now I need to decide what to do with those two before I undo the spell."*

"I am glad that you did not see everything that took place. This young fairy was about to physically attack the female before I stepped in to stop him. He has much ability, but he does not have much strength of character."

Soren *suddenly looked very old. "What you have recognized in Dagan is something that we all saw three and a half years ago. We had hoped we could change him. I knew when I first saw him that he had great potential to be a powerful fairy. Now, I wish he would use his ability for good."*

Elan looked thoughtful for a moment. "Let me train him during the respite between terms. The training of a soldier, combined with his mental abilities, may prove just what he needs."

"Yes . . . I suppose it might just be what he needs."

Samantha felt a frigidly cold touch to her hand. She pulled herself away from the mirror with a gasp. Dagan stood near her, a hungry expression on his face. "Do you understand me now?" he demanded, grasping her hand tightly. "My life has never been easy. But this is an easy decision for you. Say you will be my wife."

Samantha tore her hand away from his and shook her head violently. "Never!"

Dagan's face was a mask of confusion. "But I commanded you to do it, so it must be done."

He lunged for her, but she turned and ran toward Nolan's body.

"Nolan, wake up!" She glanced around. "I need a weapon. Oh, why didn't I take one from the dungeon? Nolan, I need you to help me!"

Dagan approached with an evil cackle. "You cannot resist me. If you try, I will simply destroy you. You're only a little princess who does not have any magic or 'good fairies' around to protect her. And after you're dead, your friend here will be next. Oh, do you *love* him? Then I shall be sure to prolong his death. I'm sure the princess in the dungeon would make a lovely bride if you continue to resist my wishes. This is your last chance. Come to me!" Dagan shouted before stumbling back slightly.

Samantha stood up, trying to figure out if he was faltering to trick her into believing she was winning. *Winning what? This isn't a game. It's a battle, and I'm ill prepared to fight.* She focused on the last conversation she had with Nolan about her last blessing. *Is this the time to test it out? I have to at least try.*

Samantha squared her shoulders and faced Dagan head on. "You are a weak old fairy. You are cruel and deserve to be hanged."

Dagan sneered at her and barked out a hoarse laugh. "Is this a shallow attempt at bravery? Ha! You will leave this place as my wife or as a corpse. I will give you a minute to make a decision."

"I don't need a minute. I have already made my decision. Go ahead and try to kill me with one of your magic spells. Or do you fear a 'little princess'?" Samantha taunted.

With a throaty growl, Dagan shot both hands upward. Several bottles full of multicolored liquid rose into the air from the table in front of him. A spin of his hands set the bottles into a flurry of motion that had disastrous results. The bottles shattered on impact with each other, spraying across the room. Samantha ducked under a table and shielded her eyes. When the crashing ended, the hissing began. She peeked her head out to see the floor being eaten away in several places and a variety of a slimy objects hanging from shelves, tables, and windows.

"I know you're hiding," Dagan's voice came from across the room.

"You do not scare me!" Samantha yelled and then realized her mistake too late.

Slivers of glass flew toward her. She threw up her left arm to protect her eyes, gasping at the sharp pain and the blood flowing from the cuts. *Do not faint. That would be incredibly princessy.* She took a deep breath and exhaled slowly. Careful not to make a sound, she wrapped her fingers of her right hand with the edge of her vest and pulled out the glass shards quickly. She noticed a discarded piece of parchment under the table, and she slid the fragments onto the scroll, gathering up the bundle.

The table next to her was suddenly upended, and she heard Dagan's cackle. "Did you like my little surprise? There is more where that came from!"

Samantha jumped out from her hiding place, throwing the parchment in the direction of the voice. A screech of pain told her that she had found her mark. As she shakily rose to her feet, she noticed blood dribbling from small cuts on the side of his face. Dagan screamed out in fury as he touched his bloody face. She grasped her dagger, waiting for his next move.

Dagan snarled and thrust his hand toward her. His lips moved quickly but no sound came from them. He jerked his arm down and began to speak the tongue of the Ancients. Samantha stood fixed in her place, staring at the evil fairy.

He gave an angry shriek and waved his arms frantically in the air, spittle flying from his mouth. She watched as his eyes rolled madly in his head. Samantha listened to the words and began to translate them. *Strike yourself! Throw yourself upon the ground! Take your dagger and stab your own heart! Do as I say, foolish girl! Do not defy me! I will kill you!*

Samantha shook herself and locked eyes with him. In the tongue of the Ancients she said, "You have no power over me. You cannot hurt me in any way at all. Your evil magic has turned against you. You have lost."

Dagan gave a skin crawling shriek and pointed his index finger at her, making slashing motions with it. His scream turned into more magic curses, and Samantha struggled to understand the words flying at her. He suddenly grasped his own throat and began to choke himself, clutching tightly while the words still spewed from his mouth. Samantha watched in horror as his face turned from white to red to purple. She screamed at him to stop, but his body continued what it was doing until he dropped to the stone floor, lifeless.

Samantha turned her head and retched against the wall, shocked at what she had just witnessed. She sank to the ground and began to rock, holding her knees tightly against her chest. Hot tears streaked down her cheeks.

After a while, she gradually became aware of arms holding her. She leaned into Nolan's embrace, soaking his shirt with her tears.

"Shhh, it's fine now. He's dead." Nolan stroked her hair. "He can't hurt us anymore, Sam. We're okay."

"I killed him, Nolan. I . . . I made him angry, and he tried to curse me. I don't know exactly how it happened, but I . . . think I cursed him back. I'm a murderer!" Samantha choked out, clinging to him.

"He did it to himself. I heard the end of . . . whatever he was saying to you. Curses in a language of fairies? You don't have any magic; you didn't use any weapon against him, Sam. You are *not* a murderer."

Samantha's sobs slowly diminished and she pulled away from Nolan. "I only wanted to hurt him, to make him stop and leave us alone. I remembered that I sometimes give you a headache when we argue, so I tried to get him to argue with me. I thought—"

"You thought that if he was angry enough, he'd stop and leave us alone?" Nolan asked in a calm voice, still stroking her hair. "That was an excellent plan, Sam. You are truly the hero." He cast a look of admiration at her. "I can see you blushing under all that dirt, you know. And you're beautiful."

"No I am not. I am filthy and dirty and . . . and there's a dead body in this room! And I don't fancy being wooed with pretty words inside some crazy fairy's lair!" Samantha pushed Nolan's hand back and stood up, hiding her face.

"Would you mind if I courted you?" Nolan asked softly, catching her hand.

Samantha snatched her hand away and spun toward the doorway. "We need to free Chrissy and bind Linden more securely. After that . . . other things can happen. Or be said. Oh, you know what I mean!" She ran down the stairs, Nolan at her heels.

They were passing the large entrance door when it suddenly burst open, throwing them back from the force. Samantha squinted up at the light, seeing two figures in the doorway. Talia ran into the castle and dropped down next to Samantha.

"Sammy! Why are you bleeding? Where are you hurt? Did you find Dagan? Where is Chrissy?"

Samantha shook her head, watching Edric rush over to Nolan's side, asking the same questions. "Taley!" Samantha grabbed her, squeezing her tightly. "Help me up, please. We must get downstairs to the dungeon. That's where Chrissy is."

Nolan led the way downstairs, his dagger drawn. Edric followed him with his sword at the ready. The foursome burst into the dungeon, looking in every direction. Samantha spied the crossbow she had used earlier and reclaimed it.

"Chrissy!" Edric shouted, rushing her cell. He smashed the lock with the hilt of his sword. "Nolan, help me."

"Miss Talia, it's a magical lock," Nolan explained. "Linden told us. We did find Dagan, but he's unable to unlock it for us, courtesy of Samantha."

Talia gave Samantha an apprising glance. "I was hoping that gift would come in handy." She recited a spell to the lock and it fell from the door that was separating Chrissy and Edric.

Edric flew into the cell. He grabbed Chrissy and held her close to him. "I am so sorry, Chrissy. Please believe me."

Samantha, Nolan, and Talia turned from the couple and faced the cell Linden occupied. He had awoken and was working feverishly at untying his knots.

"I will be free from this prison soon, so you better watch your back," Linden shouted at Nolan. "No one is safe from Lord Oblex! You will all bow to me."

Nolan hit the bars fiercely. "Your master is dead, Linden. His own words killed him. His magic, the magic you so trusted in to rule this land, has turned against him. You will pay for your crimes."

Samantha laid her hand on Nolan's arm. "Let's leave him here with the magic lock on *his* cell. Or, perhaps a lock on the entire castle. Talia, can you do that? That way he can never leave, but he will be the king of one castle."

"A fitting punishment, Sammy. I will do it," Talia assured her with a smile. "Leave him here in the cell. He'll remove his bonds soon enough. I'll cast a binding spell on the castle doors."

Nolan signaled to Edric, who led Chrissy up out of the dungeon. Nolan pulled on his brother's arm and Edric reluctantly released Chrissy to Samantha. Samantha hugged her tightly and helped her up the stairs.

"How did you get here so quickly?" Nolan asked his brother. "Are you fully healed?"

"Talia decided to take a risk and heal my ribs after I kept complaining that I wanted to come after you two. And then she, along with several other fairies, cast a spell on our horses to make them fleet of foot. It seemed like we were flying over here."

"No matter how she did it, I'm glad she did," Nolan answered as they exited the castle. "Did you find the hidden tunnel?"

"A tunnel?" Edric repeated. "No, we came up over the mountains."

"Well, if you brought horses, they won't fit through the tunnel. Why don't you and I fly, er, climb down the mountain with the horses while the ladies go through the tunnel? We'll meet them on the other side. Chrissy will be safe. She's with Samantha and Talia."

"And where's Dagan? Or was it Lord Oblex?" Edric asked quietly, glancing over at Chrissy.

"One and the same. Somehow Samantha killed him. It had something to do with magic, but Sam doesn't have any magic. All I know is that he's dead and we aren't."

The group surrounded the horses that were wandering about the area in front of Dagan's castle. Nolan quickly outlined the plan and Edric led Chrissy and Talia to the hut with the entrance to the tunnel. Nolan kept his eyes on Samantha, willing her to look at him. She glanced up and then back down quickly, keeping Edric's horse between them.

Nolan spoke over Chester's back. "Why did you kiss me in the castle?"

Samantha looked up at him and held his gaze. "I thought I might die, and I wanted you to be sure of me."

"What do you mean, sure of you?" Nolan asked, a puzzled expression on his face.

"Don't make me say it here, Nolan. You know what I mean," Samantha ducked her head and began to walk toward the hut.

Nolan dashed around the horse and caught her hand. "I think I know what you mean, but I want you to say it."

"It is not my place to speak first," Samantha whispered before pulling her hand away and running to the hut, almost knocking Edric to the ground in her haste.

Edric gave a low whistle as he approached his brother. "What did you do to make her cry?"

"She was crying?" Nolan stopped short, turning towards the hut.

Edric grabbed Nolan's arm. "Just mount up. You'll see her soon enough. Plus, I don't think Sam likes being chased. She's the kind of girl who needs to work through things in her head first. What did you say?"

Nolan adjusted the stirrups on the horse Talia rode and then pulled himself up. "I don't remember, exactly. I wanted to tell her that I love her and that's she beautiful. No, wait. I did tell she's beautiful, but she told me to not say that when there's a dead body in the room—"

Edric's laughter cut him off. "Do you even *have* a romantic bone in your body? No wonder she ran away crying."

The laughter continued as the horses made their way down the jagged mountain until Nolan finally yelled at his brother to stop. The brothers made their way to the line of boulders where the ladies waited. Nolan was shocked to see Blaze and Windstorm waiting there.

"How?" he sputtered, looking toward Talia.

She smiled. "We found them wandering in the woods when we arrived. I set a charm on them so they would wait here until we returned."

Edric slipped down from his horse and helped Chrissy mount it. "You can ride with me. That is, if everyone else agrees that is . . . er, permissible?"

All were in agreement to Edric's suggestion. Nolan adjusted the stirrups for Talia and helped her mount the small pony. Samantha and Nolan each rode their own horses.

"Hold your horses very still," Talia instructed Samantha and Nolan. "I will place a charm on them to make them fleet of foot. We should arrive back at the castle quickly." She recited the charm. Nolan had a sudden sensation as if he was floating in the air.

"It's high noon now," Nolan said. "Could we make it back by sundown?"

"Let's find out," Edric called, his arms loosely circling Chrissy's waist to grasp the reins.

CHAPTER EIGHTEEN

*T*he sun cast its final golden rays across the grasslands behind the castle of King Aspen. The five travelers emerged from the dense forest and heard a bell ringing in the distance. As they approached the castle grounds, they could see a young guard ringing the alarm bell with all of his strength.

Almost instantly, a stream of people burst out of the castle, walking toward the weary company. One figure ran ahead of the others. Samantha recognized Dawes by his frantically pumping legs and swinging arms.

He practically strangled her in a tight embrace. "If you *ever* go off without me again, I'll tie you up!"

"I'm faster than you. You'll never catch me." Samantha squeaked out against his shoulder as she leaned from the saddle.

"Then I'll tell your *mother*." He chuckled with her.

"Dawes," Samantha whispered. "I missed you."

"I'm glad you're alive. You're my best friend, you know that, right?" Dawes' eyes glistened with unshed tears. "We better stop. Nolan's giving me the evil eye."

Chrissy's sisters began surrounding her and Edric, begging for information while trying to hug her. King Aspen shooed them away and carefully lifted his daughter from the horse. Edric nodded to the king, watching as he carefully studied his face before he nodded back. Aspen clutched his eldest daughter to him and wept openly. Queen Laurel then took her turn embracing her daughter, tears of joy streaming down her face.

Dawes helped Samantha down from Windstorm. "I was sure you were dead. I mean, I hoped you would be alive, but I was so scared—"

Samantha laughed, covering his mouth with her hand. "Enough, Dawes! What about you, tournament show off! What's that? Do I detect some perfume in the air? Who is she?" She looked over to see Cammie blushing in their direction, overhearing Samantha's question. Samantha waved at her and gave her a grin. "Good choice, Dawes. I suppose you will have to test for knighthood if you want to marry a princess. You certainly aim high, don't you?"

King Aspen approached Samantha. He patted her shoulder awkwardly before pulling her in for a hug. "I am so pleased both you and Chrissy survived your kidnappers. We were all very worried for you. I am grateful that Prince Nolan went to find you both."

Samantha stood still, gaping at the king, unsure of what to say. A crowd had grown around them, eagerly awaiting her answer.

Nolan stepped forward, a wide smile on his face. "I was very happy to go and help find the girls," he said as he shook the king's hand. He caught Samantha's eye and shook his head, his stern look silencing her. "Edric and Miss Talia arrived to help me free them. We left Dagan's body back at the castle."

The crowd gave a collective gasp and many conversations began at once. Samantha was able to surreptitiously make her escape, making her way towards the stables.

Talia rushed over to Samantha and squeezed her tightly. "Sam, dear, you need a bath. And perhaps some answers?"

Samantha nodded and allowed Talia to lead her inside the castle. *Why did Nolan lie? Why did the king think Chrissy and I were both kidnapped? I'll have to see Nolan later and we can talk about everything. Even the kiss. He asked if he could court me.*

She gasped suddenly and clutched Talia's hand. "What do I say if he asks me to marry him? Do I say yes? Do I tell him to ask my father? Taley, why did we not cover this in etiquette lessons?"

Talia laughed at Samantha's look of alarm and opened the door to her bedroom. "You'll know what to say if he asks. I can read that young man's face very clearly. He is desperately in love with you. Just as you are with him."

Talia rang for a maid to bring hot water for a bath. Samantha went behind the dressing screen to remove her filthy, bloody clothing.

"I think I should just burn these clothes, Taley. How could Nolan even stand to be near me? I reek so much. I will be so thankful for this bath." She emerged dressed in her thick robe and sat on the stool at the dressing table. Her eyes widened at her reflection. Her hair looked more brown than blonde, and there were enough sticks and leaves caught in it to create a small tree. Samantha picked up her comb and began to attack the snarls.

Talia came up behind her and began to comb her hair gently. A small pile of debris started to gather on the floor. "What questions do you have, Sammy?"

"Why do you think Nolan lied to the king?"

Talia grimaced. "I am the one who first planted that seed, I'm sorry to say. When the report came that you were both gone, the entire palace was in an uproar. I had to send a message to your parents that you had disappeared. They will be here very soon, I'm sure. Sam, don't frown at me like that. Edric told me that you went after Chrissy and that Nolan went after the two of you. How would it look if everyone found out you and Nolan spent three days together in the forest?"

"Nothing happened," Samantha protested. "He was a perfect gentleman. He didn't even kiss me. But I do see your point. He really does have the gift of convincing speech, doesn't he?"

"Are you getting moony eyed, Samantha?"

"No! Well, maybe . . ." She paused. "Anyway, this came to me out in the forest. Do you know if Osric or Elan gave me my seventh blessing? I really need to write and ask what it is. I helped Dagan kill himself somehow. I need to know what I did. I don't want that to happen again." Samantha played with her fingers nervously.

Talia sighed and tears shone in her eyes. "Neither Osric or Elan gave you that blessing."

"Then who did?" Samantha looked in the mirror at Talia's reflection. "You?" She spun around to face Talia directly. "*You* gave me my seventh blessing? What is it? Please, you must remember!"

Talia placed her palm against Samantha's cheek and smiled. "I could never forget it. It was something my mother taught me when I was very small. It's a charm to protect those you love from harm. My mother would whisper it over me every night when she tucked me in. I was hoping that it would protect you. I suppose it did."

Samantha grasped her hands. "What is it? I couldn't translate all of the words."

Talia took a deep breath and closed her eyes. "I had to change it a bit from my mother's original blessing, since I was not a princess. Translated from the tongue of the Ancients, 'No one will be able to use magic *against* the Princess of Mittra so that harm may come to her or that she would do anything to harm another.' If someone tried to use magic in a way that would harm you or go against what you desired, that charm or spell would turn back on them in some way. It only gave Nolan a headache, but Dagan truly meant to harm you."

Samantha sat there in shock, her face pale. "Dagan was trying to kill me, but his spells bounced off of me and hit him. He really did kill himself." Samantha shot up and began to spin around the room. "Oh Taley, I'm not a murderer!"

The door opened and a maid carrying a large bucket of water entered the room. She froze and stared at Samantha, her hands trembling. Talia cast a charm on the bucket to keep it from spilling, and Samantha took the bucket from the girl's hands.

"I'm so sorry," the maid apologized, nodding her head and curtseying at the same time. "I did knock but no one answered. I didn't mean to overhear. Please don't have me killed, miss."

Samantha set down the bucket with a thud and rushed back to the girl. "No, I would never do that. I was speaking of the evil fairy that trapped Princess Chrissy. He tried to kill me but his magic went awry, and I thought it was my fault—"

Talia interrupted. "Thank you, dear. That's enough water for now. Please, keep this between us."

The maid nodded violently and hurried from the room. Talia looked at Samantha and they both began to laugh.

"I believe you've had enough adventure for one day, Sammy. Time for your bath."

"Taley, thank you," Samantha said softly, hugging her friend. "Without you and your gift, I'd be dead right now. And so would Nolan and Chrissy. *You* are the hero, and I will be eternally grateful."

Talia smiled at Samantha, patting her back. "Let me heal your arm and then I'll leave you for a bit. Why don't you take your bath and then lay down for a rest?"

"That sounds like a *wonderful* idea."

‡

Nolan was changing out of his dirty clothes when Edric burst into their room.

"Are you ready to leave?" Edric demanded. "King Aspen is mounted and has at least twenty men with him. They are going to storm Dagan's castle. The king wants to see that Dagan's dead body is disposed of and deal with Linden."

Nolan grabbed his heavy cloak and his sword, heading for the door. "I was hoping to meet with Samantha, but if the king insists."

Edric shook his head with a smile. "Sam will still be here when you return. I'll let her know that you didn't want to leave her."

Nolan punched his brother's arm as he passed, smiling. "I will return as soon as I can. Don't do anything I wouldn't do."

Edric stuck his head out into the hallway. "I believe that's my line!"

‡

Samantha was roused the next morning by a scurrying sound in her bedroom. When she opened her eyes, she saw her mother pointing to the dirty pile of clothing on the floor. A young maid was gingerly picking the items up with a disgusted look on her face.

"You may burn those," Queen Adelaide said before she closed the door.

"Mother!" Samantha cried as she sat up in bed, trying to untangle herself from the bedclothes. "You came!"

"Of course I came, Samantha. Did you think that Father and I would remain in Harak once we received Talia's bone chilling letter? 'Our dear Samantha has gone missing in the forest to the north of Synterius with Princess Chrysanthemum.'" Adelaide shook her head as she sat down on the bed, patting Samantha's knee.

She threw her arms around her mother. "You memorized the letter?"

Adelaide sat stunned for a moment before she returned the hug. "Yes, it was my constant companion these last few days of traveling. Your father and I were so relieved to get here to find you alive and well." She searched her daughter's eyes. "Are you well?"

"Well enough. Chrissy is the one who went through a truly traumatic time. Tell me about Harak. I need a bit of distraction from my thoughts right now."

"If you need a distraction, I'll show you the list of Lacene's demands for her 'perfect' wedding. She insisted that I take it with me, even though I told her I would be busy worrying about my daughter." Adelaide sniffed delicately.

Samantha pulled a face. "When is Lacene's wedding? And do I have to go?"

Adelaide gave her daughter a stern look. "Yes, you must go to your cousin's wedding. You're one of the bridesmaids."

Samantha gave an unladylike snort. "Bridesmaid? She doesn't even *like* me. I know she'll pick out a hideous dress for me to wear. It'll probably be something chartreuse or mud brown."

The queen withheld a smile. "The bridesmaids' dresses are green, and I'm sure it will lovely on you. You'll blend in with the other seventeen girls."

"Seventeen?" Samantha jumped from the bed. "If she has that many, she surely doesn't need me."

"Well, the wedding is in three months. Lacene insisted on having cardoons in her bouquet and those bloom only in October. However, if you are married before October, you can't very well be a bridesmaid, can you?" Adelaide lifted her eyebrows.

Samantha ignored the comment as she took a change of clothes from her wardrobe. "Cardoons. Those are very like Lacene. Prickly, ostentatious, and unaccommodating." She disappeared behind the dressing screen.

"The wedding gown she commissioned will also take quite a while to complete. She wants the train to be as long as the aisle in the chapel," Adelaide explained with a pinched look on her face. "Samantha, I never thought I would say this, but I am very glad you are not like your cousin."

Samantha burst out laughing behind the screen. "Do not worry, Mother. I will never ask for an obscenely long train or make my groom wait several months to be married because the flowers I want are not in season."

"Groom?" Adelaide questioned with a gleam in her eye. "You have had a proposal? Your father thought Nolan might have proposed already, but I was sure that he would ask your father's permission first."

Samantha came out dressed in a simple white blouse and blue skirt. "No groom, Mother. Nolan hasn't exactly asked yet—"

A knock on the door cut off Samantha's comment. She reached to open it, but Adelaide motioned her away. "You must do your hair first. A lady should always be presentable." She opened the door and took the note from the maid standing in the hallway. "It is addressed to you." She handed the note to Samantha. "Why don't you sit down to read it while I do your hair?"

Samantha stared at her mother. "You can style hair?"

"Really, dear, how hard can it be?"

Samantha sat down and opened the note while her mother combed through her long hair. "It's from Edric. He says that Nolan left with King Aspen and two dozen other men last night for Dagan's castle. They are going to bury his body and destroy all evidences of dark magic. They've taken quite a few fairies with them." Samantha stared at her reflection in the mirror. "I hope Talia was able to stay here. There was something important I was thinking about. Something Dagan said."

Adelaide ceased her combing and looked at her daughter's face in the mirror. "How are you taking this so calmly? That man tried to kill you."

Samantha turned to her mother. "Dagan is dead, and Linden can't get out of the castle. He'd need a magic transporter to escape from Talia's charms on the doors." An odd look came over Samantha's face. "Oh, no. The mirror!"

Adelaide looked into the dressing table mirror. "The mirror is fine, dear."

"No, not my mirror," Samantha began to pace. "Dagan's mirror. He said the mirror was his window to the world. I thought that just meant he could see others in it, but what if it is a portal?"

"I do not understand what you are saying. Let me get Talia."

The queen hurried through the door that connected the two rooms. Talia returned with Adelaide only a few moments later.

"Taley, Dagan's mirror! When I was in his lair, I saw the mirror. He was able to show me his memories from the Academy in it. Dagan also said that it was his window to the outside world," Samantha said, holding Talia's hands.

"That means he could possibly travel into the surrounding area," Talia mused. "He would have to have another reflective surface to come through."

All three women glanced at the mirror in Samantha's room. "No," said Talia. "I doubt that Linden could use this. Dagan's magic must have weakened as he aged. He would only be able to journey close to his lair. If Linden managed to steal a few charms or potions, he might be able to attempt something. But I have never known a human to do fairy magic before. I will send a special message to the king advising him to examine the mirror."

Samantha noticed her mother began to tremble. "Mother, please sit down. We will work as hard as we can to solve this."

Adelaide grabbed Samantha's hand. "You were face to face with him? That *evil fairy*? How did you survive?"

Talia and Samantha glanced at each other. "Mother, I have something important to tell you." She took a deep breath. "I know what my seventh blessing is now."

The queen looked stricken. "You are not an assassin, are you?"

"No, it's nothing like that," Samantha replied. "Dagan did die, but I promise that will *not* happen again."

"How many mothers hear that promise, Taley?" Adelaide asked with a faint smile.

She turned to her mother. "Simply put, I have the gift of defying magic. If I give my permission for magic to be used on me, no harm will come. But if someone uses magic to hurt me or uses me to hurt someone else, it will backfire and hurt the one using the magic." Samantha sat on a low stool by her mother's feet.

"This does not seem so bad compared to the shock I first received at your blessing ceremony," Adelaide admitted, stroking Samantha's hair. "I fainted at that one. I am thankful that one of those old fairies had the sense to give you this gift."

"Thank Talia, Mother. It was her gift. Who knows what Elan or Osric would have given me next?" Laughter filled the room for several moments. Samantha made herself stand up and stretch from her cramped position. "Is it too late for breakfast?"

"It's getting closer to lunch time, but I suppose you can have breakfast. You are a princess after all."

"Now Mother, if you don't want me to be like Lacene, you shouldn't remind me of such things," Samantha teased as they left her room.

‡

Linden scowled from his hiding place behind a large boulder. He had managed to loosen his bonds only moments after those fools left him in the dungeon. However, he had failed to make it through a doorway before that silly fairy put a charm on the exits.

He looked down at his swollen arm, grimacing at the sight of the red streaks lacing it. The bolt Samantha had fired at him left a gaping hole that oozed yellow pus. *There was once a time when I wanted to marry that girl. Now, I shall hunt her down.* His lip curled sadistically. *She'll be begging me to kill her. But no, vengeance will be sweeter if I make her suffer. Maybe her fairy friend will be there was well,* he mused, stroking the handle of his dagger. *I will show those bigheaded princes that I am stronger than they will ever be. Dagan's power is now mine.*

He thought back to the two days he had lived in the castle, eating the rats he could stun with one of the charms Dagan had left in his work room. A sudden gleam from Dagan's mirror had caught Linden's eye. His mind remembered bits of Dagan's conversations over the last several months. Linden knew there was something special about this mirror. Dagan had shown him what his future kingdom would look like in the reflection.

Linden had touched the mirror and instead of feeling cold and hard, it was surprisingly warm and pliable. He put his hand into the mirror, feeling a mixed sensation of cold and hot, wet and dry at the same time. Linden pulled his hand out and examined it. It looked exactly the same. That was when he knew. After stuffing an empty sack with all of the potions and charms that he could find, he stepped to the mirror and pressed into it again. This time his whole body fell through.

Linden felt like he was falling through the air, but he could not see anything rushing past him. His mind spun with dizziness. He finally found himself face down in a shallow stream that ran behind Dagan's castle. He scrambled up and felt his body, relieved to find all of his body parts attached. *The mirror is a magic portal. Can I get back through it? Which one of Dagan's charms operates it?* For hours he tried each charm, but nothing worked.

He scowled again at the shelter made from the boulder and a large tree that, though dead, still provided protection from the sun. He had waited to see if anyone would arrive from Synterius to arrest him, and now they were finally here. He could hear them scurrying about in the woods, carelessly making noise.

His plan was simple. When someone approached, he would throw a potion on the enemy and see what happened. After he managed to fight them all off, he would find a way back inside his castle and prepare to raise an army to defeat his uncle and, eventually, all of Gymandrol. He knew he had the power inside him to rule, and he would not give up willingly.

‡

Nolan dismounted from the borrowed horse at the foot of the Mountains of Desolation and handed the reins to an eager groom. "Over here is a secret entrance, but we can't take our horses through there. I know that the horses have a charm on them to make them fleet of foot, but my brother did not enjoy the ride up the mountain on horseback. I suggest most of us go this way and a few stay here to stand guard."

King Aspen agreed with Nolan's assessment. He appointed two of the young grooms and five knights to remain outside while the other knights and fairies went on. Nolan led the way through the mountain pass as he had done a few days before with Samantha. He shook his head at the memory and forced himself to focus on the task at hand. They emerged into the hut and he led the way out.

As he was pointing out the known entrances to the fairies, King Bennett clapped him on the shoulder. "Nolan, my boy, I need to have a man-to-man talk with you."

Nolan's heart sank. "Sir, please allow me to explain—"

"Oh, if you could see your face!" Bennett began to laugh heartily. "No, do not worry. This is not your trial, young man, nor am I your executioner. I was merely going to ask if you had asked Samantha to marry you yet. And if you have not, why?"

Nolan stared at the king for several moments. "It is acceptable to you if I ask your daughter to marry me?"

"Boy, that's what I've been hoping for. Now that you have saved her life, I say that counts as a quest for her hand. Are we done?" Nolan nodded. "Good. We will have it announced when we return." Bennett turned away and began to speak with King Aspen.

"But I haven't even asked her yet, " Nolan stammered as the king walked away. "Oh well. We'll cross that bridge when we come to it."

A flying object caught Nolan's attention. He stared as a winged piece of folded parchment made circles around King Aspen's head.

"Excuse me, King Aspen. You seem to have . . . um, a letter?" Nolan called.

All in their party stopped and stared at the object. Finally, one of the fairies murmured a spell that made it drop at Aspen's feet. One knight stabbed it with his sword until Aspen dismissed him and picked up the paper.

"It's from Miss Talia. She says to examine the mirror in Dagan's work room. Prince Nolan?" Aspen turned to him. "Do you know anything about this?"

Nolan nodded. "I saw it there. And Sam—that is—Princess Samantha said Dagan showed her something in the mirror. It is probably enchanted. These fairies will understand that far better than I can."

"Let us go in and use great caution," Aspen boomed out.

A small movement caught Nolan's eye from a large boulder to the left of the castle. *It's probably a rabbit*, he thought as he approached the doors. He froze. *There aren't any rabbits around here. In fact, there aren't any animals around here.*

He headed to the right of the entrance, then ran around the back of the stone building. He crept out, sword at the ready, hiding in the shadows created by the afternoon sun. *There it is again.* It was too large to be an animal and was most certainly a man. *But who? We left Linden locked up in the dungeon. I'm sure he managed to get out of his bonds, but he couldn't get past Talia's charms on the doors. Maybe he had an assistant. Well, I have a surprise for him!*

With a yell, Nolan charged the enclosed space behind the boulder, his sword extended. A splash of liquid caught him in the mouth. He began to cough and splutter, dropping his sword slightly.

"It seems as if I have caught a prince. And not any prince, but my enemy," Linden crowed as he rushed toward Nolan. "Do you see what my potion has done to you now? You cannot speak. Eventually, you will stop breathing altogether. And then I will steal Samantha right out from under your nose—"

Nolan slashed out with the flat side of his sword and smacked Linden in the side of the head, causing him to stumble. As he tried to right himself, Nolan hit Linden's hand, forcing him to release the dagger.

"Don't gloat until you know you've won," Nolan taunted, ready for another attack.

Linden ran at him, head down, and tried to grab Nolan around the waist. Nolan spun easily and kicked Linden's right leg as he ran past, forcing him to fall to the ground.

Linden grabbed his leg. "Ow, I'm wounded, you animal! I should have won. I had magic on my side!"

Fairies and knights streamed out of the castle, alerted by one knight standing guard outside. One of the eldest fairies picked up the bottle Linden had thrown at Nolan and sniffed it. He read the tag and smiled. "If you could read the tongue of the Ancients, you would know that this potion heals one from warts. The prince shouldn't have any, thanks to you."

Linden turned bright red as the entire company began to laugh at him. "Shut up all of you! One day I will rule you and then who will laugh? Me! Don't sleep tonight, Nolan. I will find you and when I do, I will slit your throat. And then I will kill all of you!" His maniacal laughter spilled out until one of the fairies cast a silence charm on him.

King Aspen strode out and took one look at his nephew laying on the ground before he said, "I want a binding spell put on him that cannot be broken."

Five fairies all hurried to do as he commanded even as Linden fussed and kicked in silence, his face turning purple from his energies.

"Can someone please knock him out?" Aspen asked wearily.

Nolan stepped forward and punched Linden in the temple. He smiled apologetically at the king, who frowned at him. Finally, he nodded his approval.

"Half of you stay here with him. The other half go back inside. We will destroy the mirror and burn everything else. All traces of Dagan's magic must be erased," Aspen stated.

Nolan remained on guard by Linden's body. *There's no way he's getting away from me this time.*

CHAPTER NINETEEN

"*T*here you are," Chrissy announced, running towards the rose garden where Samantha sat.

Chrissy threw her arms around her friend, bouncing while grinning from ear to ear. "Tell me before you burst," Samantha said with a smile of her own.

"He asked me, and I said yes!" Chrissy squealed before she burst into tears. "Don't worry, these are happy tears. They've been happening ever since he asked me." She wiped them away. Then, she began to rapidly chatter. "Edric asked my father the evening we returned. He wanted to ask me right away, but my mother said I needed my sleep. Miss Talia gave me a potion to drink which made me feel much better." She sobered for a moment and touched Samantha's hand. "What happened when you found me? I have a very vague memory of Linden finding me in the forest. Then you were there. And then we were home again . . ."

Samantha looked into her friend's eyes, glimpsing a deep pain in them. *Do I tell her or let it go? She's always been honest with me.*

"Chrissy, I think you were in some sort of shock. You thought that Nolan was Edric. You also thought I was coming to get you for our ride. I don't know if Dagan put a spell on you or if your mind was trying to protect itself from the horrors of being locking in a dungeon."

Chrissy gripped Samantha's hands in hers. "*Thank you.* You are the first one who has been honest with me. I dreamt last night I was in a dungeon and it felt so real. Now I know why. Wait, did you say I thought Nolan was Edric? Did I say anything? I didn't try to kiss him, did I?"

Samantha laughed at the alarm on her friend's face. "No, you were perfectly ladylike."

"Sam, you will be my maid of honor, won't you?" Chrissy asked, eyes shining.

"Shouldn't one of your sisters be the maid of honor?"

"Cammie, Lilac, and Maggie will all be bridesmaids. They don't mind, really!"

"Then yes, I'll be your maid of honor. As long as I don't have to wear an ugly gown." Samantha declared with a wide grin.

They began to walk back to the castle. "You can wear anything you like. You and the other girls don't have to match. My mother doesn't mind, and I just want to marry Edric as soon as possible."

Samantha giggled at her friend's dreamy expression. *I'm sure I don't look like that around Nolan.*

Chrissy paused at the entrance to a side door of the castle and looked at Samantha carefully. "Any romantic news from you?"

Blushing, Samantha shook her head. "No, definitely not. I told Nolan not to talk to me about courting when we were in Dagan's lair. He was called away before he could speak to me again."

"Interesting," Chrissy said with a wicked grin. "Edric could let his brother know that a proposal would not be unwelcome to you."

"No, please don't say or hint anything," Samantha blurted. "I would rather he ask naturally. Not out of compulsion or because he thinks I'm expecting it."

"I was only teasing." Chrissy assured her as they walked through the cool hallway. "I won't say anything. Will you help me pick out a dress to wear tonight? Edric will announce our engagement tonight at dinner."

"Of course."

✣

Nolan had barely managed to dismount outside the stable when Edric ran up to him and clapped him on the shoulder. Scowling at his brother, Nolan began to unpack his saddlebags.

"Aren't you going to ask me why I'm so happy?" Edric demanded, almost jumping in place.

"I wasn't planning on it," Nolan replied. "I've been traveling for days on end, sleeping on the hard ground, and eating who knows what. Sorry if I don't leap up and down with you."

"Excuse me, I just thought my brother would be happy to know that I am getting married," Edric retorted before heading toward the castle.

"Hold on! Come back, you big lug!" Nolan cried out. He ran at his brother, trying to tackle him.

Edric met him halfway and they hugged, pounding one another on the back.

"You really asked her, didn't you? I am impressed." Nolan grinned. "Sorry for being so out of sorts earlier. I'm really happy for you two. How did you do it?"

"Well, here in Synterius, there's a tradition of hiring a minstrel to play while you sing to your lady fair in front of all the guests. I chose lunch because there were fewer people around to sing to. Chrissy said yes," Edric smiled off into the distance while Nolan laughed.

"I guess I'll have to wait to ask Sam until we get back to Mittra!"

Edric eyed him distainfully. "You're really going to wait that long?

What happens if she meets another knight on the way back home? Samantha is a beautiful girl, and she could have her pick of men. I wouldn't put it off if I were you."

"It's a good thing I'm not you, walking around all starry eyed and singing a proposal to a girl."

The brothers were walking past the rose garden when Nolan saw Samantha talking animatedly to Chrissy. He stopped and stared. *How did she get more beautiful in just a few days? Or has she always been this beautiful and I didn't see it? Edric's right. I can't wait until we get back to Mittra to ask her. It might be too late.*

"Who's starry eyed now?" Edric murmured before sauntering into the castle.

"Ouch," Nolan complained as he followed his brother. "So . . . which minstrel did you use?"

‡

Samantha entered the banquet hall that night dressed in a gown her mother had brought from Harak with her. The emerald green of the dress matched Samantha's eyes. Only a few alterations had to be made to the bodice for it to fit perfectly.

She could hear snippets of conversation as she crossed the room. Her mother and father sat at the head table with King Aspen and Queen Laurel, but her eyes flitted in every direction, looking for Nolan. She sighed. *I was sure I heard that he was back with the other men who went off to Dagan's lair.*

She shivered slightly, remembering overhearing the maid's whispers. They said Linden had been found but was locked in the cellar under the banquet hall at the present time. *I do hope he is well secured. That man is insane. Who knows what he would do if he got out? No, think of happier things right now. Like how lovely Chrissy looks.*

Chrissy sat to the right of her mother, her white blond hair caught up in curls all around her head. Her gown was a delicate shade of pink that matched the glow of her cheeks. *I wish I could be as pretty and delicate as her. Instead, I can wield a sword, scare away unwanted suitors, and face down an insane fairy. Those aren't exactly great qualities for a bride. Nolan isn't here, and I don't see anyone one else lining up to propose.*

Samantha sat down in an empty seat at the far end of the head table, half a dozen seats down from Chrissy. *No one will miss me down here. I don't know why I even came tonight. I'm not fit company for anyone.* She gave herself a sudden shake. *Stop it, Sam. This night is important for Chrissy and Edric. Just because you're unhappy doesn't mean you can ruin the evening for others.*

She made herself smile and worked on relaxing her stiff muscles. Chrissy looked down the long table and grinned at her, waving her to come closer. Samantha gestured at the other guests between them, and Chrissy nodded in understanding.

"Welcome!" King Aspen announced. "Thank you for joining us tonight as I make a toast to my dear daughter, Princess Chrysanthemum and her friend, Princess Samantha of Mittra. They have both been returned to us safely, and we owe a debt of gratitude to Prince Nolan of Lagola. Nolan?"

The entire assembly looked around the room, ready to greet the hero with a loud cheer. There was no sign of him.

"No matter, we will shout a 'Huzzah!' for him when he comes," Aspen laughed. "For now, here's to our dear princesses!"

Samantha blushed as cups were lifted towards her and Chrissy and the crowd cried out with joy.

"And we have another matter to toast to," Aspen continued when the noise died down. "Prince Edric of Lagola. Come, stand up, Edric." He looked around. "There he is! Prince Edric, the crowned prince of Lagola, has been our honored guest. He has asked for my daughter

Chrysanthemum's hand in marriage. My dear wife and I feel this is a worthy match. We wish them great joy and prosperity. And, may I say, many grandchildren?"

The banquet hall fairly shook with the loud huzzahs and cheers from the dinner guests. Samantha grinned at Chrissy's beaming face and Edric's lovesick expression as he held the hand of his betrothed. She raised her own cup to them and gave Chrissy a wink. Chrissy blushed even deeper, causing the crowd to cheer yet again.

Samantha saw the minstrel wander into the center of the room, playing on his lute. Nolan followed behind him and began to sing in a low voice. She resisted the urge to sink down in her chair. Instead, she watched him travel from table to table, singing to the guests. He was too far away for her to clearly hear the words of his song, but the laughter of the guests was unmistakable. Several pointed up to the head table, and Nolan finally glanced her way.

He walked steadily towards her, the minstrel following him. Samantha could feel her cheeks burn as she heard the words to his song.

"Have you seen my maiden fair, the girl called Samantha with golden hair? A princess so divine and pure, my heart beats with love so sure. Tell me; tell me, where can she be? I must know if she loves me. All that I have I will give to her, the one who makes my heart astir. Maiden, tell me, tell me true, will you love me as I love you?" Nolan sang out to her in his deep voice, his eyes showing the truth of his words, reaching out for her hand.

Samantha stood and skirted around the table, stepping down in front of him. She held her hand out and he took it in his. She smiled up at him and asked, "Do I need to sing my answer to you?"

Nolan kept his eyes on hers while he called up, "Excuse me, King Aspen, when the man proposes in song here in Synterius, does the lady have to respond in kind?"

A resounding roar of laughter echoed through the hall. Nolan and

Samantha stared as everyone around them heaved and turned red from their laughter.

Edric stood up, wiping his eyes. "Brother, I thought you knew I was only joking. I didn't sing a proposal to Chrissy."

Samantha glanced up anxiously at Nolan's face, waiting to see what he would do. A muscle jumped in his clenched jaw, but then he opened his mouth and began to laugh along. Even Samantha joined in.

"What do you say, Sammy? Will you have my sweet talking brother for your husband?" Edric asked.

Stepping back, Samantha looked Nolan up and down, circling him as a potential buyer would to a horse up for sale. "Hmmm, he looks like good breeding. Fine stock, I'd say."

"What are you doing?" Nolan murmured from the corner of his mouth, standing still.

"You were able to embarrass me, I'm just paying you back," she replied, fluttering her eyelashes at him.

Nolan reached out and caught her hands. "Samantha," he breathed, looking down into her eyes. "I meant everything I said in that song, as silly as it was. I do love you, and I only realized how much I love you today. I didn't want you to go back to Mittra without knowing how I felt about you. I want you to be my wife and to stand by my side for many years. Oh, don't cry," he murmured, brushing a tear from her cheek.

"These are happy tears. Apparently they happen when a girl gets proposed to," Samantha sniffed as she smiled at him. "But, which part of me do you love? The princess part or the warrior part?"

Nolan looked into her eyes with tenderness. "It's not just one part or the other. Both of those make you who you are, and I love who you are. I love your sassiness, your determination, your sweetness, your . . . Samanthaness."

"I love you too, Nolan," Samantha whispered, looking at him with shining eyes. "That's a yes, Edric!" she shouted to the head table.

Nolan's lips lowered to hers and they sealed their proposal with a soft kiss, amidst the cheers of everyone in the room.

‡

Three days later, Samantha and Nolan stood in front of King Aspen's castle, waving goodbye as Edric and Chrissy left on their honeymoon journey. Nolan took Samantha's hand in his and squeezed it gently.

"Do you want our wedding to be like that?" he asked as they walked toward the stable. "Small, not too fancy?"

"I would love that," Samantha told him. "It would suit me just fine to have our wedding outside with just our parents and close friends as witnesses. I'd carry some wildflowers picked from my morning walk. After the ceremony, you and I would go for a ride on our horses."

Nolan began to laugh and pulled her into his arms, swinging her around. "You are one of the most unusual girls I have ever met." He put her down and kissed the tip of her nose.

"Unusual in a good way, right?"

"Of course," Nolan assured her, encircling her waist with his arms. "I wouldn't love you if you were any different."

Samantha laid her other hand against the side of his face, rubbing the rough stubble growing there. "Remember back in Conti Wayo? You couldn't wait until you were allowed to shave. Edric had shaved for the first time and you were so jealous."

"You remember that now? When I just told you I love you?" Nolan's eyebrows slanted down in disappointment.

Samantha laughed as her finger pushed his eyebrows back up again. "I remember that's when I first thought you were handsome, though I would have never admitted it." She glanced down in embarrassment. "I think that's why it hurt so much when you were mean to me."

Nolan tilted her chin back up to look in her eyes. "Don't you know that when a boy likes a girl, he teases her fiercely?"

Samantha's eyes sparkled in anger. "So, if I like you, I should smash mud in your face and put worms in your dessert and crickets in your bed and—"

Nolan cut off her protests by pulling her close and kissing her deeply. "No worms, please," Nolan spoke softly against her lips when the kiss ended.

Samantha pretended to think about it and then grinned. "Fine, no worms. But I can't make any promises about the crickets."

She took off in a run toward the stable, where Windstorm was saddled and waiting for her.

"How are you able to run in a dress?" Nolan yelled after her.

"I've had years of practice running away from you!"

Nolan caught up with her and helped her mount her horse. "Do you want to get married today?"

Samantha laughed and rolled her eyes. "I think we can be patient and wait for your parents to arrive next week. Edric wouldn't wait for them, and I think they should be at *one* of their sons' wedding."

Nolan pulled himself up into Blaze's saddle. "I suppose you're right. It doesn't seem fair, though. I've known you your whole life, and Edric only just met Chrissy a few months ago."

"Oh, but there is a difference," Samantha said with a sly smile. "Edric has always been nice to Chrissy. You, on the other hand, gave me a bloody lip, muddied my gown . . . shall I go on?"

"No, please don't!" Nolan cried as they rode through the field behind the castle. "Someone might hear and get the wrong idea about me. I'm known to be a smooth talker and an ambassador. You'll ruin my reputation."

Samantha suddenly sat up straight. "I forgot to tell you something important. I've been so busy with Chrissy and her wedding and then our own engagement—"

"Slow down, Sam. What is it?" Nolan placed a hand on hers.

She took a deep breath. "I know what my seventh blessing is. Once you know, you might not want to marry me after all."

Nolan gave a short laugh. "I doubt anything will change my mind."

"It's a defense against magic. No one can use magic to hurt me or force me to hurt someone else. That's why whenever you tried to sweet talk me, it would backfire. I didn't want you to convince me, I guess. Dagan died because he tried to hurt me. His curses turned on him."

"Is that all?" he asked, his serious expression replaced by one of giddiness. "That's fantastic, Sam. Really. No one would ever guess it. You will truly be a force to be reckoned with when you're the Queen of Mittra."

Samantha blushed and urged Windstorm to continue their walk. "That's something my father said I needed to talk to you about. There's a law in Mittra that you must be of Mittran descent to rule. You would be King of Mittra by marriage, but I would be officially recognized as the ruler. This is really awkward and there's not really a precedent set for it. Queen Einara was the first Queen of Mittra to rule on her own. When she died, the throne went to a cousin. All successive rulers have been sons or nephews. I wouldn't hold being queen over your head—"

Nolan reached over again, catching her reins and holding them tight. "Samantha. Hear me now. I love you and I want to marry you. No matter the obstacles, the secret blessings, the throne of Mittra, or any other thing. I love *you*. I want you to be my wife and that's that. Do you understand?"

Samantha could feel all of her insecurities slip away as she looked into his eyes, finding the truth, love, and acceptance that she had looked for all of her life. "I do understand," she whispered. "Let's hope your parents get here sooner than a week, shall we?"

The grooms at the stable a half mile away could hear the sound of laughter ringing out over the green fields behind the castle.

EPILOGUE

"*Th*ad! Come here," Nolan called out across the courtyard to his two-year-old son. "There's someone you need to meet."

Thaddeus, prince of Mittra, skipped back to his father. He wore a wide smile on his chubby face. "Who I meet, Dada?" he asked, placing his small hand into his father's much larger one.

"Your baby sister," Nolan answered as he led Thaddeus to the bedchamber, where Samantha had endured fourteen hours of labor. "You may hold her if you promise to be very careful."

"I be careful, Dada," Thaddeus promised in a solemn voice.

Nolan smiled down at his son. Thaddeus was already showing the marks of a great ruler. He was patient and kind to all of those around him. He shared his toys with his cousin, Oakley, whenever Edric and Chrissy came for a visit. He hardly ever fussed at bedtime. Nolan could only hope the same could be said for his new daughter.

Nolan blinked back tears as he thought of the little person he had held just a few minutes ago. Her small body fit so nicely into his arms, her cheeks pink, her chin as stubborn as her mother's.

Nolan knocked softly on the door, and Talia opened it with a smile. "I've brought the proud big brother in to see his baby sister."

Talia led the way to Samantha's bedside. Thaddeus stood there staring at the baby lying in his mother's arms, his mouth a perfect "O."

"Mama, is that my baby?" Thaddeus asked in wonder.

The adults in the room smiled in amusement. "Yes, Thad, this is your baby sister. You'll help us take care of her, won't you?" Samantha asked with a twinkle in her eye.

"Yes, I help you, Mama. I big!" Thaddeus stated, standing on his tiptoes.

Talia took the boy's hand and started to leave the room. "Let your mama and sister rest for awhile. Would you like me to tell you a story?"

"Yes, Taley. The one with Dada and Mama and the mud," Thaddeus exclaimed as the door closed.

Nolan crouched down next to Samantha and lightly touched the baby's head. "Apparently my deeds live on in infamy."

"I did warn you," Samantha teased with a tired smile. "Before I fall asleep, I wanted to ask you what you finally decided to name your daughter."

Nolan grinned at her. Thaddeus had been born two weeks early, and Nolan had been away on a hunting expedition with Edric. Samantha used his absence to name their son with her top pick of boy names. Nolan told her that he would get to choose the next child's name without any input from her.

"I was considering either Meredith or Emmalyn—my grandmothers' names," Nolan explained.

Samantha's eyes lit up. "I love both of those names. What about Emmalyn Meredith? I know she'll have a few other middle names to satisfy both sides of our family, but I think she looks like an Emmalyn Meredith. What do you think?"

Nolan kissed his wife softly. "I think you're beautiful and you're right."

"I've taught you well," Samantha teased before she kissed him back. "Would you put our daughter in her cradle, please? I need to get a little sleep before all of our visitors arrive."

"The blessing ceremony is in three days, isn't it?" Nolan asked as he covered his tiny daughter with a blanket, a look of awe on his face.

"The private one, yes. The public ceremony is the day after that. And Talia and I are hoping that it will be as calm as Thad's was," Samantha replied.

Thaddeus had been born in January, following a heavy snowstorm. Very few fairies arrived for the ceremonies and Talia had given him his only fairy blessing: that of wisdom. Samantha sighed when she thought of little Emmalyn Meredith's ceremony.

"Why did I have to have a baby in November? Eleven blessings . . . Eleven chances to go wrong . . ."

"With Talia as her fairy godmother, nothing can go wrong," Nolan assured his wife as he tucked her in. "I love you, Samantha, queen of my heart."

In a sleepy voice, Samantha replied, "And I love you, my Nolan, king of mine."

The End

Upcoming 2011 TLT Releases

Dartboard by JD Gordon

Reaching Riverdale by Geeta Schrayter

Valren by Kerry Castorano

Demons Are Jackasses by SM Blooding

Concealed by Sang Kromah

Little Red Wolf by Paul Schumacher

Melissa's Charity

Melissa has chosen the Young Adult Library Services Association (YALSA), a division of the American Library Association, as her supported charity. This charity combines several of Melissa's favorite things: reading, libraries, young people. YALSA believes strongly that teens deserve the best, yet many libraries do not have enough trained staff and resources to meet the needs of teens. Studies also indicate that many teens do not possess critical literacy skills. Therefore, YALSA's mission is to advocate, promote and strengthen library service to teens. They do this by advocating extensive and developmentally appropriate library and information services for young adults, supporting access to the full range of library materials and services, including existing and emerging information and communication technologies, for young adults; and encouraging research and is in the vanguard of new thinking concerning the provision of library and information services to youth.

Get Involved - Participate in YALSA

http://www.ala.org/ala/mgrps/divs/yalsa/getinvolved/participate.cfm

Melissa Buell

CPSIA information can be obtained at www.ICGtesting.com
Printed in the USA
LVOW081626260413

331118LV00001B/154/P